ACCIDENTAL FAE

FAE WAR CHRONICLES

JESSICA WAYNE

B.A.D.
PUBLISHING

B.A.D.
PUBLISHING

Fae War Chronicles, Book 1
By Jessica Wayne
Copyright © 2022. All rights reserved.

Edited by Dawn Y
Proofread by Rachel Cass
Cover Design by TwinArt Design

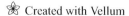 Created with Vellum

This one is for Heather.
Thank you for talking through the crazy with me.

ACCIDENTAL FAE

A life on the verge of death isn't living.

When the doctors mention hospice, I know it's time to take what's left of my life into my own hands. Stumbling through a portal into the fae realm wasn't part of the plan.

But then I see *him*—the man who claimed my dreams with glimpses of his piercing golden gaze and sculpted body slick with sweat as he fought bloody battles. Seeing him once gave me strength; now, he gives me hope.

The creatures here claim he's a rebel. A murderer. A traitor to their crown—a crown they say I'm tied to in irrevocable ways. I say he might be my only path to salvation.

I refuse to waste another life waiting for answers to secrets no one dares speak. It's time for me to break free of my prison and claim the life that was always meant to be mine. My warrior has been broken by circumstance, though, and if I can't give him a reason to fight, it could mean the end for both of us.

CHAPTER 1

EMBER

Death.

A fun word, right? After all, what other word consisting of five ordinary letters possesses the ability to ground the dreamers, cripple the strong, and bury the hopes of all who hear it? Dramatic? Maybe. Probably. But as I sit here, staring at four stark-white walls boasting various degrees that still didn't give the man before me the knowledge to save my life, I feel like I've earned that right.

The right to be a tad dramatic.

Even if I have no more tears to cry.

Dr. Alexander, a man pushing seventy, closes my file and leans back in his chair. His white hair has lost all its pepper, and his blue eyes appear haunted by failure. "I'm so sorry, Miss Hall. We've checked everything and—"

I don't need him to continue because I've heard it all before, using one phrasing or another. Over and over again these past five years, they've all said the same thing.

We can't figure out what's wrong with you.

We've run every test.

Triple checked every scan.

I'm so sorry.

There's nothing more we can do.

Let me refer you to my colleague.

We can make you comfortable.

We can treat the symptoms.

The suffocating lump in my throat grows larger; every breath burns with the force of my grief. My anger. I'd let myself get my hopes up. Let myself believe that even though I've been fighting this battle for half a decade, this time, things would be different.

This time, they'd find what was wrong with me.

Boy was I wrong. How damned fitting—a girl with no past lacks a future as well. It all feels so pointless, doesn't it? So completely and utterly pathetic. After all, what the hell is the point of my life? I haven't done anything of notoriety.

Never saved a life.

Never fallen in love.

I won't get a chance to mother the next President or a scientist who can cure diseases like mine.

So what the hell has the point of my life been? I'll answer that one: there is none. I'm one of the few who literally has no purpose. Fun deck of cards I've been dealt. A family who abandoned me, an orphanage who never wanted me, and now a disease that is killing me.

One, two, three, and the blows just keep on coming. My gaze drifts out the window to the people laughing and strolling through the park across the street.

A couple sits beneath the shade of a thick, towering tree, enjoying what looks to be a picnic lunch while their kids run and play near a pond dotted with different colored ducks. The serene scene should make me smile. Instead, I'm filled with an over-whelming jealousy that just pisses me off.

Forcing my attention away, I scan the park, doing a double-take when I see the massive wall of muscle standing on the other side of the street, staring directly toward the office. Cars pass, but he remains on the sidewalk, staring. My pulse hammers as my throat goes dry. *Holy cow, that man is gorgeous.* And half-naked.

Tan skin stretches across muscles I didn't even know could exist—you could *literally* wash clothes on those abs. Was he running? I crane my neck around to try and get a better look; I mean, I may be dying, but I'm not dead, yet. And something about him is almost—*familiar*? I swear I've seen him somewhere before—

Dr. Alexander tilts his head, obscuring my view. "Miss Hall? Ember?"

"Huh?" I stretch out further, only to see that the man is already gone, likely finishing his run toward some gorgeous girlfriend who is just as healthy as he is. Ugh, I'm being such a downer I'm even annoying myself.

"Ember," he says my name again, so I swallow hard and refocus entirely.

Hazel eyes train on me through thick-rimmed glasses, and the doctor leans back in his seat, running a hand through his silver hair, sighing as he does it.

"I'm sorry. What did you say?"

He smiles softly, revealing a look of pity I know all too well. It makes my stomach churn. I don't want pity. I want help. *Answers.* I want a chance to live a full life—to get a man like the one outside to take a second look at me.

Is that really too much to ask?

The doctor sighs. "Maybe it's time you meet with a grief counselor. Someone who can help you come to terms with what's happening."

I snort. *If I had a dime…* "Come to terms with

dying at the ripe old age of twenty-six? I'll pass, thanks."

"You know, it's normal to be angry. Afraid. Learning that you only have six months—"

"Thank you for your help," I interrupt him, not wanting to hear another damned word. "I really appreciate everything you tried to do for me. I won't ever forget it. In fact, I'll remember until the day I die." Pushing to my feet, I sling the olive-green strap of my messenger bag over my shoulder.

Dr. Alexander stands as well. "Think about what I said."

Uh-oh. There's the problem with not listening. "Which part?"

"Going into hospice care could keep you comfortable until…"

That's a new one. "Until I die?"

He purses his lips. "I truly am sorry."

Forcing a smile, I step forward and offer my hand. He takes it, holding it softly, as though the slightest pressure might break me. That's been the worst part of dying. Having everyone treat me like I'm made of glass. "I really do appreciate everything you've done. But I won't be going into hospice care."

"Ember, you don't have anyone. Accepting help is not—"

"I'll be fine," I interrupt. *Thanks for the reminder that I'm all alone.*

Thankfully, he seems to have the good nature not to argue with me. "Please, just think about it. While you do, we can continue the cold therapy. It seems to help keep the spells at bay."

I know he's just looking out for me; after all, we've spent the last year running every test, trying every possible route to manage my symptoms, and so far, nothing has worked. But he's the only doctor, out of the sixteen I've seen over the last five years, who I believe has actually given it his all.

Yet, he still found nothing. No one can tell me why I pass out at random, why my hot flashes make me feel as if I'm about to spontaneously combust. And so far, no matter how many tests they run or how many 'specialists' I see, not a single doctor has been able to tell me why my temperature runs over a hundred degrees...or why my organs are shutting down, one by one. How, one moment, I feel totally normal, and the next, I can be nearly positive that I'm about to draw my last breath.

"Thank you for everything. Sincerely. But I won't be needing the cold therapy anymore." I offer him a hug then force myself to leave his office before he can bring up hospice again or ask me why I turned down the one treatment that brought me any relief.

Sarah, the receptionist, glances up from her computer to offer me a smile and a wave. "See you later, Ember."

Once upon a time, right after I'd started seeing Dr. Alexander, we'd gone out for a girls' night. Drinks at the club. She'd gone home with a man she's now engaged to. She'd been the closest thing I'd ever had to a friend…until I'd confided in her that my prognosis had worsened.

Wasn't long after that she'd pulled back. Stopped inviting me out, stopped returning my messages.

Not that I blame her. There aren't many people who'd want to be friends with a walking dead woman. After all, why would you want to grieve someone you just met?

"See you around," I say. "Good luck with the wedding."

"You know you're invited."

I tap my bag. "Have my invitation right here." Neither of us mentions the giant elephant in the room. Her wedding is in just over a year, and according to the good doctor, I have less than six months before my entire body shuts down and I join the dearly departed.

Sunshine warms my bare shoulders as I step out into the bright early-summer afternoon. Texas summer came early this year, and with my hot flashes, I'm already rocking cut-off shorts and a tank top in the seventy-degree weather. Since my temperature runs at one-hundred-and-four on average, one-ten during a spike, there aren't many opportunities for me to be cold.

I step up to the curb and force my attention away from the handsome businessman waiting for the crosswalk beside me. Not that he pays me any attention, at all. Since I can't keep anything down, putting any kind of weight on is impossible. Add that to my flushed skin, thinning hair, and gaunt appearance—let's just say I know I'm less than noticeable.

It's embarrassing to have the body of a pre-pubescent teenager, but at least I don't look healthy. Pretty sure that would be false advertising.

The pedestrian light turns green, so I step out onto the street with the businessman as his stride carries him farther and farther away from me. I've made this walk more times than I can count, so as I head home, my mind drifts to the moment that started all of this.

I was twenty-one when I passed out for the first time. Right in the middle of teaching a self-defense class at the Y. I had my first dream then, too—a vision of me running from something that I now believe was a subconscious message about trying to outrun the reaper. Maybe my brain knew I was going to die before my body did.

When I woke up, they told me my temperature and heart rate had both skyrocketed and they weren't sure how I was even still alive. A 'miracle' they'd called it. And when a week passed and neither vitals changed, they told me there was nothing more they could do for me there, and they sent me to a specialist. The rest is history. One doctor after another, one bad news meeting after another, and here we are.

Bitter acceptance.

As it always does after an appointment, numbness consumes me, blocking out my ability to care. Who knows? Maybe I'll be abducted by one of those supernatural creatures claimed to have been outed in Montana a few months ago.

I snort. *Leave the fiction to the fairy tales, Ember.*

My apartment building looms ahead, and I pause on the sidewalk for just a moment. The decent trust fund set up for me by the family I never met is nearly gone, as is the savings I'd managed to earn working two jobs.

Not that it matters, can't take money with me when I die, right? With a deep breath, I make my way inside. Before I even fully step foot into the lobby, I'm rushed by Amber and Heather, the two women working the front desk. Never too far behind looms Wally, the door man.

Cue the rapid-fire.

Heather's first. "Well?"

Then Amber. "What did he say?"

Finally, Wally. "Anything?"

I smile softly, hating that I have such crap news to deliver. They are the only three who haven't run from me, despite my worsening condition. And I'm pretty sure that's because I was already sick when I moved here seven months ago to be closer to the hospital.

They've never known me any other way.

Then there's the shit fact that Wally has found me passed out on my floor in a pool of my own blood more than once. They've all seen me at my worst, and never my best. Maybe I should be grateful because Dr. Alexander was wrong.

Even though I have no family, I know I'm not alone.

I look at each of them individually, letting my gaze travel over their faces, absorbing the hope in their eyes.

Hope that I'm about to crush. Honestly, as shitty as it is for me to think this way, it was almost easier when no one cared. When everyone pulled away from me. "He said there's nothing more they can do."

One by one, their expressions falter. Wally sniffles, and Heather gently touches his arm as she glances at Amber.

"I'm so sorry, Ember." Amber—a woman I bonded with at first because of how close our names are—grips my hand in hers.

I shrug, forcing off the onslaught of emotion welling up inside me and making its way past the numbness. "It's nothing I didn't expect."

"But your last treatment, it was working," Heather insists. "You haven't had a spell in nearly a month."

"Symptom management," I tell her. "That's all the cold therapy was ever supposed to be." I cast my gaze to the floor a moment before looking up and delivering the final news. "The doctor wanted me to check into hospice."

"Fuck that," Wally snaps. We all turn to him.

"Wally," Heather says, admonishingly.

"No," he says. "Ember is *not* going into hospice. We can take care of you, Ember. Make sure that you're comfortab—" His voice breaks as a tear slips down his wrinkled cheek. "I can't bear the thought of you withering away alone."

I pull back from Amber and wrap my arms around Wally. "I know I won't ever be alone. I turned it down."

"Good." Wally crosses his arms. "We'll find you someone else who can actually figure out what's wrong. Damned doctors—good for nothing, that's what they are."

And now to deliver more crappy news. With a sigh, I add, "There's more. Last night, I decided that if the news was bad, I wasn't going to see any more doctors."

All three of them gape at me.

"You're giving up?" Amber's voice cracks. "Just throwing in the towel?"

"I've been at this for five years. I've spent nearly every cent of my savings on hospital bills I will probably never be able to pay off. I'm exhausted with it. And if the best doctors in the States can't find out what's wrong with me, I doubt anyone else will."

"But you have to try. There's still time," she insists.

"He gave me six months." They all fall silent, each in varying stages of disbelief.

"Six months?"

"According to Dr. Alexander, I won't see this next Christmas."

"Well, screw him. What does he know?"

I smile at Wally. "He's the best auto-immune specialist in the world," I remind him. "And he spent a year testing me for everything under the sun."

"Six months," Amber repeats. "I just...I don't know what to say."

"Whatever you need from us. We're here. Just tell us what you want to do."

I offer Heather an appreciative smile. "I actually think I want to take a trip. I've never left the state, and honestly, I want to see something other than the Austin skyline before I die."

They're quiet a moment. Then Heather finally breaks the silence. "Where will you go?"

Straightening, I reply, "I'm going to go to Ireland."

Amber's eyes widen briefly. "That's a long trip, Ember."

"It is. But it's where my finger landed on the map when I closed my eyes and spun around in a circle last night."

Heather shakes her head. "You're *kidding* me. Tell me that's not how you decided."

"I wish I could. But it's the truth. I want to see so many places; that was the only way I could really decide."

Amber's lips turn up in a half-smile. "Just like that, huh?"

"Just like that. I've spent my entire life doing things on other people's terms. The orphanage, shelters, and for the last five years—countless doctors. I want to spend what's left of my life on *my* terms. Doing what I want, when I want, how I want. No more tests, poking, prodding—none of it."

"But you'll be alone," Wally insists.

"Technically, I will. But I know that when I really start to go downhill, I can come back here." The lie is bitter on my tongue. The truth is that if I leave this place, the only way I'm coming back is in an urn. Hell, I probably won't come back in an urn. I have no family. I'll more than likely end up cremated and shoved in a back closet somewhere.

Not really sure how all that works, but I won't give a shit because I won't be breathing anymore.

Heather's gaze softens. "Are you sure you're up for it, Ember?"

"Not really. But if I don't go, I'll always regret it." I take one of her hands, then one of Amber's, and look up at Wally. "I've never been anywhere but this city, never done anything because I was always waiting for the right moment. But I think I've run out of time." My eyes fill, and a tear slips down my cheek. "I can't wait any longer," I tell them. "I need to go, to see the world—or at least, another part of it."

I release Amber and Heather.

Wally takes my hands in his. "There is a plan for you, Ember. You have to believe that."

"I do believe that," I reply, yet another lie. "But I think that maybe whatever I was supposed to do has already been done."

The elevator dings, and a woman steps out, offering me a tight smile before heading out into the sunlight.

Alone again, I turn back to them. "I hope you guys know just how much you mean to me. You've been like family to me over the last year, and I never would have made it this far without you."

"Yes, you would have," Amber insists. "Because you're a badass, Ember Hall. A badass that I'm so grateful to call my friend."

Tears spill down my cheeks as I accept her hug. She squeezes tightly, and I breathe in her Jasmine perfume, the same perfume she spritzed on me when she'd helped me get ready for her engagement party because I'd been too weak to do it myself.

The memory sends more grief washing over me, and my throat tightens, burning from tears I refuse to shed.

Amber releases me and steps back.

"When do you leave?" Heather asks, after pulling me into an embrace of her own.

"As soon as I book my flight." I release her then look up at Wally.

He'd only known me a month before he practically adopted me as a granddaughter. Now, he's the closest thing to a father figure I've ever had.

"Thank you for everything, Wally." I wrap my arms around him and bury my face in his chest as he runs a hand over my back.

"You are fire, girl. And fire is indestructible."

It's the same thing he's said to me before every doctor's appointment over the last year that I've known him. Ironic, really, that my name is Ember. Because it's exactly how I feel. A spark that's slowly and steadily losing its luster. Soon, it'll go out, and so will I.

Pulling away, I wipe my face and force a smile. "I better go get packed."

"We're praying for you, Ember. Praying for a miracle."

"Thanks, guys." I turn away and head for the elevator, hitting the button for the seventh floor before anyone can say anything else. My life has never been easy, but I've always gone with the flow, rolled with the punches. I didn't complain, didn't argue, just looked out for myself because I *always* believed something better was waiting around the corner.

But I just don't have it in me to hope for the best anymore.

Maybe this is my fate. My destiny.

If there's one thing I truly believe about destiny, it's that you can't change it. Whatever is meant to happen will—inevitably—happen, no matter how hard you try to fight it.

And I'm so damn tired of fighting.

CHAPTER 2
EMBER

The sun sneaks through the clouds, briefly illuminating me as I step out of the Dublin airport and onto the sidewalk. Cars move by on the street while people fill the sidewalks. My stomach churns, and my chest tightens as the voice in the back of my head telling me this was a huge mistake, that I need to turn around and go home, grows louder.

No. I deserve this trip. My entire life, I've erred on the side of caution and done what was expected of me. This is my time to be reckless, to do whatever the hell I want.

Besides, what's the worst that could happen?

After scanning the cars parked, drivers standing outside with signs, and seeing that my ride has yet to arrive—thank you, early gate arrival—I move off to the side and set my carry-on down so I can slip my bright yellow sweatshirt off and over my head.

I get a few weird looks after I shove it into my suitcase, but I'm guessing that's probably due to the fifty-degree weather and the fact that I'm now rocking a t-shirt boasting a chicken and the words, *What's up mother cluckers.* A gift from Amber who'd recently ventured into the hobby of screen printing.

Speaking of... I withdraw my cell phone and connect myself to the guest Wi-Fi, then Facetime audio my friends back home.

Amber answers on the first ring. "Hey! Guys, it's Ember."

"Put her on speaker." Wally's request makes me smile.

"You're on speaker. We're all chowing down on some lunch. How are you?"

"I'm good. It's really beautiful here."

"Have you made it to your room yet?"

I shake my head even though they can't see me. "Not yet, waiting on my ride."

"So you're still at the airport?"

"I am."

"How are you feeling?"

"Good, actually. I think the fresh air is good for me. It's cooler here, too."

"Maybe the trip is exactly what you need to come back refreshed," Heather says into the phone.

"Maybe." A black town car pulls up in front of the airport, and a man gets out with a sign that reads *Ember Hall*. "There's my ride now. Call you guys when I get to my hotel."

"Okay, girl, talk soon." The call ends just as he's approaching me.

"Are you Ember?" His accent is thick, and I know it's silly, but it only increases my excitement. Wearing dark wash jeans and a sweatshirt, he looks more like a grad student and less like a professional driver.

A very attractive grad student, I add to myself when I get a closer look at his sharp features. "I am." I smile, suddenly feeling very underdressed.

"I'm Sullivan," he says as he reaches down and retrieves my bag, then gestures toward his car.

"Nice to meet you."

"You, too." He opens the door for me, and I slide onto a warm leather seat. The heavy scent of pine fills my lungs as he closes me inside and puts my bag into the back. When he climbs into the driver's side, he glances over at me and smiles. "This your first time in Ireland?"

"Yeah."

"And how's the impression been so far?" He pulls out onto the street. I grip the strap of my messenger bag as I fight the urge to shut my eyes while he merges into traffic. I really didn't think it would bother me being on the opposite side of the car...but here we are.

Sullivan chuckles knowingly. "I take it you're going to need some time to get used to being on that side of the vehicle."

"You could say that. It's been good, by the way. The impression."

"Glad to hear it. How long are you staying?"

Until I die. "Not sure yet. Open-ended."

He casts a curious glance my way, eyebrow arched. "Oh? Are you meeting friends? Family?"

"Nope. Just me, myself, and I."

"Interesting. A bucket list visit, then?"

"It is."

"Well, I truly hope your visit is exactly what you were eager for."

"I'm sure it will be."

He merges onto a road that—according to the map I browsed while on the plane—should take us to my rented room in the Academy Plaza Hotel, which is close to a lot of the pubs I researched in the few hours I had before boarding the flight I booked last minute.

As we pass by various shops and restaurants, my anxiousness begins to fade away, making room for excitement. Butterflies flitter in my stomach, and for the first time in years, it's not due to nerves over bad results.

This is my time. If I'm going out—if that truly is

my fate—then it's going to be one hell of an exit. Bungee jumping, mountain climbing, surfing—I'm going to do it all. Maybe Ireland is just the start, after all. I could stay for a week then move on. Maybe go to Greece or head to Rome.

So many possibilities and nothing to keep me grounded.

"I like your shirt, by the way. Mother cluckers. Good one."

"My friend has decided she wants to wage a war on non-funny t-shirts. So, she's on a mission to single-handedly fill the world with 'ExpresShirts.'"

He laughs, a deep sound that makes me grin like an idiot. "I like your friend."

"She's something else, that's for sure."

"So you're truly just here to take in the sights of Dublin?"

"I am. I wanted to see the place before…" I trail off, swallowing hard. This is a new place, a new country, and here I can be anyone I want. Here, I'm not Ember Hall: dead woman walking. "Before I lost the chance."

"I understand that. We only live once, right?" He throws me a wink.

How true that is. "Right."

He pulls off the road and in front of the hotel. "Well, Ember Hall, here we are." With a grin that borders on too sexy for work, he climbs out of the car and rushes around to open my door. "I'll grab your bag."

"I can get it."

"Nonsense, it's all part of the package, love." He winks at me again, and heat rushes to my cheeks.

No one ever flirts with me. Not anymore. And even though I know he's doing it for a tip, it doesn't diminish the impact. Or the fact that he's one of the most attractive men I've ever seen. Dude could model on book covers and make a killing.

He comes around the car, and I start to grab my bag, but he shakes his head. "I'll carry it to the front desk for you."

"You really don't have to."

"I don't mind at all."

Enjoying the feeling of being pampered when it doesn't come with a side of pity, I resign myself to the idea of accepting his help. "Okay. That would be great, thanks."

He opens the door for me, so I step inside. The lobby is warm, welcoming. Maroon carpet adorned with white petals covers the floor, while chairs, in leather a shade of maroon that's slightly brighter than the carpet, are arranged throughout the room along with small brown tables. We move farther in, walking on polished white tile floors, and I'm greeted with warm smiles from the two women working the front desk.

"You have an Ember Hall here," Sullivan announces as we walk up to the desk.

"Miss Ember! Yes, I have you right here." A woman with silver hair and a bright smile waves me over. "Will you be using the same payment method you booked with?"

"Yes, thank you."

She taps something on her keyboard then reaches across the desk and hands me a key. "This is for you. You're in room twenty-seven. We have a complimentary breakfast each morning, and the Wi-Fi password is written here on your pamphlet." She hands the pamphlet over along with the room key. "If you need anything else, all you have to do is ask." She smiles widely at me then gives Sullivan an appreciative glance.

"Thank you so much."

"You're welcome. Elevators are right over there."

I smile and step away, moving off to the side with Sullivan following. Pulling out my wallet, I do my best to hide all the converted cash inside. After pulling some out, I offer it to him. "I'm sorry. I'm not entirely sure how much to give you."

He glances down at the wad of bills in my hand then shakes his head. "You can do me the honor of letting me show you some of the finest pubs Dublin has to offer tonight instead."

Shocked doesn't even begin to cover my reaction. "I'm sorry, what?"

He blushes. "I'd like to take you to dinner tonight. I know of a great pub that serves the best fish and chips in the entire city."

"Oh." I start to turn him down, start to explain that when I eat things, they tend to come back up, leaving me exhausted and sick for two days. But the grin on his face, the hopeful way he's watching me, it's a new kind of thrill. And one I haven't experienced since my twenty-first birthday when my entire body decided to revolt against me. "That would be great, thanks."

His answering grin is blinding. "Lovely. I'll fetch you about eight, then?"

I nod. "I look forward to it."

"Me, too." He stares at me a moment longer then offers me a wave before turning away and heading out the front door.

My smile carries me all the way to the elevator and up to my room.

A date.

I'm actually going on a date. It's been *years* since I had one. Five years, to be exact.

When I reach room twenty-seven, I slip the key into the lock and open it. The room is small, boasting only a twin bed, a flat-screen TV, and a small desk where I leave my messenger bag. Since I know I'll be here at least a week—possibly more—I drop my carry-on onto the bed and unpack the few items I brought with me.

Tomorrow, I'll venture into the city and hit up the shops with the money I have for clothes and other essentials to get me by until… I trail off. *No.* This trip is not about death or dying.

It's about life. Shutting the dark thoughts out, I happily unpack then study the outfits I did bring so I can decide what I want to wear tonight.

What does one wear to an Irish pub with a handsome stranger?

"You're going to get yourself murdered," I whisper to myself as I stand in front of the mirror and stare at the summer dress I've chosen for the evening. The fabric is not form-fitting but, instead, falls down my body in a cascade of floral print.

In the last two hours, I've talked myself out of tonight at least half a dozen times. Even after calling Amber and Heather and having them tell me to stop overthinking it, I came within inches of calling down to the front desk and requesting they ask him to leave when he shows up. I mean, I just met this guy. In another country. Hell, what if he were only asking me out to screw with me. Could be he's planning on not showing up at all.

Wouldn't that just be perfect?

The darker voice inside of me—though, the morbid one—reminds me that even if he does kill me, it's not like I have a full life ahead of me, anyway. I could die within a month—or two—so what do I really have to lose?

And with that dark thought, I shrug a light, white, knit sweater onto my shoulders and grab my purse.

It would be dumb of him to kill me, right? The front desk people saw us together; they could tell the police all about it.

"Stop being a psycho," I whisper to myself, after doing one last turn in the mirror. I rarely wear makeup, but tonight, I applied a little bit of concealer over my red splotched skin and some dark liner beneath my eyes. I may be sick, but at least now I look mildly healthy. "You got this, Em." With a roll of my shoulders and a check of the time, I force myself to head out into the hall and downstairs.

Habitually early to everything, I'm not expecting to see Sullivan sitting downstairs in one of the maroon armchairs. He doesn't see me first, so I take a moment to appreciate the way his dark hair curls just above his ears and the way he sits up straight, shoulders back, completely confident in himself.

He glances up from the magazine that he's reading, and his brown eyes meet mine. "Ember Hall, you look absolutely stunning." Setting his magazine aside, he stands, and I breathe a sigh of relief that he's dressed casually.

Dark jeans and an olive-green sweatshirt are a lot more relaxing than a suit.

"Thank you. You look nice yourself."

"Thanks." He grins and crosses the floor toward me then holds out his arm. "Shall we?"

"We shall." I let him lead me outside.

"I figured we'd do some walking tonight if that's all right?"

My stomach churns with unease, but I nod anyway. I'm used to walking to and from the hospital, but long distances tend to wear me out. "That sounds great."

We fall into companionable silence as we stroll down the street alongside other couples and groups of friends out for a fun night in the city. Lights shine brightly through panes of glass, proof of Dublin's nightlife as patrons file in and out of other pubs and buildings dotted alongside the street. The whole scene is gorgeous and exactly what I'd been expecting. For someone who has lived the last five years in a perpetual state of death, this proof of life alone makes the trip worth it.

"Can I tell you a secret?" he asks.

"Sure."

He leans in, eyes sparkling beneath the twinkling fairy lights of a building we pass. "I'm really glad you were early."

I laugh, the sound completely foreign to me after years of suffering through grief and anger. "I'm really glad you were, too."

"I barely wanted to drive home and change." He gestures to his clothes. "I made myself do it, of course. Can't be showing up to a date looking the same as when ya asked, but part of me just wanted to hang out until you were ready. That's a tad creepy, though, isn't it?"

The laughter grows, making my sides ache as I shake my head. "I think it's sweet."

"That's good, then. Sweet, not creepy. Noted."

"What's the plan for tonight?"

"We're going to head over to Murray's for a bite and a drink, and then I can show you Dublin City Centre if it suits you."

"That sounds wonderful." I swallow down my nerves and mentally tally everything I've eaten today. If I overeat, even a single bite past my normal, I end up sick for days. Since I only managed to eat a mini garden salad before boarding the plane, I figure I'm okay with a piece of bread or so.

Anything else and I might be ending the night early in a mad dash to my hotel.

The night air surrounds me, a comforting blanket

that allows me to breathe deeply. It's moments like this I think I'll miss the most. When the world is active, people happy, the night air crisp.

"Are you cold?"

"Not at all." I smile at him as he pulls me toward a building with *Murray's Grill* on the front. Thousands of lights hang from strings, illuminating the name. The patio is covered in plants that spill out onto the sidewalk, and I can hear music playing from the speakers while people chat happily at their tables.

This is a place of life, of joy, and I am so ready to be a part of it, if even for a sliver of a moment.

As Sullivan gets us inside and to a table, I let my mind drift while studying the other patrons. My gaze travels over men and women dining together and a couple of friends sharing a larger table. They briefly glance toward me, and I offer them a smile before turning my attention back to the hostess.

But as I'm shifting my gaze, it lands on the shadow of a man in the corner, and all the air is sucked from my lungs. My heart rate increases, the heavy pounding all I can hear. He's huge, brooding in the corner, his muscles bulging from beneath armor plates that don't look like they belong anywhere near this century. I can't make out his features, but based on the set of his shoulders, the way he hovers in the corner, I'd say he's pissed about something.

Yet, what's even crazier is the overwhelming feeling that I've seen him before. And then it hits me.

Muscle man outside the doctor's office. Except, why the hell is he here? *Who are you? Why are you following me?* I start toward him, ready to demand the answers to both of those questions, but as soon as I do, Sullivan grabs my hand gently. I turn back to him, and he smiles while the hostess leads us away.

"Who's—" I start, but as I turn back toward the man, my voice breaks. He's gone, no sign of him anywhere, leading me to wonder if I hadn't just imagined him. And if I had—why? It's not like I have a taste for muscled, brooding men. The opposite, in fact, as they intimidate the hell out of me.

But twice now, I've seen him. Am I losing my damned mind on top of everything else? Has the heat of my body finally seeped into my brain like they'd been so worried about?

"Here ye' are," the hostess says with a bright smile as we take our seats at a table in the corner.

"Thank you," Sullivan says, fondly. The waitress nods to him then leaves us alone. "You okay?"

I nod, cheeks flushing with embarrassment. "I'm fine. I just…I thought I saw someone I might know."

His brows furrow. "All the way in Ireland? I thought you didn't have any friends here."

"I don't." But even as I speak the words, my gaze drifts to the now-empty corner. Sullivan starts chatting idly about dinner, and I force my attention off the man no longer in the corner and onto the one sitting before me.

All through dinner, though, I find myself glancing back at the corner, hoping for one last glimpse of him. Though, I imagine, one last glance may never be enough.

CHAPTER 3
EMBER

S ullivan and I step outside onto the brightly lit street; while he appears calm, wearing a smile stretched across his handsome face, my brain is going over the ticking time bomb that is my disease. It's a constant distraction, a consistent pull back into reality.

"Dinner was lovely," I say. "Thank you."

I'd tried to get away with just a bit of bread—I really did. But Sullivan had insisted I eat more, not letting up, and I hadn't had the heart to tell him why I couldn't shove my face full of delicious beer and stew.

For purely selfish reasons, of course. I could have been honest, but where would that lead? Sullivan would just be added to the long list of people who pity me, and I really, really don't have any inclination of adding to it.

"You're welcome. I'm glad you tried the stew. It's amazing, isn't it?"

"It is," I agree. The flavor had been fantastic. Almost worth the pain it will likely bring me.

"Shall we venture to Dublin City Centre?" he asks, curiously.

I shake my head and force a yawn. "Honestly, I'm exhausted. Jetlag and all. Think we can get a rain check for that?"

Arching his eyebrow, he studies me. "Are you okay? You're looking a bit pale." Reaching forward, he brushes a strand of my red hair out of my face.

Perfect. Ember, you idiot. "I'm fine. Just exhausted."

"Totally understandable. I'll walk you back to your hotel. We can always venture there tomorrow. That's if you're not just trying to get away from me because I was awful company." He winks at me and I smile, this one not forced, despite the gurgling in my stomach.

"Not horrible, at all. I really enjoyed myself." Sweat beads on my forehead, but I don't shed my light wrap because I don't want him to notice that I'm burning up. Just ahead, the hotel looms, and hope blossoms in my chest that we just might make it before I completely fall apart.

Though, if the heat keeps smothering me, I might just pass out before we reach the front door. "Do you have any siblings?" I ask, forcing my attention away from the fullness building in my stomach.

"I do. A brother. He's a *Garda Síochána*."

"Garda?"

"I believe they're called police officers in the States."

"Oh, okay. That's neat."

"It is. He hoped I would follow him, but I'd really rather not." Sullivan chuckles. "He lives a serious life, and I prefer to live my life one day at a time. You never know when a day will be your last."

If only you knew. "I think that's a great outlook."

"Yeah?"

"Why are you so surprised?"

"You seem like the planning type to me. Calendars, notebooks, and all that."

I smile as the first of many waves of nausea wash over me. Years of 'fake it till you make it' have conditioned me to hide it while I can, though. Won't be long before I'm unable to. "I used to be."

"What changed?"

"Let's just say I got a lesson in just how short life can be."

"I'm sorry to hear that. Lose a loved one?"

We reach the front door of the hotel, and I turn to

him. "No, just a close call. Thank you so much for dinner."

"You're welcome, Ember Hall." Leaning forward, he presses a light kiss to my sweaty cheek, though he doesn't draw back and note it. "I'll come fetch you tomorrow evening, then?"

"Sounds great, thanks."

"See you then."

I watch him walk away then turn back toward the hotel and make a mad dash to the elevators. I'm nearly there when the first wave of pain slams into me. I double over, my gut feeling as though someone drove a dagger into it.

Not that I've ever been stabbed, but it's the only description I can think of that might be close enough to the way I'm actually feeling. The lights above the elevator show it will be a bit before it reaches me. Tears burn my eyes as my stomach heaves, threatening to send its contents from dinner back up.

Finally, what feels like hours later, the elevator dings, and the doors open.

"Are you all right, lass?" An older man wearing a cap steps off with his wife on his arm.

"Fine, thanks. One too many beers; you know how it goes."

"That I do. Get some sleep, and don't discount the hair of the dog," he says with a wink as I rush past him and onto the elevator. I press the door close button over and over again, trying my damnedest to not puke all over the elevator.

One.

Two.

Three.

Another wave of pain slams into me, and I grip the bar alongside the back of the elevator cart to keep myself upright. Sweat slicks my body, making my hair wet and forcing the fabric of my dress to cling to me like a second skin.

The doors open, and I rush out, doubled over as I try to run to my room. I can't even bring myself to care if someone sees me, though the hall is empty as I dash down to my room. I fall to my knees in front, unable to stand any longer as my stomach heaves again. Bile burns my throat, but I force it back down as I unlock the door and crawl inside, straight to the bathroom.

I barely make it before everything in my stomach comes right back up and into the toilet bowl before me. It burns, and my body shakes. *Why did I let myself get talked into it? I knew better.* I throw up again, and I know this is just the start of what will probably last a few days.

Though, I suppose, if I die tomorrow, then at least I lived a little tonight. Isn't that what this trip was for? To live before I die?

His body gleams with sweat as he swings a monstrous blade. It glints beneath the blistering sun just before meeting its mark and tearing through the abdomen of another man.

His opponent falls, and blood soaks the ground. Then, the brutal man turns to me—and smiles.

"Are you well?"

"I am." My response is lacking all empathy for the dead and all shock over the murder. It makes no sense because inside—inside I'm screaming.

The man moves closer to me, and I am helpless to do anything but stare at his brutally handsome face. Not that I would run at his approach, even if I could.

There is something about him— He reaches up and cups my cheek, letting his rough thumb caress the skin just below my ear. "Nothing will harm you, Ember. Not so long as I breathe."

My own breath catches, and a tear slips from my eyes because I know he's wrong.

I'm already hurt, and there's nothing that anyone can do about it.

Breathing raggedly, I wake, completely naked on my bed. The air conditioner is set as cold as I can get it, and still, my body might as well be aflame. I can barely move; my muscles still ache from the two hours it took my stomach to realize there was nothing left to purge.

My dream plays on repeat. The brutal savage had taken the same form as the man I saw outside Dr. Alexander's office—the same one I saw tonight at dinner. Both of those things, combined with what I just dreamt, tell me that the man was not real.

He's little more than a figment of my dying mind. How sad is that? Not wanting to focus too much on the why's of the whole thing, I close my eyes and whimper.

Outside, cars pass by, and I focus on the sounds of them rather than the pain still lingering in my gut. The air in this room is stifling already, more so since I know I'll be trapped in here while my body recovers. Needing some fresh air while I can get it, I force myself to roll to my side since my stomach muscles are too sore to sit straight up.

Perched on the bedside table, the clock reads eleven-forty-seven. Because this is nothing new to me, I know I have maybe another hour before my stomach needs to empty again—even though there's nothing left in it. But it will still be like that, every hour on the hour, for the next two or three days.

Woohoo for predictability.

Taking advantage of the brief reprieve, I pull on

black leggings and a white tank-top before quickly braiding my hair to the side. Then, I grab my room key and wallet and head out into the hall to make my way down to the lobby.

I pass no one in the hall or elevator, most either still outside or having already turned in, and the quiet eases a bit of my anxiety. I may have the strength to make my way outside, but idle chatter is not anywhere close to being on my mind. It takes energy, and I have very little these days.

Offering the lady working the front desk a slight wave, I head out onto the street and suck in a deep breath. The night air surrounds me, the chill in it temporarily beating back the heat. The relief is, as I said, temporary though, and within minutes, I'm already sweating again as I set out for a walk. Sometimes, if whatever is wrong with me is feeling lenient, a walk can help alleviate some of the discomfort. It can also exacerbate it, though. A gamble—fifty-fifty at any given point.

But given my options are pain, or more pain, I'll take those odds.

As I walk, I offer smiles to passersby, keeping my eyes trained straight ahead so no one gets a good look at me and forces me into a hospital bed for fear I'll die on the sidewalk.

An older man with salt and pepper hair curling

from beneath a black cap turns onto the sidewalk and offers me a wave. "Too many pints there, lass?"

"Yes," I reply with a smile.

He nods. "Been there a time or two myself. Hair of the dog is what you need." He winks at me and continues on his way.

My head begins to pound, yet another wonderful side-effect from the increase of blood flow caused by any type of physical activity. Just ahead, an iron gate stands tall, drawing my attention. Huge trees flank either side of it, and as I move inside the lush green park, it feels as though I'm entering another world entirely.

A world consisting of me and the trees. No people, no lights, just the stars overhead. The farther I walk, the less debilitating the pain becomes, so I continue to wander. What is it they say of nature? It's rejuvenating, right? Isn't that why people pay thousands of dollars for mountain retreats?

Shit, I'd pay thousands of dollars for five minutes of feeling the way I do now.

The garden is magnificent and full of luscious topiary and bright flowers, and the only structure is an empty gazebo with a single dim light dangling from the pitched roof.

Turning my attention to the bordering trees, I take another idle turn, feeling more like myself than I have in years. The pain is gone, the sweat dry on my skin.

What is this place? I turn in a slow circle, expecting to see the city at my back, but there's nothing.

Nothing but more trees. *What the—how did I get here?* Shifting my attention forward, my gaze catches sight of a light shimmering just ahead. Focusing on it, I'm overwhelmed with a feeling of calm; of peace that I haven't experienced in far too long. So, I continue forward, curiosity pulling me closer and closer. *Has it always been there?*

Humming builds steadily in my ears, blocking out all other sounds until I can hear nothing else but the steady tune. The light hovers just in front of the trunk of a large tree. Which, if I were thinking logically, I would know makes absolutely no sense.

But I'm not thinking logically. Not anymore.

I reach out and touch it. The thing sparks beneath my fingertips, shooting a jolt straight through my arm. I cry out and try to withdraw my hand, but I'm unable to. Before I can open my mouth and call for help, or even try to get away, my vision swims, and my body overheats once more. The fire slams into me, an inferno in my veins.

The world begins to fade away, my vision blackening as I slip into the abyss of unconsciousness. But before I'm completely gone, a deep baritone breaks through the overwhelming humming.

A throaty voice mutters three words that send my already panicked heart racing. *"There you are."*

CHAPTER 4
EMBER

Warmth on my face has me easing my eyes open. I raise a hand and shield my face from the bright sun as I force myself to sit up. My stomach muscles ache as I move, sore and probably torn from all the vomiting I did last night.

Birds chirp around me, their happy, sweet songs filling me with confusion.

Where am I?

I try to get my bearings, to stand, but I'm met with weak legs, and I fall back to the ground. Ground that is made of plush grass and brightly colored flowers dotting the meadow I find myself sitting in.

"Well, this is new," I say aloud.

I've passed out in quite a few different places. But managing to stumble into a meadow and then pass out? Definitely a new development. I touch a hand to my aching head. Still, there are worse places to wake up.

A gutter being one of them—and I've been there, done that.

Surprisingly, though, my body doesn't feel as battered as it typically does after an attack. Normally, it's not just my abdominal muscles screaming in protest with each movement. And shouldn't I be throwing up again already? How long have I been passed out?

Taking a deep breath, I force myself to stand, stumbling over toward a tree to use it as a temporary crutch as I look for the path that will take me back to my hotel. I'll shower, sleep for two days, then hope-fully get this final vacation back on track.

"Hello?" I call out, not seeing a path anywhere. And I mean *anywhere*. The entire meadow is surrounded by thick trees and brush with no break in between. My heart flutters, and panic surges through me as I realize I have literally no clue where I am.

This is not Dublin City Centre, that's for damn sure. I may not know much about the country, but I did have a lot of time on the plane, and it was one of the places I cyberstalked before arriving. So if I'm not there, then how did I get here?

Shutting my eyes tightly, I try to focus on the last thing I remember.

A gazebo.

A bright light.

A voice.

My eyes snap open, and the scene I'm greeted with is a much different one than moments ago when I closed them. A thick, heavy fog inches toward me as clouds overhead block out the sun. I back up, pressing my back all the way against the tree as I scan the space for the gazebo.

A structure, I now see, is nowhere in sight.

"Hello?" Fresh fear pulsates through me now. "*Hello?*"

Get yourself together, Ember. Not wanting to close my eyes again, seeing as how the last time brought me to where I am now, I focus instead on the heavy fog pouring over the grass like controlled liquid. I take deep, steady breaths, focusing on what I can change right now.

Which is pretty much nothing, so that's a fantastic realization.

Lightning splits the sky, the bolt slamming into the ground a few yards away from me. I scream and force my way back, farther into the trees, now using my temporary crutch as a shield. The ground is scorched, the grass boasting a blackened circle now.

Thunder booms, and I jump just as a man roars overhead. Metal clashes, and someone grunts. A body slams into the ground, and I cover my mouth with a shaking hand, trying not to scream at the bloodied, broken corpse. Wide eyes stare directly at me; there's no life left in them.

Another battle cry and I try to move backward into the trees. Vines woven together behind me make it impossible though. I grip them and try to rip, to tear my way through the foliage, but it's useless; the things might as well be ropes for as pliable as they are.

Something slams into the ground behind me again. I don't want to turn around, don't want to see another broken body—but I also don't want to be caught off guard, so I turn, slowly, and have to cover my hand as I cry out.

A man stands in the clearing, hovering over another who glares up at him.

"You miserable bastard," the man on the ground sputters, spraying blood over the white armor of his attacker.

"You chose the wrong side, Paulson." He raises a leg and brings it down—slowly—onto the throat of the other man.

The man he called Paulson grips his ankle with both hands and tries—unsuccessfully—to shove him back. "You. Have. That. Backward."

Metal clashes above me—*how are they doing that? Is there a building up there I can't see?*—briefly pulling the attention of the man pinning

Paulson to the ground. "I truly am sorry you are meeting this end. But I must defend our world, and that includes defending the crown." In a blur of movement, he draws a blade and drives it down into the man's chest.

I swallow back a scream as I shut my eyes tightly and scramble back into the brush, trying to get as far as I can away from the man.

He killed him! Where the hell am *I?*

"Who's out there?" The man wipes his blade on the shirt of the now-dead Paulson, then looks out into the trees—almost right at me.

I hold my breath, focusing only on keeping as quiet as possible. The last thing I want is to meet my end by way of sword in a random-ass place I accidentally stumbled into.

After a moment, he turns away and jumps, disappearing from sight.

I gape at where he'd been standing.

Where in the actual hell am I? Am I dead? Is this some kind of purgatory? I don't—another body slams to the ground, this time followed by a dozen living ones. They land heavily, boots like thunder claps against the ground, blades raised as they fight.

In some scene straight out of a fantasy movie, they battle; swords clashing, eyes wide, expressions furious. The man from earlier is back on the ground, facing off with one wearing the same bright green leathers as the ones currently getting their asses kicked by men in white.

They fight, and I try to shield myself, not wanting to see anyone else die but also not wanting to be caught off guard. The last damn thing I want is to close my eyes, only to open them and have a sword in my face.

A man in green roars and rushes toward the man who killed Paulson. "In the name of the one true king! Long live Raff—"

He doesn't even hesitate as he spins his blade and rotates around, impaling his attacker. Grinning the entire time—sadistic bastard—he yanks his blade free and starts in on another man, then another, until the only ones who remain are men in white and the ground is littered with the dead bodies of the men wearing green leather.

"Well fought, men." The man in white puts his blade back into its holster—if that's what you call the thing that holds a sword—then turns to face his men, who all snap to attention like they do in cheesy military movies.

Only, where I might find it amusing if these men were acting, the dead men on the ground make it impossible to see anything but the horror. Where in the world am I? There's no way I'm still in Dublin... right? I'm pretty sure murder is outlawed here, and I would have known if there were some kind of war going on.

Both of those things lead me to wonder—am I actually dead?

Something cool presses against my wrist, and I glance down, stifling a scream as an immense red and black snake slithers out of the brush, wrapping itself around my arm. I try not to move now, for fear I'll scare it and it'll sink its fangs into me.

But it seems I'm either facing the blades or the snake.

I'm choosing the snake.

"Head back to the castle, and take pride in knowing you stopped yet another uprising of rebels!"

Loud cheering breaks out amongst the men, and the snake wraps even more tightly around my wrist. I stifle a sob. *A little longer, Ember. You got this.*

Inner pep talk aside, my heart is hammering so loudly against my ribs I'm sure it's going to lead the killers right to me.

As if on cue, the leader turns toward me, eyes narrowing as he studies the trees. It seems luck may be on my side, though, because he turns away a moment later and jumps into the air again with the other men following him.

I wait a breath of a moment then slowly try to remove my wrist from the snake. It clings to me, and I whimper, not wanting to move but also desperately needing to get away from the situation I'm in now.

Death by snake? No freaking thank you.

It raises its head toward me, looking at me with beady eyes as it opens its mouth, showing two huge, barbed fangs. Do snakes have barbed fangs? Why the hell does it have barbed fangs?

Unable to hold it in any longer, I scream, the shrill sound sending birds retreating up into the sky from the trees around me.

In a blur of movement, a hand reaches down and grabs the snake by the throat, flinging it back into the trees and pulling me up at the same time. My back slams into a tree trunk, and I find myself staring up into the impossibly golden eyes of the man who murdered another by the name of Paulson.

"Well, well, well," he says softly, releasing me and stepping back so I can get my bearings. "What have we here?"

"PLEASE, LET ME GO." I SQUIRM AGAINST HIS HOLD as he drags me up marble steps and into a foyer so crisp I can see my reflection. And what a reflection it is. Hair wild, one strap of my tank top torn, I look like I spent more than an hour in the woods.

I don't even know why I'm fighting, to be honest.

It's not like this is reality. We *flew* here. As in, the guy stretched two huge, massive wings and flew us here like he's some kind of man-bird. I'd say Angel if he weren't a murderer.

Angels aren't evil, and I watched this man slaughter a handful of men less than ten minutes ago.

"You aren't going anywhere, pet. The king will be the one who decides what to do with you." His accent is thick, Irish, which only adds to the illusion that I'm probably still passed out in my hotel bed.

The only reason I have to doubt that particular explanation, though, is the pain radiating through my arm from where his large hand wraps around it. But I'm trying my damnedest to not pay any attention to that development.

His boots pad softly on the floor as he carries me down a corridor then shoves open two gigantic golden doors and tosses me inside. My knees hit the floor with a slam, causing pain to shoot up into my thighs. I try to stand but stumble down again, my body still sore from my traipse in the woods and the sickness that I honestly believed would be what killed me.

Now, I'm not so sure—present company considered.

"What is this?"

I glance up as a new man speaks. My red hair blocks part of my view as I appraise the new member of what is quickly turning into the strangest nightmare

I've ever had. His long, golden hair falls down his back, and a golden crown encircles his head. Emeralds are embedded in the ridged gold that matches the color of his eyes.

I wish I could laugh, but the terrifying way he's watching me has me swallowing hard and looking back down.

"I found it lurking in the woods."

It?

"Where?"

"Near Mossy River. It was hiding just out of view, tucked back into some trees with a serpent wrapped around its wrist."

A woman, who I didn't notice until now, clears her throat and steps up to the king's side. Her hair is dark—nearly black—her nose crooked, as though it's been broken more than a few times. She whispers something into his ear, and his gaze flies back to my face.

"Come here," he orders me, but I don't move.

"The king gave you an order, thing," the man kicks my side, and I wince, biting down on a sob.

"You will not touch her, again," the king orders, his voice stern.

"Yes, Your Majesty."

The king's golden eyes shift back to mine. "Come here, woman. You will suffer no more at his hand."

Nothing about yours, though. Still, not seeing

much of a choice given—and I really, really do not want to get kicked again—I stagger to my feet and cross the distance to him. To my dismay, he stands, coming down the steps to greet me at the bottom. Slender fingers grip my chin, and he tilts my face up. His eyes are kinder now, and he holds my face gently.

I don't look away. If I'm going to meet death, it will be head-on. After all, I'm already expecting it to come for me, aren't I?

"You are exquisite," he whispers, voice calm. Releasing my chin, he brushes strands of my thick hair from my face.

"Who are you?" I manage, my voice barely audible.

He smiles softly. "I am Taranus. King of Faerie. And I have been waiting for you."

CHAPTER 5
EMBER

I can't help myself. I snort, completely unable to hide the humor at my imagination. Faerie? Seriously? How sick am I right now? Or, a better explanation, maybe I hit my head on the edge of the toilet during one of my heaves and am currently passed out on the floor. Still, I feel like my imagination could have come up with a better name than Tar-anus.

I snort again, earning a glare from the guard.

Brow furrowed, the "king" watches me with the intensity of a hawk. "Why are you amused?"

For one, your name ends with anus. "You just told me that you're the King of Faerie. And since you're standing in front of me, that means you want me to believe that I am in Faerie. As in, the mythical land from old fairy tales and Celtic mythology." I shake my head. "I must have really hit my head when I fell."

Taranus turns away from me to glance back at the woman. She nods, smiling softly before crossing the floor toward us. Her white gown brushes against the floor, making it appear as though she simply glides over the marble.

"The woman has suffered from the elements," she says, softly. "There's no telling how long she was outdoors. Perhaps she could use a meal and a soft bed to rest in."

Taranus's expression softens. "Yes, we will see that you are fed, bathed, and well-rested. Come." He turns to the guard. "Conary, see to it that our guest has fresh clothing, and have a bath drawn for her."

"Yes, Your Majesty." He bows his head and disappears right in front of my eyes.

"What the—where did he go?"

At my obvious surprise, Taranus chuckles. "He will see to it that you have fresh linen and a warm bath. Come, my dear, we have much to discuss." He tucks my arm through his and guides me back down the corridor as the woman follows behind us, gliding soundlessly across the floor.

"Okay, but where did he go? How did he vanish like that?"

The "king" evades my question. "You are not from here, are you?"

I snort. "Understatement of the year."

"Excuse me?"

Clearing my throat, I nod. At this point, I'm just curious how much more my imagination can come up with. Maybe I should switch from ghostwriter for hire to full-time novelist. "No, I'm not from here."

"My advisor tells me that you are human."

How handy that she would just know that. Cheap writing, imagination, cheap writing. "That is correct."

"Where do you come from? I've never visited, but I'm fascinated with the worlds beyond this realm."

I bet you are. "I'm originally from Austin, Texas. It's in the United States." I humor him, studying my surroundings as we move through the castle. "But I recently took a trip to Ireland."

"Ireland. I've heard of that place. It is the closest gateway to ours."

Yet another cheap writing job. "It must be since that's where I was before I ended up here."

"And how did you find yourself here, I wonder?"

"Apparently, it's my punishment for taking a midnight stroll."

"Punishment. You believe this place to be a punishment for your indiscretions?"

"And why wouldn't she after the way she was treated upon arrival?" The woman's soft voice carries toward us with authority and power.

"Yeah. Conary—or whatever his name is—was a real asshole."

The king stops walking, gaping at me with complete surprise. Eyes wide, mouth slack, it's almost amusing. And when he throws his head back and laughs, the velvety sound puts me even further on edge. "Asshole. I truly enjoy that word. Come, let me show you to your room." He takes my hand and guides me up the stairs.

The other reason I'm pretty damn positive this is a dream? My body doesn't hurt. Well, not in the way I'm used to. Where the bastard kicked me still stings. But that's not all. For the first time in half a decade, my temperature feels regulated—though I won't know that for sure without a thermometer—and my stomach is actually growling with the force of my hunger.

It's *growling*. That fact alone makes me smile. Maybe living in my dream world is not such a bad thing. It's been years since I was actually hungry. Anytime I eat, it's because I have to force myself to choke down whatever bland food I have in my apartment at the time.

"You said you were waiting for me? Care to elaborate?"

"Ahh, yes. A prophecy was delivered recently; speaks of a fiery woman who will come from another world and will finalize my seat on the throne."

"So it's a prophecy about you?"

He chuckles, "Yes. I believe it is about me."

"And you believe I am that woman?" *Interesting plot twist, imagination.*

"How can you not be? Your fiery hair, fierce eyes, and mode of arrival all speak to that truth."

Fierce eyes, huh? "What do you mean she will finalize your seat on the throne?"

"It is believed that she is the missing piece, the one true queen who will help to unite the realm under the current hostile conditions. I believe that she is to be feared; that none will risk crossing her."

I snort. "I think you have the wrong person," I reply, dryly. "I've never scared anyone in my entire life. Unless, of course, you count the orphanage director and the plastic snake I snuck into her bed."

"Orphanage director?" he asks curiously.

"I never knew my family."

He stops walking and turns to me. "You don't have a family?" Brow furrowed, the guy looks genuinely distressed.

"I'm sure I have one somewhere, but they didn't need or want me." The pain is fresh, despite me being in my twenties. It took me a long time to validate myself—to see that I was worthy of affection despite being abandoned as an infant.

I never knew my family, never knew of them, and after one failed adoption following another, I stopped trying to fit in. Stopped trying to be what I thought the families wanted.

"That is…upsetting. How alone you must have been." Reaching forward, he trails a slender finger over my cheek. The contact is cold, and not at all comforting as I'm sure he'd hoped it would be. "Family is so very important. I wouldn't be where I am without mine."

Clearing my throat, I fight the urge to shove his hand away. "I managed."

Taranus smiles, showing off perfectly straight, white teeth. "Of course, you did. I could sense your strength—your spark—the moment Conary brought you inside the castle walls."

We resume walking, taking the stairs slowly as if we have all the time in the world. "Have you been king long?"

"No. The world was in a great war that lasted human centuries. There were those who believed they were worthy of the throne, and it took me quite some time to claim my rightful spot."

"What made you worthy?" The words are out of my mouth, slipping right past my already fraying filter before I can stop them. "I'm sorry, that came out rude."

"A valid inquiry, my dear." Taranus chuckles. "I am worthy because I was born to rule this realm and all those who live in it. None can maintain the peace that I can." After reaching the top of the stairway, we head down a long hall, stopping just before a large, golden door.

I'm not super short at five foot eight, but this thing towers over me. Taller by at least five feet. Taranus's hand comes to rest on my shoulder, gripping me lightly. "We will speak of all things, I assure you. But for now, enjoy the food we brought up for you, soak in the bath, and rest. I will come retrieve you prior to dinner."

We couldn't have been walking for more than five minutes, so when I shove open the door and am greeted with a warm, welcoming bedroom with a tray of what smells like freshly roasted meat, still-warm bread, and cheese, I can't help but stand in the doorway and gape.

Then, I remember how the man literally disappeared in front of my face and that this is a dream, so *of course*, the room is ready for me. I step inside and close the door behind me, immediately taking a moment to drink in the plush space.

A huge window opens to the outside, letting in a steady breeze that sends the curtains floating away from it. The large bed is covered in a beautiful green comforter with golden leaves adorning it. But it's the food that really draws my attention. Or, rather, my body's reaction.

My stomach growls again, so I step closer and

take a seat in the high-backed chair directly in front of the small table boasting the tray. It's hard to describe how much I've missed food over the last few years. Eventually, after the first couple of times it sent me spiraling into the toilet, I convinced myself that I stopped craving it.

But the truth is I never did.

Carefully lifting a piece of bread, I bring it to my lips and nibble off a small taste. My stomach doesn't clench in response, so I take another bite and then another. The fresh-baked bread eases some of my hunger.

Setting it to the side, I use a fork to bring some meat to my mouth. Flavor explodes on my tongue, the smoky deliciousness so much more than I've had in the last half-decade. If this is a dream, kudos to my freaking imagination because this is delicious.

For the first time since I got my diagnosis, I stuff my face without fear of what will happen afterward. Then, I move into the adjoining bathroom and strip down, eyeing the copper tub full of steaming water. Fresh flower petals float atop the water, the shades of pink, yellow, and blue bringing a smile to my face.

Best. Dream. Ever.

The water is hot against my skin, almost bordering on too hot—but I couldn't be more thrilled. See, in addition to losing my love for food, I've also become a habitual cold shower taker. When your body runs at a whopping hundred and four degrees on average, extra heat just doesn't sound appealing.

The fragrant water fills my lungs, and I breathe deeply, relaxing my muscles with every deep breath I take. Slipping down further into the water, I take one last deep breath then sink all the way down.

My surroundings shift.

Gone is the floral scent, the hot water. Opening my eyes, I try to scream but slap a hand over my mouth to prevent myself from sucking in water. The depths are inconceivable with nothing but darkness below me.

The light above is too far for me to reach out and touch, but I kick my feet anyway, struggling to get to the surface. A hand grips my ankle, and I kick, frantically making my mad dash to the surface as the fingers tighten on me.

Looking down, I meet the sad eyes of the same man I saw in the restaurant. He stares up at me, and I notice a huge scar running along the right side of his face. Suddenly, breathing is of little necessity—the burning in my lungs ceasing completely as the water around us stills and the stranger becomes my full focus.

Something about him— He releases me and kicks his feet, putting him face to face with me. I reach out, the water slowing my movements, and gently graze a finger over the side of his face. His eyes flutter closed, and he leans into my touch as though it's been forever since he was touched. Who are you? *I long to ask him. But while I may not need to breathe, talking underwater is out of the question.*

His eyes widen and he reaches out, shoving me backward as he's ripped away, disappearing into the darkness.

I come up from the water, gasping for breath as it sloshes around me, sending flower petals and waves of liquid onto the pristine floor. *What in the actual nightmare was that?*

"Wasn't real, Ember." But my self-reassurance does little to steady my thundering heart. His pain, I'd seen it reflected in his golden eyes. So much agony, so much fear, it felt so *real*. All of this feels real. This place, the food, this freaking bathwater. I mean, I'm imaginative—I have to be with my job—but this is next-level.

Pulling my knees up to my chest, I wrap both arms around them and rest my cheek on top. "None of this is real," I whisper. "This place, that man. All products of an exhausted, dying mind."

Right?

CHAPTER 6
EMBER

I'm just climbing out of the tub when the door to my room opens slowly.

"Hey!" Squealing, I stumble back and fall right back toward the water. Before I can break the surface, though, a woman rushes forward to wrap her dainty hands around my wrists and yank me back to my feet, holding on until I'm steady.

Soft hazel eyes are wide in a youthful face, completely unmarred by life. Near-white hair is braided around her head like a crown then pulled back at the nape of her neck. Appearance-wise, she looks like she might only be in her teens.

"I'm so sorry I startled you, mistress." The woman releases me and bows her head.

It's then I realize I'm standing here in all my sickly, nude glory. Quickly, I wrap both arms around my small breasts, hoping to at least shield some of my embarrassment. I'm not modest by any means, but when you look one gust of wind away from being blown over, you tend to want to hide as often as you can. "What are you doing in here?"

Do the characters in my imagination have any manners?

"I came to help you prepare for dinner."

"Dinner."

"Yes, mistress."

Is it already dinnertime? When—

"You've been up here for nearly three hours, mistress." The woman's dainty voice is barely above a whisper, her tone sharp.

"Three hours?" I gape at her. "That's not possible. The water is still…" I trail off and reach in to touch it. "Yeah, it's still hot. There's no way I've been up here for that long." *Cheap storytelling once again, imagination.*

"The tub is spelled to remain hot until drained, mistress," she says, softly. "I am here to help you dress and to escort you down to the dining hall."

Spelled? I'm not sure why I'm surprised. I've seen people killed, fall from the sky, and fly in the matter of the last few hours. "Who are you?"

She curtsies, expression strained. "I'm your hand-maiden, mistress. My name is Flora."

"Flora?"

"Yes, mistress." She bows her head, gaze meeting the marble floor.

"And you're going to dress me?"

"Yes, mistress. I assure you, your virtue is safe with me."

I snort. After years of being poked, prodded, and having to have every inch of my body—inside and out—examined by countless doctors, I have literally no dignity left in that area. Other than my embarrassment over the skin and bones left by the half-decade of only eating enough to keep me from starving to death. "As much as I appreciate your help, I don't actually have anything other than my leggings—" Slowly, I turn in a circle, searching for the clothes I know I discarded. "Where are my clothes?"

"They have been disposed of, mistress. The king was horrified that you'd be forced to exist in such little clothing. He wanted them destroyed and has given me permission to fill your wardrobe with only the finest garments."

I arch an eyebrow and study the woman. "He destroyed my clothes?" Frustration heats my cheeks before I remember that none of this is happening.

"Yes, mistress."

"Please stop calling me mistress. My name is Ember."

"You wish for me to call you by your name?" The woman looks genuinely pained by my request.

"Yes. Ember."

She studies me a moment longer then finally nods. "Very well, Ember. I will refer to you by name within your chambers, but the moment we leave this room, I will return to calling you mistress. I will not risk punishment from the king should I not follow his law."

"Wait. Seriously? Why?"

"I am yours to command. I do not get to be on a first-name basis with you."

"That's total garbage. You call me Ember whenever you want, and if the king has an issue with it, he can take it up with me." *Or maybe my imagination will get the hint, and we can move on.*

The woman's mouth tightens as though she's trying to fight off a smile. Her eyes, though, betray pain. Something I recognize because I've seen it in my own. "Yes, Ember."

"Great. Now that that's taken care of, what am I going to wear?"

"Right this way."

She leads me over to the bed, which is now completely covered in clothing.

"How did you do all this so quietly?"

"I did not wish to disturb you." She moves closer and runs a hand over a hunter green dress boasting gold embroidered inlays on the skirt.

"It's all gorgeous."

"Only the finest," she replies.

"I'm pretty sure this is all a figment of my imagination, but it's an impressive one."

"You do not know much about fae, do you?" Her golden gaze studies me with a curiosity that nearly pushes aside her pain. *Nearly.*

"No. Until this morning, I was unaware you even existed."

Her brows draw together.

"That surprises you?" I question.

"To be honest, yes. Supernaturals were outed in your world, according to..." She trails off, and the pain returns. "According to an old friend."

"I've heard plenty about the supposed outing of vampires, witches, and werewolves."

"But you don't believe it?"

"I didn't." My admission only puts another notch in the 'maybe this is real' column. What if the creatures being plastered all over the news *are* real? Then is it really so far-fetched that this faction exists, too?

"Well, all fae have different abilities," she explains. "My bloodline can conjure." In demonstration, she snaps her fingers, and a tray of fruit appears on the bed. Plump grapes still on thick green vines adorn a golden tray. "Others can make plants grow, heal the sick. Some are warriors, others, teachers."

"But all of you can fly?"

Flora nods moments before her expression darkens. "Though some have had their wings clipped. It removes our ability to dematerialize or fly."

I gape at her. "What do you mean they've 'had their wings clipped?' That's a thing?" *Sick, twisted imagination for the win.*

"It's a punishment, a way of ensuring your help doesn't fly off to another realm."

I'm completely helpless to tear my eyes away from her. I can't even bother to care about my sickly frame still unclothed and standing in the middle of the room that apparently anyone can pop into. Mutilation? My stomach churns, and for the first time in years, it has nothing to do with what I ate or didn't eat. "That's horrible."

"It is," she agrees, sadly. "But it's our custom."

"Your custom sucks ass." Covering my mouth, I shake my head. "I'm sorry. My potty mouth is something I'm working on."

Flora chokes on a laugh. "I assure you, Ember, I've heard much, much worse in my years."

"In your years?" Now it's my turn to laugh. "How old are you? Fifteen?"

Flora beams at me. She's a ray of sunshine, and I immediately realize that I completely adore this girl. Imaginary or not, it's so nice to talk to someone who's not pitying me. "You believe me to be fifteen years old?"

"Maybe sixteen."

"I'm nine hundred and thirty-seven this fall," she says.

"I'm sorry." I close my eyes then open them again. "You're *how* old?"

"Nine hundred and thirty-seven."

"You're nine hundred and thirty-seven," I repeat. "As in, over nine centuries old?"

Flora nods. "We are immortal, my kind."

"So, let me get this straight." I begin to pace. "I'm in Faerie, which is a world separate from my world. Faerie is full of fae—did I say that right?" She nods, so I continue. "And fae are not only immortal but have different types of magic, and most of them can fly."

"All correct."

"I must be dead."

Her brow furrows. "Dead? Why would you think you're dead?"

"Because it's only a matter of time," I whisper.

"A matter of time? I'm afraid I don't understand." Flora's face twists in confusion.

"It doesn't matter. We're all going to die someday, right? Well, maybe not you. But I will."

"Not if the king chooses to make you a fae," she says.

"He can make me a fae?"

"If he chooses you for his bride, he has the power to do so."

"Woah, woah, woah." I throw up both hands and back away. "Bride? No one said anything about getting married."

Flora smiles and retrieves a white chemise from the bed. Then, she walks over to me and starts to lift it over my head, but I snatch it out of her hand before she can.

"I can do it."

"I don't mind. It is my duty."

"Not with me, it's not." I slip it on, the silky fabric smooth against my skin. It chills me—a welcome sensation given my typical hot nature. "So, tell me more about this bride business. He wants to marry me?"

"He'll try to court you first," she explains, hands folded in front of her. "Then, if he declares you a good fit for queen, he will propose a deal for you. After all, you can't very well lead at his side if you're human."

"Obviously." I snort, not failing to see the irony in my current situation. I went to Ireland because of my mortality. And now, I've apparently fallen into a rabbit hole where I may be offered immortality.

"Are you okay, Ember? You're looking a little pale."

"I'm fine. I'm pretty sure this is all just some crazy dream, anyway."

Flora smiles softly then turns her back a moment

to retrieve the beautiful hunter-green gown. I am unable to tear my eyes away as she carries it over to me and holds it up, eyeing it against my skin. "Just as I thought. Perfect for your tone. May I help you?"

"Sure."

She unlaces the back then raises it as I duck slightly, and she drops it over the top of my head. The fabric is soft, cooling, just as the chemise was. Only, unlike the undergarment, it cascades down to the floor, pooling at my feet. She tightens the laces, and it hugs my body, giving me the appearance of a woman with a full figure.

For the first time in five years, I actually *feel* like a woman.

"Oh my gosh." I stare at myself in the full-length mirror across from me as she attaches a molded, golden plate over my shoulder and links it to the dress with straps. "I look like a warrior princess."

"No, Ember, you look like a warrior queen." Flora winks at me then comes to stand beside me so I can see her reflection in the mirror. "You are much kinder than I thought you would be," she admits.

"What? How did you think I would be?"

"The king is—"

The door opens, interrupting her, and the woman I saw earlier with the king steps in. Lips pursed together, she studies Flora with a scowl. I glance over and see that my new friend has dropped her gaze to the floor.

"Leave us, handmaiden."

"Yes, ma'am." She curtseys.

"Bye, Flora!" I call after her. She smiles softly before disappearing into the hall.

"We didn't have a chance to meet properly earlier," the woman says as she moves farther into the room. "I am Lloren. Advisor to the king." As she turns her sharp gaze on me, I get the sudden urge to shrink down as though to not be seen as a threat.

Thank you, Animal Planet, for that visual.

"Ember."

She purses pale lips. "As the king mentioned, we've been awaiting your arrival."

"And why is that, I wonder? Because he expects to marry me?"

The woman's eyes narrow. "I would beg of you to not believe everything you hear from the staff. They have their own opinions, but they are opinions of the uneducated."

"That's harsh." *I don't like or trust you one bit.*

"It is our way." She smiles, but it looks forced; unnatural on her face.

"I'm dressed and ready to go," I say, eager to get out of her presence and somewhere less private. The woman makes my skin crawl.

"You will change your gown. White is the color of the king."

I take note of her pristine snowy dress, the way there's not a single stain on the fabric. Heck, I once wore a white t-shirt to a barbeque and ended up with a brown sauce stain the size of a softball within the first ten minutes. "I will not change. As it happens, I like this dress and don't appreciate being told what I can and can't wear."

There's that smile again. "You will do as you're told, Ember. Because it is our custom, and you are a guest in our world now."

"A guest that can leave?"

With a chuckle, she turns to leave. "You don't wish to change tonight. Fine, but after tonight, you will no longer wear that rebel color in our presence. Come with me. I shall show you the way to dinner."

Rebel color. I don't miss her non-answer or the chill that shoots up my spine as I start to follow her. *But none of this is real, right?* Out of curiosity, and to put my mind at ease, I reach over and pinch my arm. Pain shoots through my nerves, and I wince.

But it's no match for the panic that steadily begins to build upon itself in my gut, settling in deep like boulders in a lake. When supernaturals were supposedly outed last year, I'd dismissed it. I mean, come on. Vampires, were-wolves, witches? Those belong in stories, not reality.

And let's be honest, I had much bigger things to worry about than what is or isn't lurking in the dark.

However, for the first time, I find myself wondering if maybe, just maybe, this isn't some dream. And if it's not, just how much danger am I in?

CHAPTER 7
EMBER

Somehow, I have to get through dinner without losing my mind. Obsessing over how much danger I might be in won't help with that, so instead, I try to focus on my surroundings. At least, then I might learn enough to figure out what to do next.

A feat much easier said than done.

Since I'm not much of a chef—being able to make a mean box of Mac-N-Cheese doesn't count—I don't know exactly how long it typically takes to prepare a feast. But seeing the spread covering the twelve-seater table before me, I can imagine his employees have been working the majority of the day. Golden flatware flanks a pristine white porcelain plate with a cloth napkin of the same color folded on top of it.

Unfortunately, none of this tells me how to get out

of here, though. Or if what's outside these walls is more dangerous than being trapped within...

The moment we approach the table, the king stands. His blond hair has been tied back at the nape of his neck, and his golden eyes practically light up when he sees me. "My dear, you look lovely."

"Thank you. I heard I should have worn white, though." I glance back at Lloren, whose tight smile makes me want to shrink away.

"One night is no trouble," he explains with a brief glance at his advisor. "Come, sit." He gestures to the chair to the right of his seat at the head of the table. After a man wearing a white shirt and matching pants pulls it out, I slide onto the wooden seat.

Manners I only have thanks to old movies remind me that I need to put my napkin into my lap. So I do that then stare down at the two different forks, trying desperately to remember which one I need for salad and which is for the main course.

"Did you have a nice rest?" he asks, pulling my attention from the fork debacle.

"I did, thank you. Flora is very kind."

His brows draw together. "Flora?"

"Her handmaiden," Lloren interjects.

"She's a sweet woman," I tell them.

"Ahh, yes. I have known her for quite some time." After glancing over my head, he nods, and a man appears with water for my glass. "Please, fill your plate, Ember. Enjoy your meal."

"I—" I stare out at the food, prepared to explain that I can only handle a few small bites, when my stomach growls loudly. My cheeks flush in embarrassment, but Taranus only looks pleased by my obvious appreciation for the food in front of us.

"Eat, my dear. Enjoy yourself. I assure you, there is plenty."

Not needing to be told a third time, I lift my plate and start piling food onto the top of the porcelain. Meat, cheese, bread, broccoli, and some carrots round out the largest meal I have ever eaten.

As soon as I set my plate down in front of me, the king and Lloren fill their own plates, though, admittedly, they take much less than I did.

Enamored by the idea that I may not have an adverse reaction to the food, I cautiously take my first bite. The flavor of the meat permeates my mouth, the garlicky taste one of the most amazing things I've ever tasted.

I follow it up with carrots, my favorite vegetable, then move to the bread. No matter how much I eat, how full I feel, my stomach does not cramp. My body does not heat, and the lack of symptoms for my disease leads me to believe that perhaps this really is a dream.

That, or I'm already dead.

The door bursts open, and Conary stalks in, his boots hitting the ground with heavy thuds.

"What is the meaning of this interruption?" Lloren gasps as she jumps to her feet. The king stays silent, and his eyes harden when he sees the man Conary is dragging in beside him. A bloodied face is barely recognizable, but the green leathers are identical to those of the men from the clearing this morning.

The same color as my dress.

"We found this one lurking near the queen's chambers," Conary growls as he tosses him to the ground.

The man hits the marble with a thud, and he looks up at me. The moment my gaze locks with his golden one, his eyes widen. "Can it be?" he whispers. "You are her."

Before I can ask what he means, Conary kicks him in the back, and he falls forward with a whimper, smearing his blood over the white marble floor.

"Hey!" I yell as I jump to my feet and rush toward him. I fall to my knees beside the man. No one makes a move to stop me as I try to pull him up.

The king stands now, slowly. "You say you found him near the queen's chambers?"

"I did."

"And what was he doing?"

"Peering in the window."

The king nods and walks around the table to the

man. In defense of him, I attempt to pull him behind me. With my slight frame and his much more muscled one, though, it's useless.

"Why were you looking for a queen, I wonder? This realm has had no queen for quite some time."

"You must find him," the man chokes out, his eyes on me. "Find Raff—"

Lloren grabs my arm and rips me back. "Hey! Let me go!"

"You know nothing of our customs. That man was looking to harm you."

"No."

The man forces a smile. "Find him," he whispers, moments before Conary grips him by the hair and yanks his head up, pressing a blade I hadn't even seen before to his throat.

"What the hell are you doing?" I try to rip my arm from Lloren's grasp, but it's no use. "Let me go! He's a person!" I attempt to free myself again, but when I look at her hand on my arm, I'm taken aback by the colorful mist along her fingers. Is that magic?

"He's a dirty rebel," Conary spits back.

"Why are you here?" the king asks again, his voice level and eerily calm.

The man doesn't speak.

"Just tell him!" I plead. "Whatever it is, it's not worth your life!"

His golden eyes meet mine, and a soft smile plays at his lips. "I cannot, Your Majesty. Because it is."

"You call a complete stranger Your Majesty, but not your own king?" Taranus clicks his tongue.

"She is of the prophecy," the man replies. "But you are no king."

Blood spills from his throat, pouring onto the floor as a deafening scream fills my ears. It's not until I clasp a hand over my mouth that I realize it was my own. Taranus moved so fast, so precisely, that I hadn't even seen the blade in his hand until now as he wipes it clean on the leathers of the dead man.

"What…why?" I choke out, feeling my stomach churning now, though it has nothing to do with my disease. "You killed him!"

"He's a rebel who would have killed you."

I may be new to whatever world this is, but, dream or not, I saw nothing but kindness in that man's eyes, and I know, without a doubt, that he would never have hurt me. "He didn't do anything," I choke out. "He was helpless!" Hot tears stream down my cheeks.

"This is the way of our people, Ember," Taranus says calmly as he takes his seat. "Please, let us continue eating. They will clean this up."

Lloren takes her seat again, but I'm rooted to the spot as those who served us rush in with tears in their eyes as they clean the dead man from the floor. A woman sniffles.

"Are you not pleased there's another dead rebel?" Conary snaps at her.

"Yes, of course. I merely wish he hadn't ruined dinner." She coughs to mask a cry, and I ball both hands into fists.

"I'm no longer hungry," I growl. "I think I'll just go to sleep." *So I can wake up and be free of this disturbing nightmare.*

"You will go nowhere until the king releases you." Conary steps up behind me, blocking my exit.

I turn, meeting his gaze head-on as a wave of nausea that has nothing to do with my disease hits me. "Unless you want to wipe vomit off your uniform, you'll get the hell out of my way."

"Let her go. She needs time to come around to our way of life. I imagine she's used to much—how do I say this—softer methods of justice," Taranus smiles knowingly at me, and I swallow down bile.

Where I'd once seen a handsome man, now I only see a monster—a murderer. He said the man meant to kill me.

But from where I'm standing? He's the threat.

With a glare, I shove past Conary and rush out into the hall. There's no one around, but I know I need to find Flora. If anyone can get me out of here, it's her. Maybe we can leave together.

Even if this is a dream, I want to spend no more time within these walls.

Gathering the skirt of my dress, I rush forward, and the soles of my leather shoes barely make a sound as I put as much distance between me and the murdering king as possible. I never cared for horror movies.

Too much blood—and honestly? Life is hard enough without adding that type of entertainment. While my friends were binge-watching bloody TV shows, I was watching re-runs of Scrubs or Cougar Town.

So, how the hell this got into my head, I'll never know. What I do know, though, is that the more time I spend here, the more I'm starting to doubt I'm dreaming at all.

Taking the corner at a run, I'm not prepared for the stairwell, and by the time I hit it, it's too late to stop. My feet fly out from underneath me, and I tumble down into the dark. The tunnel whirls around me, and my elbows slam into the ground every time I try to stop myself.

Pain radiates through my body, but still, I don't scream. My head slams into something hard, and my body stills, the fall finally over. A shadow moves in the corner of my eyes, but before I can fully understand what it is I'm seeing, everything fades to black.

CHAPTER 8
EMBER

"Woman, wake up."

A gruff voice whispering loudly pulls me from whatever unconscious hell I'd been plunged into. "What…?" Pain in my head is the only evidence I have that I'm alive, and when I finally manage to open my eyes and see stone surrounding me, I realize I'm still stuck in this damned murderous world.

All hope I've been imagining everything dissipates. I'm far too logical to think I'm still dreaming—no matter how unrealistic all of this seems.

"Sit easy," the voice orders, a thick accent making it a bit difficult to fully comprehend his order.

I do as he says, though, sitting slowly enough that my head only spins a little. Then, I study wherever it is I am. Large grey stones make up the walls, ceiling, and floor of this room. The walls are lined with torches every few feet, their fire releasing multi-color sparks that allude to an unnatural flame.

Of course, it wouldn't be natural.

Not even the fire here is normal.

Pressing a finger to my temple, I pull it back, not surprised at all to see red coloring the tip. Then, I see the stairs. "No damned wonder I have a headache." How did I miss them? Murder does distract, I suppose. Even as I think it, I want to scream. To cry. To rage about the horror I just witnessed upstairs.

"Who are y—" I turn and come face-to-face with the man I saw outside the doctor's office back in Texas. The same man I locked eyes with at the restaurant. His hair is cut so short it's to the scalp. Haunted golden eyes stare back at me with the same awe I imagine are reflected in my own. A scar runs over his right eye, making him look more warrior than man.

My gaze drops down to a bare chest marred with crusted blood, scars, and fresh wounds. He's barely clothed—only wearing a pair of ripped pants. And, as I focus on the whole picture and not just him, I realize he's trapped behind bars.

He opens his mouth to speak but stops as heavy footsteps thunder overhead. "Hide," he whispers loudly.

I obey. Why? Who the hell knows? But at least this monster is behind bars.

Crawling on my hands and knees, I scramble around a corner and into another cell where I remain behind stones I hope will shield me from view. Heart in my throat, I force myself to only take shallow, quick breaths.

"Rafferty, you're looking well these days."

Rafferty. "Find Raffe—" A message delivered on the lips of a now-dead man. But why?

"Feeling great, too," Rafferty retorts.

"Tell me, old friend, you have any visitors down here recently?"

"I haven't seen your mother down here recently, so, no."

A low growl emits from one of the newcomers. "Watch your tongue." From the voice, I can tell it's not Conary, at least, but based on the responses, I cannot imagine these men are much better.

"Or what?"

"I'll cut it out."

Tears stream down my cheeks, and I clamp a hand over my mouth.

Rafferty, however, doesn't sound the least bit worried. "You'll excuse me if I'm not overly concerned. I am however curious as to who you lost?"

A man chuckles. "That woman you were looking for before Taranus beat you? We found her."

Stiffening, I try to focus on the words. "Oh?" Rafferty questions, his response strained.

"Taranus is going to marry her," he replies.

"And just how does she feel about that?"

"Who gives a shit? She gets no choice in the matter."

"Seems like she should have a say in who she marries."

"Which is why you lost the battle. You're weak. Pathetic."

"Come on, Joaquin," a third man says. "No one is down here."

"You can sit on the other side of those bars, acting like an arrogant asshole," the man called Joaquin growls. "But we both know how truly scared you are."

"You fuckers have already taken everything from me," Rafferty replies. "I have nothing left to fear."

Joaquin chuckles. "Someday, you will realize how false that statement is. Everyone has something left to lose. And when we find that little rebel camp of yours, I'm going to take great pleasure in bleeding every single one of your men out while I fuck all of your women."

I choke on a sob as I wait to hear Rafferty's response. These men—this place—it's like I'm trapped in some horrific nightmare. Or, perhaps my initial reaction was right, only this is not heaven.

Maybe I'm trapped in hell.

"I'm going to kill you one of these days, Joaquin," Rafferty finally replies. "And it won't be slow."

"We'll see about that, Raffe. We'll see about that."

Heavy footfalls retreat, echoing up the stairs, but I remain where I am, too petrified to move. They threatened murder, torture, and rape in the span of a few minutes. What the hell are they going to do to me?

"You're safe," Rafferty whispers.

I crawl out of my hiding spot, knees scraping against the stone as I stand and move to the outside of the cell. "Am I?"

"Are you?" he asks. "You're dressed in rebel colors, bleeding, terrified—how did you get here?"

"I don't know."

Dark brows draw together in a concerned expression. "Do you know where you are?"

"Flora said I'm in Faerie."

"Flora? You saw Flora?"

I nod. "She's my—she said she's my handmaiden?"

He breathes deeply and leans back against the stones behind him. "I have not seen her in a few days, so I was growing concerned."

"You know her?"

"I do. How did you get here?" he repeats his

earlier question. "I was under the impression the Veil was warded closed."

"Warded? Veil?"

"Spelled to remain closed. So no one can pass between Faerie and your world."

"I don't know anything about that. I wasn't feeling well. Went out for a walk. Ended up face down in some forest while men died above me." Frustrated, terrified, and exhausted, I press the heels of my palms to both eyes. "Please wake up," I whisper. "Please wake up."

"I fear you are not dreaming, woman, though I do commend you for your efforts to make this disappear."

"Listen, asshole," I snap. "First of all, my name is Ember. Not woman. Second, I just watched a man murdered in front of me, then fell down who the hell knows how many flights of stairs. The last thing I want to deal with is you behaving like a prick."

His expression softens nearly instantly. "Who did they kill?"

"I don't know. Wasn't really time for pleasantries." My voice cracks as my eyes fill, the image of his terrified gaze sinking in. "He told me to find you," I tell him. "Any idea why?"

"He was likely a rebel," Rafferty replies, as though it's the most normal thing in the world. "And the rebels wish to dethrone Taranus."

"Why?"

"Because he is a bastard unfit to rule." His reply is coated with so much hostility it charges the air around us.

"Is that why you're down here? Because you do not want him as king?"

Rafferty stares at the wall past me, his gaze haunted. "Something like that."

"Flora knows green is a rebel color?"

"She does. While I believe she never meant for any harm to come to you, Flora can be quite vindictive, and it appears as though you got caught in the crossfire."

"Of a fight that isn't mine!" I retort, a bit louder than I meant.

"Taranus murdered Flora's brother right in front of her. He removed her wings and bleached her hair as punishment. Trust me, Ember, she has every right to hate him."

Every bit of anger I'd felt at the woman disappears nearly instantly. I have no siblings, but if I did and someone killed them, I wouldn't give a shit whether or not a random person was caught in the middle. "Why is she still here?"

"Because I have no choice."

I whirl as Flora steps down off the bottom step. Shit, I hadn't even heard her! But based on Rafferty's lack of surprise, he had.

"Why are you down here?" All of her earlier appeasement is gone down in the depths of this dungeon. As though she's finally out of the presence of a king she refuses to bow to.

"I fell."

"You look a mess." She shifts her gaze from me to Rafferty. "And you're likely filling her head with all kinds of rebellious notions."

"Kind of similar to how you dressed her in green?" he asks.

"Taranus cannot control every aspect of my life, Rafferty."

"You dressed me in rebel colors, knowing it would piss him off?" I ask, even as I understand why she did it. I need her to see me as more than a weak human because I imagine I can't escape without her.

"Taranus would not harm you, that I was sure of. But seeing his future bride in green did piss him off."

I ball both hands into fists. "I am not marrying him."

"That's not what he believes," Flora replies as she moves closer to Rafferty's cell. As she does, she unwraps a fabric napkin and holds it out.

The man behind bars stands for the first time, and my mouth goes dry as I cannot help but stare at the wall of muscle reaching for a napkin full of fruit.

"Can't you conjure more than that?" I ask. Surely a man of that size needs more—

"The walls are lined with iron. My power does not work here." She accepts the now empty napkin as Rafferty eats the fruit. Then, she turns to me.

When she crosses the distance, I instinctively take a step back. So far, I haven't met a single person who cannot be seen as a threat in one way or another. Taranus literally murdered a man in front of me, Rafferty has been imprisoned, and Flora? Well, she seems to have her own brand of violence.

"I won't hurt you," she says.

"Says the woman who might as well have dressed me in red and put me in front of a bull," I snap.

"I did not know whether or not you were a threat. Had you turned your nose up at the green dress, I would have known you were not on our side."

"You let me wear it. Let me put it on even when you saw I had no idea what it meant."

"I was curious." She shrugs. "Don't worry. I took my licks for allowing you to wear it." Flora turns her back toward me and drops her left shoulder, using her right hand to pull the fabric down far enough that I can see thick, red wounds sticking out from the top.

My stomach churns, and my heart aches for the pain she must have suffered. "What did they do to you?"

"Nothing I couldn't handle," she replies as she straightens her gown.

"You have to stay alive, Flora. You cannot taunt him."

Her eyes are full of tears when she turns to Rafferty. "I don't have a choice. Serving him after what he did to my brother—" She chokes out, and rage burns hot through me.

"He forces you to stay here," I say, recalling what she said when she came down. She doesn't have a choice—not any more so than Rafferty chooses to remain behind those bars.

"Part of my sentence," she snaps.

"He—" I choke out, my voice not wanting to form the words.

"Taranus is a monster," Flora tells me.

"You need to get her out of this castle," Rafferty tells Flora.

"It's impossible. They watch her like a hawk."

"Not right now. They can't find her."

Flora narrows her gaze at me. "True."

"So get her out. Now."

"Um, excuse me, I'm standing right here." Feeling like a third party in a conversation that directly involves me, I raise my hand. "Literally, right here."

Neither bothers to look at me. "Get her out. That's an order."

"In case you've forgotten, we're both here because of one of your orders. You'll excuse me if

I'm not jumping to follow another that would lead to us both dying."

"Flora—"

"No," she interrupts. "I'm not leaving you. Besides, they took my wings, Raffe. We won't make it past the gates before we're both so full of arrows we'll make the quivers jealous."

Rafferty reaches through the bars and grips Flora's hand. I watch, feeling like a third wheel, yet again, as her bottom lip quivers. "My fate is sealed. Yours is not. Perhaps you don't get her out tonight. Play the game, stop with the rebellion, and sneak her out at your first opportunity."

"Your fate is not sealed. I will get that key, and I will free you."

"Key?"

"To the cell," Flora replies. "Conary carries it with him everywhere."

"He spends a lot of time with Taranus?"

"Yes."

"I can get the key."

Flora stares at me a moment before crossing her arms. "You can get it."

"Yes. As it happens, being a hungry orphan earned me some skills as a pickpocket."

Rafferty grips the bars, and my pulse increases quickly when his eyes meet mine. Probably not a good thing, given I'm pretty sure Flora and he are a thing. "Doing so could get you into trouble," he says.

"Staying here seems like it will do the same. I'd rather take my future into my own hands." *Besides, it's not like I have long left to live, anyway*, I add silently. Just because I'm feeling better doesn't mean I'm not still dying.

"If you free me, I will get you out of here."

"I want to go home."

"As I mentioned, the Veil is warded closed, but if you can guide me to the portal you came through, I can get you there."

"Deal." I hold out a hand, and he stares down at it. I'm ready to pull it back when his large hand envelopes mine. Something in the air around us shifts as his hand warms mine. I swallow hard and force myself to pull back despite how damned right the contact felt.

I'm no fool, though. Taranus may be the larger threat at the moment, but Rafferty is no innocent man. That much I can see.

He just so happens to be the lesser of two evils.

"Flora, get her back to her room. They will be here soon."

"Be here for what?" I ask him, then turn to Flora.

"I've faced much worse, Ember. Come get me when you find the key, but no sooner. The more you come down here, the more risk you face."

"Let's go." Flora grips my arm, but I'm hesitant to leave.

"You are a powerful woman, Ember."

"No. I'm not."

He smirks. "You possess the power to move this world. So long as it doesn't destroy you first."

CHAPTER 9

EMBER

This is real.

Those three words run through my mind on repeat, a brilliantly illuminated marquee reminding me that I am no longer in control of anything that happens to me in this place. How can I be when I'm human and these damn things can fly?

"Stay close," Flora warns as we reach the top of the stairs. She peeks out, and her hair becomes wispy in a breeze. "Come."

I follow her out into the main hall, and we slow our pace to normal. As we walk, our leather shoes padding softly are drowned out by heavy footfalls just ahead.

"Follow my lead," she warns as two men rush forward.

"Flora, I see you found our guest."

"Joaquin," she says as she drops into a curtsey. Now, I see the stiffness in her movements. She hates this—every single bit of it. "I found her wandering outside in the roses."

His golden gaze shifts to me, and in it, I see disbelief. "Funny, we looked there."

"Not hard enough," I say as I gesture to my dirty gown. "I fell and hit my head on a rock. Flora found me."

He smirks. "You'd do well to show more respect."

"You'd do well to do the same," I reply. After all, if they think I'm to be the queen, doesn't that earn me some right to say what I want?

At that exact moment, Taranus and Conary round the corner. Taranus holds out his hands and takes mine. "Ember, my dear, what happened to you?"

"I fell in the rose garden. Hit my head. Flora rescued me."

Taranus glances at Flora.

"It's true, My King," she says as she curtseys once more.

"Then I am grateful to you for a safe return of Ember. You may leave. We have matters to discuss."

Flora looks reluctant, but I smile at her. "Thank you so much for rescuing me."

"Of course, mistress." She curtsies at me and moves quickly down the hall and out of sight.

Forcing my attention to Taranus, I swallow hard.

It's impossible to see anyone but a murderer now, but if I'm to get the key from Conary, I need to earn their trust. "I apologize for my quick departure. Flora explained to me that the rebels are looking to hurt you and anyone who is loyal to you."

He arches a blond eyebrow. "Did she now?"

"She did."

"I am grateful, then, that she was able to explain that to you." He puts my arm through his, and we begin walking. Conary lingers behind, but I can sense his presence just behind us. "I do apologize for my crass nature, though. I was so afraid for your safety that I fear I lost my head a bit in there."

"I appreciate your concern," I say.

He guides me down another long hallway lined with windows. Just outside, I see a vast garden overflowing with bright blooms. Red, pink, and white roses shine beneath golden rays of sunshine. Heart in my throat, I allow Taranus to guide me outside. "Tell me, my dear, where did you fall?"

"Huh?"

He stops and turns me to face him. "I wish to see where you fell so we can prevent it from happening again."

Shit, shit, shit. I turn from him and study the flower garden. "I was honestly disoriented," I tell him as my cheeks heat. "I'm a bit embarrassed, to be honest."

Taranus's grin spreads, and I know, without a doubt, that both mine and Flora's future depends on me convincing him of the truth in our lie.

"Maybe, if we walk around, I'll see it?"

"Very well." He tucks my arm through his again and we begin to walk. The gravel path crunches beneath our steps, but all I can hear is the heavy thundering of my nervous heart. "As we walk, why don't you tell me of how you got here?"

"I don't really know. I was out getting some fresh air, and I saw this light. I followed it, and then woke up in the woods where Conary found me." *Don't lay it on too thick, Ember*, I remind myself. The best lies are layered with truths, but you get caught when you try to be too detailed—too fake.

"You must have stumbled through the only portal up between our worlds."

"Portal?" I feign innocence since the only person who gave me any information is one I should never have met.

"Our worlds are separated by a veil. It is impassable by anyone but a light fae."

"Are you a light fae?"

"I am." We turn a corner. "Not too long ago, that veil was warded closed by a fae who wanted to trap her brother on your side. Seems she left a portal open, though." He smiles at me. "Does anything look familiar, yet?"

"Not yet," I reply. "But I do love these flowers."

"I am happy to show you all of the gardens should you wish to see them."

"I do. Being out here calms my nerves."

"Good." He pats the hand looped through his arm, and his touch is like sandpaper. We turn another corner, and I see it. Somehow, someone messed up the gravel. A rock juts out of the ground, and it's tipped with a bit of crimson.

"This is it. This is where I fell!" I yell loudly. Birds take to the sky around us, and Taranus glances back at Conary.

"Why has this not been tended to?" he asks.

"I'll find out."

Victorious in solidifying my lie, I smile at them both. "It really is not a big deal."

"You are bleeding, Ember. That is a big deal. Your fragile state needs to be tended to. I will escort you to the healer."

"I really am okay."

Taranus grins at me, showing off a row of impossibly white teeth. "While I am grateful you think so, I'd much rather have our healer take a look at you."

"If it will make you feel better, I will do it."

He beams at me. "I am grateful for that. This way." He loops my arm back through his and guides me back down the path toward the castle. Out of the corner of my eye, I see Flora in what looks like an herb garden. She doesn't spare me a glance, but I know it was her.

Somehow, she fixed it so Taranus would not recognize my deceit.

Getting the key is about more than freeing Rafferty or myself. I can also free Flora, and that alone is worth the risk.

"Can I ask you a question?" We step inside where the sunlight is replaced with flaming sconces on the walls.

"Of course."

"The man you—"

His grip tightens. "I truly am sorry I killed him in front of you. That was very unkind of me."

Not an apology for taking a life, just for letting me see it. "I understand why you did it, though it did bother me to see it."

"Won't happen again. You have my word."

"Thank you."

"Of course. Now, what was your question?"

"The man told me to get Raffe? Who is that?"

Taranus stops and turns me to face him. His expression darkens, eyes hardening. I almost regret asking at all, but I need to know everything I can. And if Taranus can give me anything at all about the prisoner beneath the castle, I want to know.

"Rafferty is—was—my brother. He tried to have me killed when he was not chosen for the throne. His jealousy—" Taranus closes his eyes tightly, and I find myself even more grateful that I met Rafferty first. Because this show? It's damned convincing. "He was killed when he led an army to our castle in an attempt to kill me."

I feign surprise, covering my mouth with one hand and gasping for an audible effect. "Your own brother tried to kill you?"

He nods. "We'd lost our sister a few centuries back, and Rafferty was never the same afterward. Seems he lost his mind."

"I am so sorry, Taranus. That is horrible."

"I appreciate that, Ember. While I never wished for my brother's demise, I truly am grateful he is not here to threaten you."

"Why would he be a threat to me?"

"Because I adore you, and my adoration makes you a target for anyone who wishes me harm. It's why I took the threat earlier so seriously."

"You adore me? But you barely know me."

He stops in front of a door. "You are a kind woman, Ember. I can see that much in your gaze, and you would treat my people with kindness they have not known in quite some time." Leaning in, he presses a kiss to my cheek, then knocks on the door. "I will escort you back to your room when you are ready."

The door opens, and Taranus steps aside as an

older woman with a hollow smile answers the door. "May I help you?"

"Heelean, so good to see you. Ember is in need of an exam. I fear she tripped outside in the garden and injured herself."

Heelean swallows hard and nods. "Then I shall see to her." Stepping to the side, she gestures for me to enter. The soothing scents of lavender and vanilla fill my lungs as she quickly closes the door and moves swiftly across the room to a table on the opposite side.

As she messes with something in jars, I study the room. A small bed sits on one wall, a countertop on the other, and an empty tray that looks as though it was brought to her in here with food sits on the countertop. "Do you live in here?"

"I do," she replies. "Come sit so I can take a look at you."

Obeying, I sit down on a chair beside her countertop. The short woman is the only one I've seen not wearing white. Instead, she wears a black gown that hugs her waist and falls down to her feet. "You aren't wearing white."

"I am in mourning," she replies as she tilts my head to the side and dabs something on my injury. The sting shoots through my head, and I wince. "You poor dear, seems you took quite a fall." She reaches for a pair of tweezers then plucks something from my wound.

"What is it?"

Heelean doesn't say a word as she studies it for a moment. Then she takes a seat across from me. "Where did Taranus say you fell?" she questions, her golden gaze narrowing on my face.

I clear my throat. "The gardens."

"Hmm." She studies the dark shard between the tweezers. It's no bigger than the end of a pen, but I get the impression that it completely undid my lie. Heart in my throat, I can only hope that she is not loyal enough to rat me out. "This is iron-laced graphite," she finally says. "The only place you can find this is in the dungeons below the castle."

Fucknugget. "I—"

"Don't panic. This room is soundproof, even for fae hearing. It's just you and me."

"Maybe some managed to make it outside."

"Doubtful," she says as she stands and moves across the room. After messing with some bottles, she comes back with a small vial in her hand. Then, she drops the sliver into a clear liquid, and I watch in awe as the evidence disappears. "Now, how about you tell me how Rafferty is doing."

"You know him?"

"I do."

"He's not doing great," I tell her, honestly. "He's pretty banged up."

She mutters something in a language I don't understand then gets to her feet and moves back toward her bottles.

"How do you know him?"

"I worked with the rebels," she replies. "Until Taranus got a hair in his ass and decided to overthrow his brother."

"Is that why you live in here? Is this your cell?"

She stops and turns toward me. "My daughter made him promise not to harm me. Why? I've no clue since she murdered my husband—her own father—without so much as the blink of an eye." Tears spring to her eyes, and she takes a deep breath.

I reach out and touch her arm. "I'm so sorry."

"Taranus cannot harm me unless Sheelin gives him the go-ahead. Which she likely won't do until she can come here and deal with me herself."

"Where is she?"

"In your world, trying to kill her brother."

Maybe I should be glad I never knew my family. "That's so awful," I say, keeping my other multitude of thoughts inside.

"We have a long, dark past, dear. Nothing for you to fret about. Frankly, you have problems of your own at the moment."

"I know. Taranus thinks I'm the woman from some prophecy."

"You are," she replies. "And he believes wedding you will make him the one true king."

"So I hear." I groan. "Seriously, though. One true king? What is this, Camelot?"

She stops and turns toward me. "I'm not sure I know what you mean."

So much for a King Arthur reference. "Nothing. I just…I don't understand what I have to do with any of this."

After a few moments of silence as she works, Heelean turns toward me and offers me a vial with green liquid. "Can you get this to Rafferty? It will heal him."

"He made me promise not to come back."

"You need to get this to him," she says. "Or give it to Flora so she can. I'm not allowed to see anyone but those Taranus allows near my room. And I cannot leave."

"Did he cut your wings, too?"

Her cheeks flush. "No. Though I am warded in this room and it is lined with iron. There's no leaving for me."

"There's no way to remove a ward? What is a ward?"

She smiles softly and pats my cheek as a mother would dote on a child. "You are sweet. Far too kind for the fate set out for you. Do yourself a favor and escape from this place, Ember. As quickly as possible."

"How can I get you out?"

"You can't," she says, softly. "But you can save yourself, and that will be just as satisfactory."

"I have a plan—"

A heavy knock on the door interrupts me, and Heelean shoves the vial at me. I take it and put it down within what little cleavage I have, hiding it from view—barely. Then, she applies a bit of cream to my forehead. "Be well, dear," she whispers, before shuffling over to open the door.

Taranus stands on the other side. "Feeling better?"

"Yes. Thank you." I turn toward Heelean. "I appreciate your kindness."

"Of course." Heelean bows her head slightly and shuts the door the moment I'm in the hall.

"Heelean treated you well?"

"Yes."

"What did you two talk about? She can be quite the chatterbox," he says with a laugh.

"Nothing really. She asked me what happened then applied something to my temple."

"Surprising. Normally she has much more to say."

"Maybe she was tired?"

"Maybe." He stops walking and takes both of my hands in his. They're cold, and the contact makes my skin crawl. Especially when he begins massaging the tops of my hands with his thumbs. "Speaking of, you must be exhausted."

I glance out the window at the setting sun. Truthfully, I'm wired. So much has happened today that I doubt there will be any sleep for me, at all. But if it gets me away from Taranus, I'll agree to damn near anything. "I am wiped," I reply.

"Wiped?"

"Sorry, tired. It's a phrase we use where I'm from."

His smile spreads. ", I understand and am looking forward to learning more about where you come from." Taranus releases my hands before looping one of my arms through his. We begin to walk, and I pay close attention now to the way the servants watch him. Those daring enough to look our way study him with a grimace, those not brave enough—they do everything possible to avoid him.

It's heartbreaking to see.

As he guides me up the stairs, my throat tightens. The idea of being so far from anyone but the man I watched slit a throat without so much as the blink of an eye is nerve-wracking—to say the least.

"I can sense your nerves," he says. "I assure you, you're safe in my presence."

Can fae read minds? "I'm sorry, this is all new to me."

"I can understand that." We stop outside my door. "You will have a good life here with me, Ember. I can assure you that. A long, happy life at my side."

"A long, happy life sounds nice," I reply with a smile.

Taranus beams at me, but all I see is a nightmare dressed in a daydream. "Have a good night, Ember."

"Thank you, Taranus." For good measure, I lean in and press a kiss to his cheek. When I pull back, he is smiling widely at me. Before I hurl in front of him, though, I rush into my room and shut the door behind me. The trip to the bathroom is easy, thankfully, and before I know it, I'm bent over a bucket with the contents of my stomach coming right back up.

I heave while sweat beads on my brow, and my stomach clenches when there is nothing left. As soon as it relaxes, I sit back and take a deep breath. Now that I'm done vomiting, I can smell the scented water from the full bathtub right in front of me.

It's alluring, that's for damned sure, but the suffo-cating panic in my chest has me remaining right where I am. As a child, I'd been alone a lot. That loneliness bred a ton of anxiety about what could happen to me. In an attempt to cope, I'd devised a plan for coming to terms with my reality while not focusing on all the what-ifs.

So I use that tool now.

I am here in another world, surrounded by creatures with abilities I cannot even begin to understand. My sickness may have subsided, but as it turns out, there are much bigger things to worry about than my impending doom.

I've been seeing what must have been visions of a man Taranus claims is dead; a man I saw less than an hour ago imprisoned below.

In the last twenty-four hours, I've seen more death than I've seen in my entire twenty-six years, and the worst monster of them all thinks he's going to marry me.

Oh, and how could I forget to mention the murdering bastard holding the literal key to my escape? Running both hands over my face, I groan.

How the hell did I draw this shit card? Dinner with a handsome man turned into a flare-up of my illness, which led me here. Fucking wonderful. I must have done something truly awful in a past life to get this deck handed to me.

Reaching between my breasts, I withdraw the vial Heelean gave me. I know I shouldn't take it to him. After all, even he asked me to stay away, but the idea of seeing him again—it's far too enticing than it should be. And who knows how badly he needs it? It was pretty dark down there. Could be he's injured more than he let on.

Mind made up, I push to my feet and head to the basin full of clear water on the counter. I reach in with both hands and drink some of the water to rinse my mouth out. Then, after splashing some on my face, I strip down to climb into the bath that's already waiting for me.

Warmth surrounds me, and I sink down beneath the surface. I've never been overly heroic, but I always believed I'd do the right thing if given the chance, so as I sit here beneath the surface until my lungs begin to burn, I add Heelean to the list of people I want to free from Taranus.

All I need is a key.

CHAPTER 10
EMBER

U nder the quietness of night, I creep out into the hall. Wearing a white dress and cloak, I slip down the stairs as silently as possible. I even remained barefoot, not wanting to make any sounds as I move through the castle.

Vial tucked securely between my breasts, I hope that if I'm caught, I can simply say I needed some fresh air. Maybe they'll believe me…maybe they'll slit my throat like they did that other man. Who knows, really, but at this point, inaction is what will surely drive me mad.

Reaching the bottom of the stairs, I glance to the left and right just to make sure no one is near. The hall is empty, so I creep out and head toward the entrance to the dungeon. It's dark. A gaping hole seemingly leading to nowhere, and yet, to me—this is the only place I can be where I don't feel vulnerable.

And isn't that insane.

Moving as quietly as possible, I reach out and feel for the next step before moving down. Each time, I'm careful not to fall. While my heart thunders, I listen for any sounds that would tell me someone was coming or that Rafferty was not alone in his prison.

So far, nothing but silence, so I continue.

One step. Then another.

When I reach the bottom, I breathe a sigh of relief. Until I see him. Curled in the corner, his back to me, he shivers. Every inch of his back is covered in lacerations. With his flesh torn completely open, his pain must be unimaginable, and before I know it, I'm rushing forward. "Raffe?"

He doesn't say a word, and the only evidence he's not dead his constant quivering—likely from the pain.

"Come on, I have something that can help you, but I need you to come here."

"Ember?" my name is a growl leaving his lips, but it's something.

"Yes. Come here. I can help you." Reaching into the top of my dress, I withdraw the vial. "Heelean gave it to me."

"Heelean?"

"Yes. Come here," I repeat. "I don't know how much time we have."

"Moving is—" he hisses as he tries to sit, "difficult at the moment."

I study the cell then gather my skirts and rush around into the empty neighboring one. "Dammit, Rafferty, who did this to you?" As I kneel beside the bars, my stomach churns at the sight of his torn flesh.

"Looks worse than it feels," he whispers, but the words are a lie. Even I can see that.

"How is your front?"

He groans and pushes himself up on the back wall then grips the bars and faces me.

A tortured cry leaves before I can stop it. Just like his back, his entire abdomen is covered in the same lacerations. The fact that he's even alive when his entire torso looks like it was just run through a shredder—that in itself is a miracle.

"Rafferty," I whisper.

"I don't want your pity."

The way he spits the words out gives me the impression that this is not a man who cares to be seen as weak. What he can't seem to understand, though, is how familiar I am with that very same need. "I don't pity you," I reply. "But I can help you."

His golden gaze locks on mine, and we stare at each other for a moment. My need to help him, to save him from this pain, is so overwhelming it brings tears to my eyes. I don't say another word, though, because doing so would be too much. Something else

I know from my illness—sometimes the compassionate thing to do is remain quiet and allow the other person to make the decision for themselves.

Finally, he does. Each movement is slight, and his face remains contorted in agony until his back is to me. I remove the lid from the vial and wait, holding my breath until he finally settles his back to the bars.

"Are you ready?"

He grunts, something I take for consent as I dip my finger down into the vial. I honestly don't even know if one is going to do the trick. I should have convinced Heelean to give me ten of the damned things.

Just in case it isn't enough, I start on the worst wounds, gently touching the torn skin and slathering as much on as I can. I remain conservative with it, though, not wanting to use too much and risk not having enough for the front.

Before my eyes, his skin begins to knit back together, and with each one healed, he shakes a bit less. Working quickly, I finish his back within minutes —though, it feels like hours of watching him suffer. With my breath held, I watch as the final lines knit back together, leaving nothing but jagged pink lines where once there was torn flesh. "Okay, turn around."

He does, easier this time, and breathes deeply as he kneels before me, resting his face between two bars, eyes closed. It takes all my focus to remain attentive to the wounds when all I want to do is study every line of a face I somehow already know as well as my own.

The gashes are not quite as bad on his front, but the flayed skin shows thick cords of torn muscle beneath it. They may not be as bloodied, but they are deep. I use more this time, not as worried about not having enough. Just like his back, his front knits back together before my eyes until I'm staring at a blood-crusted but otherwise nearly healed chest.

His eyes remain closed, his breathing ragged as he grips the bars. My blood pounds, the hammering of my pulse all I can hear as I stare at him.

The connection I feel—it's something I've read about. Something I've written about but never actually believed in.

As if this man before me can heal every wound I've ever suffered. As if I've been waiting for him my entire life.

With a shaking hand, I reach out and touch him again, needing to feel the warmth of his body beneath my fingertips, even as I know it's an incredibly stupid move—especially if he is, in fact, in a relationship with Flora.

But I can't help it.

I saw him only twice before arriving here. How?

I've no clue. But I'm drawn to this man—this warrior —in ways I can't even begin to explain.

"Thank you."

Resting my palm against his chest, I look up at his face. He's watching me, expression softer now that he's no longer hurting. I swallow hard. "You're welcome."

"You risked a lot to bring that to me." With every word, his chest vibrates beneath my palm.

"Taranus took me to see Heelean about the cut on my forehead. When she realized I fell down here and not in the gardens, she wanted me to bring you this." I remove my hand and show him the vial in the other.

"I'd truly hoped she'd escaped." He sits back on his legs so I do the same. Inches apart, but with these bars, it might as well be miles.

"She told me her daughter will not allow Taranus to harm her."

"Sheelin is a monster all her own. If she's forbidden Taranus from doing anything to Heelean, chances are she has something much worse in mind."

"She told me she's trapped in her room—that it's warded? Is that the right word?"

A grin plays on the corner of his mouth. "It is. You're learning."

"Adaptation is one of my skills."

"As is thievery?"

"When you're an orphan with very little to eat, you make do."

His expression falters, and I see the ghost of pity on his face. "I'm truly sorry you suffered."

"Just like you don't want pity? Neither do I. Life happens; cards are dealt; we move forward or risk being trapped in the present."

Rafferty nods. "That is an excellent outlook."

Swallowing hard, I force my gaze away from the intensity of his own, if only for a moment. "Taranus told me you were dead."

He arches a dark eyebrow. "You inquired of me?"

"I did. Like I told you earlier, that man they…" Trailing off, I fight back tears at the memory of the panicked victim. "He told me to find you, so Taranus knew I'd heard your name."

"And he said I was dead?"

I nod.

Rafferty scoffs. "Not surprising. Taranus has always been an asshole. I was warned—most recently by our other brother—but I chose not to listen."

"He said you lost yourself after your sister died."

Rafferty's eyes turn so hard it steals my breath. In the blink of an eye, he goes from the calm, collected man I first met, to an angry, murderous warrior. "Taranus has no business speaking of Niahm."

"I'm sorry, I didn't mean to bring it up."

"Not your fault." He closes his eyes and breathes

deeply, nostrils flaring. Then, he appears to calm once more when he looks at me again. "He's not wrong about me losing myself, though his issues with me were always more about jealousy."

"Yes. He said you came after him because you were angry over losing the throne."

"Do you believe him? Do you believe there is truth in the accusations that I am a dirty, murdering rebel?"

I don't even hesitate. "No."

"Why? You met us both at the same time, so why do you believe me over the man on the other side of the bars?"

"Does it matter?"

"It does to me."

Taking a deep breath, I get to my feet and begin to pace. "I saw you," I admit. "Twice. Once back in Texas outside the doctor's office, and again in a restaurant during a date."

"A date?" His brow arches. "Have you someone back home?"

"No. Not like that; I'd just met him. And he likely has already forgotten about me."

"I very much doubt that. You don't strike me as a forgettable woman."

My cheeks flush. *If only you knew.* "Anyway, I dreamt of you, too, the night I came here, and while I don't understand how any of that is possible, I feel like I can trust you. Which might be dumb, but hey, what do I have to lose?"

His smile falters briefly. Then he clears his throat. "I know why you saw visions of me," he says, softly.

I whirl on him. "Why? How?"

"Our destinies are entwined, Ember. See, I dreamt of you—bathed in fire. I believed you to be a figment of my imagination. That was until a seer told me of your prophecy."

I don't even focus on the one part of that conversation I probably should—prophecy and all. Instead, I move closer to the bars. "You dreamt of me?"

"Many times."

"And I was on fire?"

He shakes his head. "You'd caused the fire."

The words are more of a gut punch than they probably should have been, but after coming here, seeing all I've seen, prophecies don't seem too far out of reach. "I caused the fire? What does that even mean?"

"I don't know," he answers, honestly. "But I do know that you are going to change the world, Ember. One way or another."

"You all have the wrong person. I'm no one. A woman who—until recently—had never even left Austin, Texas."

"The prophecy claims you will make the one true king."

I step back. "That's insane. I don't have a magical vagina or anything. How the hell is marriage to me supposed to make someone all-powerful?"

He gapes back at me. "Magical vagina?"

I'm too shocked to be embarrassed. "You know what I mean." Pinching the bridge of my nose, I shake my head. "This is all insane."

"You're standing in a dungeon beneath a castle in Faerie, and a fortune seems insane?"

"Yes. Fortunes are nothing but fake money-making schemes at carnivals. They aren't real."

"Ember, in my world, if one sees the future, it is cemented."

"So my fate is laid out for me, then? I'm supposed to burn something then marry someone so *they* can be king? What kind of garbage is that?"

Expecting him to show yet another look of pity, I'm not prepared for the frustrated expression on his face. "You may not believe that your fate is to marry the king, Ember, but I do know this will play out the way it has always been meant to. Whether you run or not."

"I wish I would have just died already." The words are out of my mouth before I get a chance to stop them. *Thank you, shit filter.* Covering my face with both hands, I shake my head and attempt to rein in my anger. Truthfully, Rafferty is not the reason I'm here. Therefore, taking it out on him isn't fair.

Don't shoot the messenger and all that.

"What do you mean by that?"

"Nothing. Just that I wish I wasn't here, that's all."

"I truly am sorry you have been pulled into this. It's not too late to just run, Ember. Wait until they are not looking, and go."

I shake my head. "There's no way I can find my way back to the portal. Not without your help."

"You could try."

"And I'd probably die before I made it even halfway there. I'm sticking with the original plan. I'll get the key, and I'll get you out."

"It's risky."

"I'll take it." Silence surrounds us until all I can hear is the sound of water dripping somewhere in the distance. We remain like that, in complete quiet for minutes that stretch on until, finally, Rafferty clears his throat.

"Thank you, for helping me."

"You already thanked me."

"I know, but I—I'm not great at accepting aid when needed."

Arching an eyebrow, I cross my arms. "You don't say."

He chuckles and runs a hand over his shaved head. "It's a weakness of mine."

"I'm the same way," I admit. "Never wanting anyone to see you at your weakest has its negatives."

"Very true."

"I'm sorry you lost your sister. And that your brother is an asshole."

Rafferty throws his head back and laughs. The deep baritone is such a surprise it catches me off guard. *Damn, he's handsome.* My stomach warms, and my pulse quickens. "You are an enigma, Ember. And I am really looking forward to getting to know you."

"What about Flora?" I ask, yet again, before realizing the words are prepping to leave my lips.

"What about Flora?"

"Aren't you two a thing? Boyfriend? Girlfriend? Spouses? Mates? Whatever you call it?"

Rafferty's face falls slack a moment before he begins laughing again, only this time, he doesn't stop with one bout of laughter. The bastard actually bends at the waist and laughs so hard he has to steady himself against the bars.

"Why is that funny?"

"Flora is my closest friend," he says as he straightens. "She was once betrothed to my middle brother, Ridley, but he found his mate in your world."

"Wait, they were betrothed but not mates?"

"Correct. My kind does not choose to mate often, though marriage is common practice. To bond with your true mate—the one whose soul yours chose—is actually quite rare. Because, a lot of times, even if we do find our mate, we won't complete the pairing."

"Why?"

"If you complete the pairing, you become irrevocably tied to the other being. Meaning if they feel something, you feel it. If they die—"

"You die. That's so sad."

"It is our way. Having a true mate is a weakness, and as you can see, my kind does not like to feel weak."

"But to spend eternity with someone who is not your soulmate, and knowing your actual soulmate is there, that must be so sad."

"Sometimes. But fae tend to be selfish creatures, as I imagine you've noticed. If they choose to marry someone who is not their true mate, they've chosen to remain untethered. At least in that sense."

"Taranus and Conary certainly are. Selfish," I add.

Rafferty's mood shifts, altering the very air around us. "Conary killed his mate before they had the chance to form a union."

I gasp. Surprised that I am, well—surprised. It's not that the bastard has been anything but a monster. "That's awful."

"It was. He will die a painful death. I assure you that."

"You hate him."

"More than you can even begin to imagine."

"Well, when I get you the key and we get the hell out of here, I'll help you come back and kill him. Maybe it's him you saw me light on fire."

Rafferty chuckles. "You do not have a violent bone in your petite frame, Ember."

"You'd be surprised. I've broken quite a few noses in my life."

"Oh?" Crossing both arms, he leans against the bars. "Tell me of these broken noses."

"Well, to start, there was Levi Karlon. He pinched my butt in the ninth grade."

Rafferty laughs as I continue recanting my first trip to the principal's office. It's so easy to talk to him —so easy that before I know it, sunlight begins to illuminate the stairs. It carries down, making tiny dust particles visible throughout the dungeon.

"You'd better get going," Rafferty tells me. "Everyone will be waking soon if they aren't already."

"Are you going to be okay?" I'm hesitant to leave him, hesitant to go anywhere he's not.

"I'll be fine," he tells me. "I assure you."

"I'll come back tonight."

"You need to be cautious, Ember. If they catch you—"

"They won't. Sneaking around happens to be one of my specialties."

He pauses for a moment then finally nods. "I would love to see you again."

"Then I'll be back. And I'll bring more of this." I hold up the vial before tucking it down in between my breasts. I do it without thinking, so when I glance back at him and notice the way he's watching me—the dilation of his pupils, the heaviness of his breathing—it spurs my own lust. Something I think he realizes.

"You'd better go." His tone is gravelly now—as if strained—so without another word, I turn and head back up the stairs.

After checking the hall and being grateful there's no one there, I step out.

I haven't made it five steps before I hear a deep voice behind me. "What are you doing up this early, I wonder?"

CHAPTER 11
EMBER

S lowly, I turn until I'm face to face with Conary. "I'm an early riser."

His golden gaze does not waver from my face, even as he cocks his head to the side in a move that's so fast it's not the least bit natural—at least, not for a human. "Oh? I am, too. Would you grace me with a walk and early morning conversation? I can offer you coffee."

Coffee. It's been so damned long since I was able to drink it. Still, if I didn't need his trust to obtain the key hidden somewhere on his body, I would have turned him down. "Coffee sounds great, thank you."

He smiles and reaches out to thread my arm through his. Simply touching him makes my stomach churn. The man is a damned snake, something I need to remember every moment I'm in his presence. "I wish you nothing but apologies for my behavior upon our first meeting. I assure you, had I known who you were, I never would have been so hard."

Sure you wouldn't have been. I bet you're a big ol' murdering teddy bear, aren't you? "Not a problem. I didn't exactly look innocent when we met."

He chuckles. "No, you didn't." We move down the hall and into the kitchen. It's not bustling with people, though there are a few women inside. All three of them eye Conary with an uncomfortable wariness that tells me damn near everything I need to know about him. "Ladies," he says, softly. "Have you met our guest, Ember?"

All three women lift their gazes to me. "Good to meet you, Ember. I am Bonny." A slender woman who looks to be in her early twenties—human years, at least—is the first to greet me.

A woman with dark hair and a scar on her cheek offers me a nod. The third woman, short and stocky, forces a smile. "We're happy to make your acquaintance, miss. Should you need anything, the name is Annie."

"So nice to meet you guys."

"Great. Coffee is this way." Conary guides me to the other side of the room, and as soon as he's turned away, I glance over my shoulder. All three of the women are watching me with concern in their bright gazes.

I offer a tight smile, hopefully reassuring them I know what I'm up against. I can smell a perverted bastard a mile away, thanks to more experiences brought on by never having anyone to protect me.

"Do you enjoy cream in your coffee?"

"No. I don't like cream," I lie. I know it's ridiculous, but I don't want to leave any room for interpretation with this man—not even a simple possible innuendo.

"Wonderful." He smiles and fills two ceramic mugs with steaming dark liquid from a glass carafe.

"I didn't realize you had access to coffee here."

"We grow it. A few decades ago, a traveler to your world brought back a plant. Ever since, we've harvested our own."

"That's neat."

He offers me a mug then retrieves his own and takes my free arm again. "I enjoy taking my coffee in the garden. Interested?"

"Yes. Thank you."

Together, we move out through the side door and into the early morning sun. The air is crisp, the light bright, and morning dew drops dot the greenery surrounding us on either side. This is not the same garden as yesterday. Here the hedges are taller, the plants so high no one can see us.

Fuck.

"So how are you enjoying your stay?" he questions as he releases me and takes a drink of his coffee.

"Murder aside?" I question, and he smirks at me. A monster shielded by a handsome exterior.

"Yes, again, my apologies."

"Not necessary," I reply, with my own forced grin. "I am beginning to see that this is very different from where I'm used to." I take a drink of coffee and nearly groan as the potent flavor hits my tongue. Even without cream, there's a sweetness with a hint of what I believe to be vanilla. Maybe some cinnamon?

"The coffee is to your liking, then?"

"It is. Very much so. How is it so sweet?"

"We took your methods and made them better. When we roast ours, we add cinnamon and vanilla beans. The combination gives us quite a sweet flavor."

"It's delicious."

"Glad to see you're enjoying it."

We fall into a silence that makes me even more uncomfortable than I am when he speaks, so I decide to start setting myself up for earning his trust. I simply need to get close enough to grab the key. Problem is I have no idea where he's hiding it.

"So, Conary, how did you become the king's right-hand man?"

"I've known King Taranus since we were boys."

"You knew Rafferty, then?"

A muscle in his jaw twitches. "I did. He and I were close friends until their sister was killed. After that, he was never the same. I adored their sister. While she was not my true mate, we'd grown—close. And then she was gone."

"Oh, I am so sorry."

He shrugs. "It was a long time ago, and we'd never become anything but friends."

"What of your mate?"

He glances down at me. "My mate?"

"You said Rafferty's sister was not your true mate. Did you ever find out who was?"

Something flickers over his gaze, and had I not already known the destiny of his true mate, I might have missed it.

"She was killed not long before Niahm. We obviously never completed our pairing, which left me free to love whoever I wish without the risk."

What's even worse than his callous words is the fact that I can see he feels nothing for the woman who was lost.

"Pairing?" I force myself to ask since I'm not supposed to know about it. Alluding that I know anything about anything in this world is a mistake I plan not to make. There's no way I want to give him any reason to question my motives.

"Our kind mates very rarely because having a mate is a weakness we wish to avoid. When the pairing is complete, you are tied to the other person. If they die, you, too, succumb to death."

"That's sad. And kind of romantic."

"Tragic is what it is," he replies instantly. "Rafferty was mated, though."

"He was?" I stiffen. I don't know why, but the fact that he didn't say anything bothers me. It's not like we're overly close, but everyone here has a damned agenda. Is it possible he hid her from me to shield me from his?

"Yes. She was beautiful…ethereal, even. But along with that beauty was a need that he was unable to sate. She stepped out on him, sleeping with many others—shifters from your world as it happened."

Ouch. "What happened to her? Is that what killed him?" I add, remembering Taranus's lie about Rafferty's death.

"No, it's not what killed him. He was in my position at the time, serving the royal family that held the castle prior to Taranus's appointing. To save him, they sent her into the Veil still alive. She's trapped there now, destined to live alone in a state of decay that continues to repeat itself."

I'm horrified. While I don't condone what Conary is saying she did to Rafferty, condemning her to a life of rotting away alone? That's barbaric. "That's horrible."

"That was the family. They were savages, and Rafferty was their henchman."

Even as he says the words, I have to swallow down my returned anger. The blatant lies—they're exhausting. And all of this was coming from a man who murdered his own mate. "The rebels don't seem to think so. I wonder why that is?"

He doesn't miss a beat. "It's easy to manipulate the weak-minded. The rebels have craved to be free of laws, of a ruler. Rafferty gives them that."

"Gave them," I correct. When he glances down at me, I add, "He's dead, isn't he?"

The very brief twitch of his eye is nearly unnoticeable before he's nodding. "Yes, though his movement is still very much a threat as you saw yesterday."

I don't bother to add anything to that particular comment—mainly because revisiting seeing a man die brutally in front of me is not something I feel like doing. "It's nice that you get to work alongside your close friend—Taranus. That you support him in his bid to be king."

"I do," Conary replies. "He was chosen by his predecessor."

"Who was that?"

"You ask a lot of questions, human."

"I am curious. If I'm stuck here—which it seems like I am—I'd like to know the history."

"Very well." He sighs. "The family was over-thrown by a much stronger fae. He mated their daughter, and after his death, she took the throne. Recently, she decided she'd much rather retire to your world, so she chose Taranus as her successor."

A twisted tale compared to the one I've heard. I don't speak that aloud, though, as doing so would likely put a target on more backs than mine. "That was kind of her."

"He was her only choice."

"Is that why she warded the Veil? So no one could leave if they didn't agree with him?"

His savage grin is bone-chilling. "That, my dear, is a story for another morning walk, I'm afraid."

"Why?"

"I've duties to tend to, though I would much rather continue reveling in your company." Reaching out, he grabs my free hand then bows down and presses his lips to it. My skin crawls near the point of contact, sending prickles of awareness running up my spine. *Is he trying to seduce me?* "Perhaps we can have coffee again tomorrow morning? Given that we are both early-risers."

"Sure," I somehow manage despite the bile in my throat. "That sounds nice."

"Splendid. Do you need to be escorted to your room?"

"No, thanks." Turning on my heel, I head back toward the house.

"Ember?"

I stop and close my eyes tightly before opening them and turning back to him, wearing a fake smile on my face. "Yes?"

Conary holds out his mug. "If you're headed to the kitchen, would you mind taking my mug, as well? Saves me a trip."

"Not at all." I start toward him and pluck the mug from his hand.

"You will make a beautiful queen," he says, quietly.

I'm grateful my skin doesn't turn green from the disgust churning my insides. "Thanks. Have a day as pleasurable as sharing your company has been." *As in, I hope you fuck right off.*

"What a kind notion. Same to you, Ember." He rolls the 'r,' and it's all I can do to not roll my eyes.

Quickly, I turn and head back into the kitchen, moving as fast as I can without arousing suspicion. The moment I'm inside, though, I lean back against the door and suck in a few steadying breaths. My legs begin to feel more solidified now that I feel safer, but the unease in my belly—that remains.

"Are you all right, love?"

I open my eyes at the soft, feminine voice. All

three of the women are staring at me, so I nod quickly. "He makes me—"

"Uneasy?" The blonde questions.

"That's one word for it."

"Try not to be alone with him," Bonny warns, her tone low. "Conary has a taste for all women, and he cares not if you feel the same."

I'd suspected it, but to hear her say it— "He's—"

"Yes, and we cannot be speaking of these things!" The third woman, who never gave me her name, scolds.

"Just be wary is all I'm saying," Bonny retorts. "I can take those."

I hand her both mugs and watch as she dips them in a silver tub full of soapy water. "Can I ask why you all stay here? If you're not safe?"

"We have no choice."

"Were your wings clipped?" I whisper loudly.

"Of course, not!" Annie says quickly. "But we've families to feed, and working here gives us enough gold to do just that."

"You can't find somewhere safer?"

"Honey, you've seen nothing but what's within these walls. The things out there, they can be far more terrifying than twenty minutes with a man who can't keep his hands to himself."

It burns my soul to hear her mention it so callously. As though she's forced to choose the lesser of two evils. "What of the rebels? Will they not take care of you?"

Bonny hurries across the room and covers my mouth with her hand. "Hush, will you! You're going to get us all killed!"

"Uncover her mouth at once," Annie orders.

Bonny hesitates, but then slowly pulls her hand back.

"I'm sorry, I didn't mean anything."

"You're fine, dear. This is all new to you, yes?"

"You can say that."

"How about you have a seat and we can get you some food. What do you like to eat?"

"Anything and everything," I reply as I accept her offer and take a seat on a stool at one of the many counters.

"How about some biscuits, then? Some eggs?"

"That sounds wonderful, thank you." My stomach chooses that exact moment to growl, and Annie laughs. Even Bonny and the third woman look far more relaxed. "I didn't get your name?" I ask the woman kneading bread.

She wipes her floured hands off on an apron and offers me her hand, though she doesn't speak.

"Her name is Petal. She cannot speak, though."

"Oh, I'm sorry." She releases my hand so I raise it and sign, *It's nice to meet you, Petal.*

Her eyes light up in complete delight as she replies, *You as well, Ember.*

"You speak in signs, too?"

"I do. How did you learn it?" I ask, redirecting my attention to Petal.

My brother went to the human world to try to find a witch to heal me. When that didn't work, he brought me back materials to teach me how to communicate.

"That was so kind of him."

She nods as her eyes shimmer with tears. *He died a year ago. Joined the rebels and was killed in a fight.*

"I'm so sorry. What made him do that?"

"Petal, you're going to get yourself killed!" Bonny scolds.

"I won't say anything," I assure them. "I'm not happy with how things are here."

Petal swallows hard, then, after looking at Annie, who nods approvingly, she begins to tell me the story. *I came to work here when it was run by the previous family. Fearghas the First and Heelean were so kind. But when Odhran took over the kingdom, things grew colder. Still, I worked, and all was well. Until Taranus was appointed king. Conary—* she shuts her eyes tightly. *When my brother learned what he'd done— what he continued to do—he tried to force me to leave, but I have family to care for. I refused, and he swore to get vengeance for me. Conary killed him in a fight. He told me about it during...* She trails off, and Bonny wraps an arm around her shaking shoulders.

"Our lives are not as hard as they could be," she says, softly. "But they could be a lot better."

"A lot better. You are living a nightmare," I tell them.

"Someone is coming," Annie warns. Within seconds, all three women are back tending to their other chores.

A second later, the door opens, and Conary strolls in. "Petal, I need to speak with you."

She stiffens. "Actually," I interrupt, standing. "I would love the escort to my room if you are still offering. I'm quite exhausted."

"Absolutely," he replies. "Let us go, then." He heads for the door. When his back is turned, I use my hands and sign, *Be gone when he comes back.*

Thank you.

Trust shows on all three faces, and the women offer me smiles as I head into the hall with a monster.

CHAPTER 12

EMBER

The mid-morning sun is high in the sky, bathing the grass below my window in bright light. Snow-capped mountains in the distance are so similar to my world that it hurts my heart. If given the chance, I'd leave here and return to my death bed in the blink of an eye.

And isn't that saying something. Right after Conary escorted me here, he received a summons to see Taranus, so I'm really hoping Petal was bought more time—perhaps all the time she needs to realize that this place isn't worth what she's going through.

No amount of gold is worth the exchange of her body. Her soul.

I haven't seen Flora, though there was a fresh dress waiting for me when I arrived back into the room. I've been waiting for her, hoping to pump her for information on Rafferty's mate.

His mate. Why the hell didn't he tell me about her? We talked all night—about mates even—and he didn't even think to mention it? Is he embarrassed about what she did? Ashamed of the hand he had in her punishment?

A knock on my door pulls me from my thoughts, and I turn, running both palms down the stark white dress I'd changed into. It's exactly like the one I took off, but I suppose that doesn't really matter as long as it's not green.

"Come in," I call out.

The door pushes open, and a woman in white steps in. "Good morning, Ember." With her dark raven hair up in a tight bun, she looks like an evil headmistress at a boarding school you'd see in a cartoon.

"Lloren."

She pushes the door open all the way and moves into my room. "I'm happy to see you're wearing the king's colors."

"What do you want?"

"Were you perhaps expecting someone else?" she asks, with eyebrows drawn together.

I instinctively take a step toward the bed, wanting to put some distance between us. "Yes. Flora. I thought she would come to show me around."

"Flora is otherwise indisposed at the moment," she replies. Her tone, though, gives more away than I want to hear.

I stiffen as alarm bells go off in my head. "Where is she?"

"You'll see her soon enough." She clasps her hands together. "In fact, how about we go see her now?"

"What did you do to her?"

"Why would I do anything to her?" Lloren clicks her tongue. "Come, I'll take you to her." She holds out a hand and gestures toward the doorway. Slowly, I move toward it, my need to make sure Flora is okay overriding my own self-preservation.

Lloren guides me down the stairway at the end of the hall then leads me toward what I now know is the entrance to Rafferty's prison. We move past it, and I can't help myself. Sparing the darkened hallway a glance, I swallow hard, imagining him down there, in pain, alone.

"Right this way." She approaches the throne room door, and two guards flanking either side shove the doors open.

Taranus stands in the center of the room, his eyes hard, lip drawn up in disgust. Conary stands beside him, and directly in front of them is a woman on her knees. "Flora!" I scream her name as I rush inside and fall to my knees beside the bloodied woman. Her face is crusted in crimson, and her bare back is covered in lash marks, both fresh and partially healed, though based on the amount of blood— "What the hell did you do?" I roar at the king while hot tears sting my eyes.

He stares down at me, eyes hard. "You did this to her, Ember," he says softly, as he gets to his feet.

"What?" I reach for her head and pull it into my lap.

"Run," Flora whispers as she falls to her side, no longer strong enough to keep herself up. "You have to run."

I look down at her broken face and run a hand over her cheek. I've been here for a day. One damn day, and the first kind person I meet ends up bloodied and half-dead on the floor. Why is this happening to me?

"Yes, Ember. Please, try to run," the king says. "I will continue to do this to anyone you offer even the slightest smile to. I noticed you took quite a liking to Petal, Annie, and Bonny, too. Shall they be next?"

"No. Please, no. Leave them all alone!"

"You will understand something." He kneels before me. "Your future is here. With me."

I look back down to Flora—I want nothing to do with this. I'd rather die. And as long as I live in this place, I will search for a way to fight back.

"Why?"

"Flora was caught stealing supplies from the kitchen. It came as quite a shock to us as we've been nothing but kind to her." Lloren moves closer to the king, her feet gliding across the floor.

"Kind to her? You sliced off her wings, you fucking monsters!" The second I say it, I realize what I'd done. Covering my mouth with a shaking hand, I wait for the lashing.

"So, she told you of her punishment?" Conary demands.

"Figured I'd warn her of you arseholes," Flora chokes out.

"I'm so sorry, Flora."

She smiles at me, and I see her teeth, cracked and bloody. "You are fire, Ember. Burn them the moment you get the chance."

"Yes, Ember. Try," Conary taunts.

"Your place is here," the king repeats, ignoring her words. "You belong to me now, and it would do you good to remember that."

"Fine. I'll do whatever you want. Please, just don't hurt her."

The king nods to someone behind me and before I have a chance to fully glance over my shoulder, two men are gripping my arms painfully and dragging me backward. "Let me go!" I scream, fighting back against their hold as I cling to Flora.

"It's okay," she whispers.

"No! No, it's not! Don't hurt her!" I scream until my lungs burn, until my throat is so swollen with emotion that I can barely breathe.

Conary stalks forward, wearing a sick smile on his face. "I truly will enjoy this," he says as he kneels down and grips Flora by the hair, exposing her throat.

"No!" I scream again as I make eye contact with the king. "Please, I swear, I'll do anything you want. You can have me."

"You'd sacrifice your future and stay here with me, to save the life of a fae you just met?"

"Yes. A thousand times, yes. Please, just let her go."

The king regards me curiously, giving me hope that I reached a part of his heart that's not stone. But then, to my complete and utter horror, he turns to Conary. "Kill her."

"No!" Sobs break free from my chest, and I shake as Conary murders Flora right in front of me. Blood spills from her throat as she falls to the ground, face turned toward me. Her golden eyes are wide as she stares straight at me, and I lose the ability to stand.

My knees buckle, and I fall forward as bile surges up from my throat, allowing the contents of my stomach to splatter all over the marble floor. As my stomach heaves, tears burn down my cheeks.

Boots click across the marble, bringing the king closer and closer to me. A guard grips my hair and yanks my head back so I'm forced to stare up at him. With a slender finger, he reaches forward and touches my jaw. "I can be your best friend, lover, protector, Ember. Or, I can be your worst enemy."

At his use of the word 'lover,' my stomach churns all over again. "I want nothing from you, you miserable fucker."

He smiles. "You will. Toss her in the pit. A week down there should do her some good."

They drag me backward as I scream, kicking and hitting the fae who lifts me and tosses me over his shoulder. Another grips Flora by the legs and drags her, spreading her blood all over the floor. Seeing her lifeless body dragged away like trash breaks something in me.

Never, in my entire life, have I ever seen such horror. And to be honest, I never thought I would. But in the last day of being trapped here, I've seen nearly a dozen people die. Two of which were directly in front of me, and the others—well—they literally fell from the sky.

We descend steps, and I let my body go limp. Whatever the pit is? It can't be worse than what I just lived through.

Hot tears stream down my face.

"What the hell did you do to her?" Rafferty's voice fills my ears. A door squeaks open, and the guard drops me. My back hits the ground with a thud, but I don't cry out. Not even as pain shoots up my back and into my head. I bring my knees up to my chest and bury my face in between them while he slams the door shut.

"Keep your head in your own fucking business, Raffe," the guard grumbles. "Though, you should know, your little fae bitch is dead."

"Flora?" Rafferty's choked voice brings a fresh wave of grief over me, and I choke on a sob.

The guard chuckles. "Have fun with that one. Hope you enjoy the sound of whining. She's pretty damned pathetic." His boots carry him away, and I hold myself as tightly as I possibly can, trying to get the image of her lifeless eyes staring back at me out of my head.

"Ember," Rafferty says, softly. "Look at me, please."

I shake my head. "I got her killed," I choke out.

"No, no you didn't, Ember. Flora knew what she was doing."

"If I hadn't been here, she wouldn't be dead."

"Yes, she would be," he assures me. "Sooner or later, they would have killed her for what she was to me."

"They caught her getting supplies."

"Ember, look at me, please."

His voice cracks on the please, so I swallow hard and force myself to look up and meet his eyes across the narrow hall in our prison. His hard body presses against the bars as he grips them, and his eyes glisten with emotion. "Are you okay? Did they hurt you?"

I shake my head and look down at my once white dress. It's stained with red.

"Flora wanted to get out of here," Rafferty says. "More than anything. And now, she's free of this place. This hell."

"How can you say that? She was alive while she was here."

"There is a vast difference in being alive and living, Ember. Trust me. The things Flora faced within these walls were a lot more horrific than meeting death."

"I don't belong here."

"No, you don't," he agrees. "This is no place for anyone with a kind heart."

"You don't even know me," I shoot back, angrily.

Rafferty doesn't even hesitate. "I can see your kindness, Ember. And it's going to be what gets you killed."

CHAPTER 13
RAFFERTY

Ember's cries are daggers to my chest.

Hours have passed, and still, she sheds tears over the loss of a fae she'd only just met. That guilt—anguish—it's evidence enough of how kind she is. Not that I'd needed to see it to believe what I know to be true.

Despite the dreams predicting her to be a woman of destruction, I can sense her goodness, her innocence, and the fact that part of it was stolen from her today makes me angrier than I've been ever since getting tossed into this fucking pit. The things I've seen since being down here—there are no words apt enough to describe them.

And still, knowing this woman is hurting brings me more agony than I care to admit.

Taranus is a plague on this realm, and it's my fault

he is where he is. My people suffer day after day—being murdered, tortured—because I made a fucking mistake and trusted the wrong person.

Flora is dead because of me.

And the woman I've been dreaming of for the last few weeks is trapped down here because of me.

I shake my head and force myself to stand, pacing across my cell as I try to come up with any plan at all to get her out of here in one piece. But without my magic or anyone who can come save me, I'm at a complete loss.

A door opens, and boots hammer against the stone as they descend.

"Get away from the bars," I tell Ember.

She lifts her head, her amber eyes wide, but after a heartbeat, she nods and pushes to her feet, backing as far away as she can just as Taranus comes into view.

He smiles at me, lips pulling back from white teeth. "Rafferty. I see you've met my future bride."

Ember chokes on a sob.

"So this is how you treat your betrothed?" I shoot back. "Pretty fucking sure you were raised better than that."

Taranus chuckles. "You would know, brother."

"You told me he was dead," she whispers.

"He might as well be. Isn't that right, big brother Raffe?" Taranus grins at me, and his eyes glitter with amusement. "The perfect son, finally seen for what he is. A criminal." He spits the last word at me as though it's poison.

"I'm only a criminal because you're too afraid to let me out."

Taranus rolls his eyes. "Afraid? Not even in the slightest."

"Then let me out."

"You only want out so you can rip me away from what is my rightful position."

"Being king was never your right."

"It should have been."

"Fearghas was to be king." Mention of the true Prince of Faerie reddens Taranus's cheeks.

"He didn't want it."

"No," I agree. "But you never would have been anywhere near the line of succession."

"Because you'd planted yourself firmly at the top."

"Being head of the king's guards is what placed me at the top." I'd spent centuries serving the rightful king—Fearghas the First. Centuries of service, and I'd failed him when his daughter betrayed him. He'd lost his crown, his throne, and we'd all become outlaws.

Taranus snorts. "When bedding Sheelin didn't work as planned, you'd gone—"

I snarl, clenching my hands into fists. "I never bedded Sheelin. You know that."

"Not for lack of trying, eh, brother? Before Odhran, you had eyes for her, despite having a mate rotting away in the Veil, did you not?"

Back when Sheelin had been little more than an innocent princess, there had been moments between us, though they never would have amounted to anything. Even if Odhran hadn't manipulated then raped his way into her life. "You've no idea what you're talking about."

"Odhran saw what he wanted, and he claimed it. He was the strongest king this realm had ever seen, and yet you sought to overthrow him."

"He was a fucking monster."

Taranus shakes his head. "Even still, when Sheelin was queen, you did everything you could to get the crown. Tell me, how was what I did any different than you? You're simply angry I reached the top first."

"I never would have rested my crown upon the deaths of innocents," I snap back, enraged that he'd even attempt to compare the two of us. The truth is, Taranus was always a psychotic bastard, but I'd chosen to ignore it because I'd foolishly believed our blood bond was enough to keep him in check.

And every death, every atrocity carried out by his hands or the hands of his men, rests firmly upon my shoulders because, by the time I realized just what he was capable of, it was too late.

"You've always been weak, Rafferty. It's why you would never have been king." He turns away from me and moves toward Ember. Pressing her back against the stone, she's helpless to get any farther away.

I know that if I show fear on her behalf, he'll use it against the both of us, so I grip the bars and keep my mouth shut as they open the door and he moves into her cell.

Ember's eyes clamp shut, and she turns her head to the side as he reaches forward and trails a finger along her jaw. "What to do with you, my dear?"

"Let me go."

He chuckles, and I want to smash his face into the stone walls surrounding us. Over and over again, until he's nothing more than blood and broken bones.

"You won't be going anywhere."

"Why not?"

"Because you will give me sons, who will continue on with my legacy, making us the most powerful fae in all the realm."

She turns to him now, jaw hard, eyes glistening with unshed tears. "I will not go to bed with you."

He grips her chin, and she whimpers. It takes every bit of my restraint to keep me from losing my shit. The only reason I remain calm, though, is because my outburst would cause her nothing but more pain.

"You will come to bed with me after we are wed, human."

"No."

He shoves her back then opens his hand and slaps her. The crack echoes through my ears. "Taranus!" I roar, unable to keep myself chained any longer. Ember crumples to the floor, holding her face, and I use all the strength in my arsenal to try my damnedest to pry the bars apart.

He glances over his shoulder with amusement showing in every line of his arrogant face. "You are so predictable." Chuckling, he reaches down and grips her arm, yanking her up as she whimpers. He drags her out of her cell, careless of the white dress scraping against the stone floor.

"Let her the fuck go," I growl.

"She's a human."

"She's a person," I snap back.

Taranus slams her against the bars, and her eyes shut as her cheek is pressed against the cool metal. "Open his door," he orders Conary.

"Your Majesty?"

"You heard me. Open. His. Door."

Jaw tight, Taranus's little pet reaches into his pocket and pulls out a key then does as he's told and opens my cell door. I clench my fists, waiting for my chance to rush out and kill them all. But before I can, he throws Ember inside.

I rush to grab her before she can fall, but my movements are slowed by my still-healing body. Reaching her moments after she hits the ground, I kneel and glare up at Taranus as he slams my cell door once more.

His sharp jaw is tight; his thin lips pulled into a snarl. "You care so much, you do with her what you wish. After she spends some time with you down here, she'll be begging me to take her." He laughs and turns on his heel, marching toward the stairwell with the other fae behind him.

"Are you okay?" I reach for her, but Ember scrambles away from me, pressing her back against the far wall. I clench both hands into fists at my sides to keep from reaching for her again.

Her eyes are wide, terrified, and she stares at me, holding her hand against her cheek still red from Taranus's palm. "What are you going to do to me?"

"Nothing. I won't put a hand on you."

"No? This isn't all some sort of sick, twisted game to get me to do what you want? To free you? Let's manipulate the weak human girl, huh?" She sniffles. "You two are brothers after all."

The accusation is clear as day, pissing me off even more. "By blood, yes, but in no other way."

Her face breaks, and she sobs, pulling her knees

up to her chest. I reject the urge to rush toward her and, instead, scoot back and lean against the opposite wall to put as much distance between us as possible.

I can't even imagine what she's going through, this human who found herself in another world entirely.

"Why is this happening to me?" she whispers.

"I don't know. But I'm sorry."

"I should have just let myself die in Austin."

The words are muttered, barely audible. "Die? Why?" It's the second time she's mentioned death to me, leading me to wonder just what it is she was suffering with before she ended up here.

Turning her head to the side, she stares out through the bars. "It doesn't matter now."

"Ember."

She looks at me.

"I swear I won't hurt you. Can I please come look at your cheek?" The need to be close to her, to ensure her safety, is so overwhelming it's all I can think about. Holding my breath, I wait for her response.

Finally, she nods. Wasting no more moments, I get to my feet and approach her slowly then sink back to my knees beside her. I raise my hand and gently touch the side of her cheek where Taranus dared redden it. "I will kill him," I promise. "One day, he will pay for everything he's done."

Ember's full bottom lip quivers as silent tears

stream down her cheeks. Her dress is ruined with what I assume is Flora's blood and dirt from the ground here in this cell. Bruised cheek aside, she looks a hell of a lot worse off than she is. Something I am incredibly grateful for.

Taking a seat beside her now, I leave only a foot of space between us. "Tell me of Austin?"

"Distracting me won't work," she snaps.

"Let me try. Let me do something. You helped me yesterday. Now let me do the same."

She remains silent and still refuses to look at me. Then, after a few moments, she sighs. "It's a city."

"Large?"

She nods.

"And it wanted you dead?"

"What?" Her eyes shift up to mine, and I'm struck dumb beneath her gaze. Never, in my entire immortal life, have I ever seen such eyes. So amber, they're nearly copper, they swirl with kindness, innocence, and strength.

And they're so much more haunting in person than they were in my dreams.

Swallowing hard, I force my gaze away. She's already been made uncomfortable enough. "You said you should have let yourself die in Austin. Twice now, you've referenced death."

Her eyes stay on mine for a heartbeat as confusion draws her brows together before, finally, she shakes her head. "Austin is a city in Texas. I—um—I was sick there," she says. Her cheeks flush, and I get the impression it's not something she wishes to talk about. "It's the only reason I'm here."

"Your illness?"

She nods. "I went to Ireland to get away from it all." Shutting her eyes, she shakes her head angrily. "I should have just accepted the truth and died in hospice like they'd wanted me to do."

The thought of this woman fading away, of dying in whatever hospice is, is more frightening than it should have been. "You shouldn't think like that. Weak thoughts will lead to your death."

Her head whips toward me. "Weak thoughts? In case you're not up to speed, I'm trapped in a cell, have seen people killed right in front of me, and was just told that I was going to be raped—repeatedly—until I produce an heir for a psychotic king. Not quite the true love, white-picket-fence I'd once hoped for."

My hands tighten into fists all over again, and I force myself to calm down, taking deep breath after deep breath until the rage is nothing but a steady flame. "He won't get his hands on you, Ember. I swear it."

"What are you going to do to stop him?" she demands. I can't blame her for asking. Truth is, I have no fucking clue how to stop him from getting to her.

I've failed every other time he's taken what did not belong to him.

"I'll think of something."

"And why do you care? It's not like you know me. Other than needing me to get a key, which, by the way, I can't get while I'm in here."

"I don't need you for the key," I reply, angrily. "In case you've forgotten, I asked you—repeatedly—to leave and not bother with me."

"Something you know I can't do."

The hostility I'm sensing from her, it's such a stark change from the woman who sat here with me all night, and it has me wondering just what lies were spread of me while she was upstairs. "Why are you angry with me?"

"You didn't tell me you had a mate."

Fucking assholes. "She is not someone I care to speak of."

"Why? Because you can't live with the guilt of leaving her to rot in the Veil? Whatever the hell that is."

"She brought that upon herself when she all but handed my sister over to a dark fae then tried to over-throw the king."

Ember stiffens, turning her gaze on me now. She scans my face, and I imagine she's searching for anything that will allude to a lie. "Are you telling me the truth?"

"Yes. She was always jealous of the attention Niahm received—even more so after I caught her sneaking into the human world to bed shifters on whims. So, in retaliation for my anger, she had my sister killed and attempted to overthrow the king. As punishment, he sent her into the Veil."

"And what the hell is the Veil?"

"You've heard me mention the Veil separating us from the human world?"

"Yes."

"They're one and the same, only that Veil is a place where supernaturals go when they die. A sort of purgatory before they pass on."

"Where she can rot for eternity."

"Something she quite deserved, I can assure you."

"But you told me your mate is tied to you irrevocably."

"Which is why he could not order her execution. She simply resides on a plane that is separate from this one. As long as I avoid the Veil and she remains there, it's as if she does not exist to me."

"So you can mate again?"

A muscle in my jaw twitches, and I turn away. "No. Never."

"Why? If she doesn't exist?"

"Because, I cannot." Sighing, I lift a knee and rest my hand on top. "I believe I am meant to protect you. To get you to the true king," I say, softly. "Not

Taranus but a strong man you can love and be loved by in return."

"And who the hell is that?"

"I don't know yet," I reply, truthfully. We have no clue who should be the next king. As Taranus pointed out, I once thought it would be me, but after the prophecy was revealed—well—let us just say I know that I am not who is to lead our world.

My future as king was a dream and nothing more.

"Who's to say another man would be any better?"

"They have to be," I tell her. "We can't be destined to be led by Taranus. It's a fate too horrible to consider."

"It could be destiny, though," she replies, "And sometimes we're just dealt a shit hand." Her jaw tightens, and I get the impression she's somewhere far away from here. Perhaps back in her Austin where life was simpler, even with her illness.

"I promise you, Ember from Austin, that I will do my best to protect you until we can get you to the rightful king."

"So I can spread my legs and give him babies? No thanks. I just want to go home."

"Then I will get you home."

She snorts. "Impossible."

"Hasn't your trip here shown you that nothing is impossible?"

Her eyes close, and she leans back against the

wall. "Maybe this really is just one horrific nightmare."

I don't reply, not wanting to rip away her false hopes that this is all a fable. Instead, I stare at her, memorizing the angle of her jaw, the shape of her nose, all while I silently plead for her to open her eyes again so I can see the honey glow once more.

Ever since my first dream of her, I've been drawn to her. Wishing for sleep so I could imagine her again. I'd never actually believed her to exist, though. I'd always assumed she was nothing more than a figment of my pained imagination. Even after the seer's prophecy, I'd been reluctant to believe she was real.

But now that she's here, I know my dreams were more than that and that I was shown her because I am destined to protect her.

To shield her.

To die for her.

And if it comes to that, I will gladly fall on my sword.

CHAPTER 14
EMBER

Though my head is throbbing, I force myself to sit up and wipe what I'm really hoping is dried blood and not drool from the corner of my mouth. My cheek aches, the bone surely bruised after that asshole smacked me last night.

And as predicted, I'm still down in a prison cell beneath a castle in Faerie.

Grief wells up in my chest as I realize I will probably never leave this place. I've never felt so helpless, so alone, as I do right now. My gaze drifts to where Rafferty sleeps a few feet from me. He's leaned back against the wall, muscled and scarred chest on full display in the dim firelight of the sconces on the walls.

If ever there were an example of a man, it would be this one. His dark hair is cut extremely short. His face is covered in stubble, making him a direct contrast to his bastard brother. And the differences don't end there, either. As I said, the man is muscle upon muscle.

And now that we're in the same cell and he's not bleeding out or suffering from horrific pain, I can take the time to actually study him. It's a nice distraction from the horrors that haunted what little sleep I got.

Lines I didn't even know a man could possess shape a chest most women would kill to get their hands on. A thick scar starts at his left hip and climbs up to his left pec, disappearing into a light dusting of dark hair.

Sporting another scar along the right side of his face, slashing through his eyebrow and picking back up beneath his eye, the man looks like he's straight from the pages of a romantic fantasy novel.

I honestly don't think he'll hurt me. If he was going to, he'd had plenty of opportunities last night. What I can't figure out is why Taranus believes spending time in here with his brother will make me accept what he wants from me.

From where I'm sitting right now, I'd sure as hell rather be down here than up there with that psychotic bastard. I draw my knees up to my chest and wrap both arms around them. There are no windows down here, no fresh air, just a bucket in the corner I really,

really don't want to look in, and an empty plate in the corner.

Rafferty groans, and I turn toward him just in time to see golden eyes flutter open. His gaze holds mine, and for a moment, neither of us move. I don't even breathe, totally unable to tear my eyes from his. What is it about this man—sorry, this fae—that renders me completely speechless?

Finally, he clears his throat. "Good morning."

"Morning."

"I'd ask if you slept well, but I'm assuming the answer to that is no."

Snorting, I shake my head. "That would definitely be a no."

He runs a hand over the back of his neck. "There's, uh, no bathroom down here." Then, he gestures to the bucket I was just attempting to avoid thinking about. "Sorry."

"Definitely getting zero stars from me."

His brow furrows as he tries to understand what I said, and it's yet another stark reminder that I'm trapped in another world. If we'd been in my imagination, he would have totally gotten my joke.

"Never mind."

"I need to—" He stands and gestures toward the bucket.

My cheeks flush as I turn toward the bars and try not to think about the fact that he's peeing a few yards behind me. Still, it's not even his pee that's bothering me but the fact that I'm going to be expected to use a bucket.

"Sorry."

"Don't apologize. Everyone pees." Awkward at best, I rarely interact with people, let alone muscled warrior fae men. The ground shuffles behind me as he sits again, so I turn and press my back against the wall. "How long have you been down here?"

"I've honestly lost count."

"How did they capture you in the first place?" When he stares at me curiously, I gesture to his muscles and immediately wish I could have a re-do. "You just don't look like someone who would go down easily."

The fae man smiles, and my breath catches in my throat, making me realize that I'm a glutton for punishment. Hello, Stockholm syndrome, thy name is Ember. "Men like me have weaknesses, Ember. Taranus knows enough about me that he was able to drop me to my knees."

"How?"

He shakes his head. "It's not something you need to burden yourself with. You've seen enough horrors over the past few days."

More curious than ever, I wish I could know—if only so I can see what power Taranus used to bring this man to his knees. Though I know that there are things I really wish not to talk about, so I let it go. "How often do they come down here?"

"It depends. Before you, I would go three days without seeing anyone but Flora." His jaw tightens after mentioning her name, and guilt slams into me like a ton of bricks falling onto my head.

"I'm sorry about her."

"She knew what she was doing. Saving you was more important."

"But why? Just because Taranus thinks I'm part of some prophecy?"

"You are the prize to be won, Ember."

"You guys have your wires crossed. I told you I'm nobody."

"And, as I told you, you're wrong." When I turn to him, he smiles softly. "Everyone is someone."

"Everyone but me. Trust me." Swallowing hard, I take a deep breath. "I'm sorry about being so angry yesterday. I shouldn't have taken it out on you."

"You're trapped in a strange world where nearly everyone you've met has lied to you."

"Have you? Lied to me."

"Never," he replies. "You'll get nothing but truth from me, Ember."

"Hmm." Drawing my knees up to my chest, I wrap both arms around them. "Surprisingly, this is not the worst place I've ever slept." My attempt at a joke is half-hearted at best, and based on Rafferty's reaction, he certainly doesn't see the humor.

"You said you were an orphan?"

"Never knew my parents. I was abandoned at an orphanage, but after multiple attempts at adopting me out, I tried to run away. Spent a month living on the streets, eating scraps from the garbage." For others who hear the story, it brings horror. But that month was the most free I'd ever felt. At least, until I became an adult. Those few years of freedom before I was imprisoned by illness were pure bliss.

"That's horrible."

"It is what it is. Just pointing out that things can always be worse."

"Worse than being held captive? I fear what your life was before here if it were truly worse."

"I'm dying." The words are out of my mouth before I can filter them. Very few times have I ever been so blunt about it, so honest—mainly because I despise the pitied looks from people when they find out the truth. "It's not just that I'm sick; the disease is killing me."

But Rafferty looks at me with no pity now. It's refreshing. "You look fine to me."

"It's different here. I've spent the last five years searching for answers as to why my body was shutting down, and no one could tell me anything. Just before I left for Ireland, a doctor informed me that my life was nearing an end. That I needed to get my affairs in order and turn myself in for hospice care." A tear slips down my cheek, and I rest my face on my knees. "I was hot all the time, sweaty, and unable to eat anything without puking it back up."

"But you do not feel that way here?"

I shake my head. "Ever since I woke up in that forest, I've felt more like myself than I have in years. Honestly, before I realized what an asshole Taranus was, I would have given nearly anything to stay."

A muscle in his jaw ticks. "And now? How do you feel now?"

It's my turn to look angry now. "I would rather die than spend another moment with him."

We settle back into silence, our breathing the only sound in the small space. Footsteps echo ahead, and I jump to my feet, reaching between my breasts and withdrawing the tonic. "Where can I hide this?" I whisper, loudly.

Rafferty reaches forward, so I hand it to him, and he tucks it behind him. I rush to the back of the cell as Rafferty remains seated. Though, even I notice how his muscles coil in preparation for a fight.

"How was your first night down here, human?" Conary's voice grates on me like a dozen tiny blades as he comes into view at the bottom of the stairs. I don't speak, though, mainly because I'm far too terrified of what his being down here means for me.

"What the hell do you want, Conary?" Rafferty questions, still not moving from his spot.

"Thought the soon-to-be queen could use some fresh clothes." He holds them through the bars, staring straight at me. "Come and get them."

"Just leave them and go." Rafferty yawns and crosses both arms over his broad chest.

"No. If she wants them, the lass can come get them. Can't she?"

The idea of getting out of this blood-stained dress is far too comforting to pass up, so I take a cautious step forward. Then another. Conary holds steady delight in my compliance, evident in his sadistic grin.

As soon as I'm close enough, I reach out and grip the fabric. Before I can pull it back, he yanks me forward, gripping my forearm and yanking me against the bars. Rafferty is at my side in an instant, his arm through the bars and gripping the arm that pins me.

"You'll want to let her go," he warns, "or I'll snap your fucking arm like a twig."

"Do that, and I'll rip her through these bars with such force it will crack her pretty little neck." Fingers brush against my throat. "And what a pretty little neck it is."

"Let. Her. The. *Fuck.* Go."

Rafferty's voice simmers with violence.

Conary grins and releases me. Rafferty lets him go and takes a step back with me. "Go on and change, little bird." Gone is his attempt at appearing charming, which makes me wonder just what he was getting at in the first place. Or is he truly bipolar?

"Not until you leave."

He grins at me. "I have all day, and I'm under strict orders to take that dress back upstairs."

My skin crawls with the idea of removing any clothing in front of this pervert, so I toss the clothes to the ground.

"Let me make this clear for you. Either you change now, or I will come in there and do it for you."

"Come in and you won't leave alive."

Conary chuckles at Rafferty's threat. "Your threats are worthless to me, Raffe."

"Then come in." Rafferty takes a step back and holds out his arms.

"Sounds fun." Conary unsheathes his blade and moves toward the gate. Fear over my cellmate kicks me into courage mode, and I shake my head, leaning down and grasping the clothes.

"No. I'll do it."

"Ember—"

"No. It's fine," I interrupt Rafferty, and Conary stops right in front of the bars.

"Go ahead, then. Don't be shy." Sheathing his blade, he crosses his arms and stares at me. Rafferty steps to the right and positions himself as much in front of me as he can get.

With shaking fingers, I untie the ribbon over my left shoulder that holds the dress in place. It flutters to the ground, revealing a chemise that barely covers anything. It's unstained, so I start to leave it on.

"Chemise, too, little bird. Prisoners do not wear silk." He grins as he says the words, licking his lips as he glances around Rafferty at me. My cellmate moves farther to the right and takes a step back, nearly completely obliterating the other man's view.

With a deep breath, I drop it to the ground and force my eyes down as I quickly slip into the fabric he brought down for me. The long skirt is tattered and torn where huge spots of missing fabric show my skin beneath. But at least, it's more fabric than the pathetic top that barely covers my breasts.

As soon as I'm covered, though, I grab the blood-stained dress and chemise and shove past Raffe, throwing them through the bars at Conary's smiling face.

"See, was that so hard, little bird?"

"Screw you," I spit back, and immediately regret my choice of words.

"Oh? Is that an offer?" He reaches down and grabs his groin. "I'll make a woman out of you."

"You got what you wanted," Rafferty growls. "Get the fuck on."

Conary chuckles and shakes his head. "I can't wait to tell your brother just how protective you are of his bride. I believe he'll find it to be quite interesting."

As soon as he's out of sight, I let out a breath. Rafferty, however, turns to the wall and slams his fist into the stone. Bones crack, and I gape at him in horror.

"What the hell! He's gone!" I rush forward and reach for his hand, but he yanks it back.

"Do you have any idea what they're going to do to you?" He whirls on me, cradling his bloody and likely broken knuckles.

"I—"

"These fae, Ember, they're monsters."

"I know that."

His expression is tortured as he looks one word away from falling over. "I'm so sorry." He sinks to the ground.

"Sorry for what? You tried to shield me from him." I kneel beside him, feeling a hell of a lot more comfortable than I should have.

"I never should have. I should have pretended not to care."

"Why? What are you rambling on about?"

His golden eyes meet mine, and in them, I see fear. "You have just become my latest weakness, Ember. And they will use you to try and break me."

CHAPTER 15
EMBER

Days pass with the speed of molasses in January—as a friend of mine at the orphanage used to say. Since I can't gauge the sunlight outside, I have no way of knowing exactly how long it's been since Conary forced me to change, but if I go strictly based on my exhaustion schedule and the single trays of food brought down for Rafferty and me to share, I'd say it's been about three days.

Three days since Rafferty has spoken a word to me.

Three days since I've breathed fresh air or seen the sunlight.

I have no idea how the man currently brooding in the corner managed to remain sane during his stay here. I'm already about to lose my damn mind.

The door above opens, but I stay where I am. Chances are it's just another tray of food. But as soon as the boots hit the stone stairs above, I'm on my feet and pressing my back in the corner as far as I can get it.

"Get up," I hiss at Rafferty, but he makes no move to either get away from the bars or to look at me. "Dammit, Raffe!"

A man appears at the bottom of the stairs, wearing the white and golden armor of a guard. Though, he's not alone. Directly behind him is Petal. The petite brunette peeks around and smiles with relief when she sees me. Shoving past the guard, she rushes over and begins signing with her hands so quickly I can barely follow.

"Easy, Petal, I can't understand. You're moving too fast."

She nods and then begins to sign again, much slower this time. *How are you? I am sorry I was unable to come see you before now. It was not safe.*

I meet the gaze of the guard before me. "Is it now?"

"I will not harm you, milady," he says. "Rafferty, I am glad to see you breathing."

Raffe moves now, if the shuffling behind me is any indication. I can feel his body heat directly beside me almost instantly. It's intoxicating. "Tommy, I'm glad to see you alive. What the hell are you doing here?"

"Getting my mate." He wraps an arm around Petal's shoulders, and she returns to me.

We ran into each other in town while I was getting vegetables for the kitchen. He is going to get me out of here, tonight. We want you to come.

Tears spring to my eyes as I reach through the bars and grip her hands. "I cannot go with you, Petal. The only one who has a key is Conary, and he's not letting us out any time soon. You guys go, now, before he sees you."

"He and Taranus are off the grounds at the moment," Tommy replies. He reaches behind him and hands Raffe a dagger through the bars. "The Rebellion needs you, Raffe. We're falling apart without you."

"I wish I could help."

"Have you seen Heelean?"

"She's here. Trapped in a warded room," I tell him.

"Shit."

"We'll find a way to get her out," Rafferty promises. "But now, you and your mate need to leave before it's too late. Once they're back, you're done. And don't dematerialize, not until you're sure you can't be followed."

"We won't. Goodbye."

"Goodbye."

The two men clasp hands, and Petal squeezes mine. "I know," I tell her. "I'll be fine, though. I'm fairly resilient."

With one final smile, they turn and leave, heading up the stairs quietly and quickly. I glance over as Raffe runs his finger along the blade of the dagger.

"Considering murdering your cellmate?" I ask.

He doesn't look at me.

"Listen, I don't know what I did to piss you off, but I'm getting really tired of the silent treatment."

Now, he lifts his gaze to me. "You cannot even begin to imagine what you being down here is doing to me." His eyes, darker now, are hard to read, his expression contorted to something akin to annoyance? Perhaps anger? "I don't even understand it."

"Seriously? You barely speak to me! What could I have possibly done to bother you?"

Rafferty takes a step toward me. Then another. I back away and swallow hard. His intense gaze is something I've never seen on his face. He looks more animal than man—a darker version of himself—and it's terrifying.

"Rafferty?"

"My name on your lips is sweet torture," he growls. The cool stone presses into my back, and I'm stopped in place. "Cool, cool torture," he whispers.

"If you're trying to scare me—"

"You? Never." He reaches out to touch me, and I whimper.

"Rafferty, what the hell is going on?"

He moves in toward me more, so I reach out and slam both hands into his chest. He stumbles back a step then glares at me. "You are no match for me," he snarls, baring teeth.

I reach up and slap him. The resounding crack echoes along the walls until Rafferty blinks rapidly, his eyes clearing. "What—"

"Back the hell off, Rafferty. Or next, it will be your balls."

"What are you—" He stares down at his hands then backs clear away, not stopping until he's on the other side. Then, he lifts the blade and, to my complete horror, runs it down his forearm, slicing it clean open.

"Rafferty! What the hell are you doing?" I scream and run forward as he sinks to the ground. I reach for him, but he shakes his head.

"No. Leave it."

Then, I turn my attention to the wound. I've seen a lot of blood recently—an unfortunately horrible turn of events—which is why I notice the shade of the blood coming from his arm is off.

Where it should have been a bright red, it's a dark crimson; far darker than I would have expected.

I move in close enough to see his expression

relax, but far enough that if he gets any ideas I have a chance to get a knee up. "What is that?"

"Dark magic," he replies.

"Dark magic? Why is there dark magic coming out of your arm?"

"My sister was sold to a dark fae," he explains. "I hunted him down and killed him, inadvertently absorbing his soul-matter."

"Soul-matter? What the hell is that?" My gaze shifts from his face, back to his arm, then up to his face again. Could my life get any more complicated?

"Dark fae exist only in the Veil unless they are freed. My mate freed him, so I killed him. Their soul-matter can be absorbed by a light fae, but it alters us, changing our magic, polluting our blood. At first, I needed to open a vein once every new moon, shortly before the Rebellion fell, though, it was once every couple of days."

"What happens when you don't?"

Rafferty's gaze levels on me. "You just saw it."

"So you turn into an asshole?"

He chuckles darkly, "Something like that. It gets harder to control."

"And if you can't control it?"

"I will become worse than anything you could ever imagine. Dark fae are unpredictable. They are driven by their desire for power—for chaos.

Embracing it, while I would be able to free myself instantly, would require a sacrifice I cannot make."

"You could free yourself?"

"I could. Once I'm away from the iron. But as I said, it would be far more dangerous."

"But why? Couldn't you just open a vein like you just did?"

He swallows hard. "The dark soul-matter pollutes, Ember. Keeping it at bay without using it is difficult enough. Should I get drunk on the power, I'd become far worse than Taranus could ever be."

"I find that hard to imagine."

"Don't."

That one word silences my argument. I may not know much about this world, but Rafferty promised never to lie to me. If I am to believe that—to believe him—keeping his control is more important than getting him out.

Especially if he becomes what I just saw.

"Why did it change? You said it was once every month, then once every couple of days."

"I don't know, but I steadily grew more volatile, so I upped the bleedings."

"Upped the bleedings...like that's some legitimate medical procedure." I stand and begin to pace. I'm two steps in when I realize exactly what Taranus had hoped for by putting me down here. "Taranus said time with you would make me wish for him."

"Yes."

"Did he know about this?"

"Yes," he repeats, this time with a bit more edge in his voice.

"Then he wanted you to attack me. That was his plan all along; his plan to get me to want to be with him." As I speak the words, a plan of my own begins to form.

"What is your point?"

"I might still be able to save us," I tell him. "But I need your help."

"Tell me what to do."

CHAPTER 16
EMBER

"How is my bride-to-be doing?" Taranus calls out as he moves down the stairs.

Rafferty takes his place in the corner, and I curl into a ball to begin whimpering. "Help me," I whisper. "Please."

"What happened here?" Taranus's question is not laced with any kind of emotion, telling me that I was right—this is *exactly* what he'd been hoping for. Time to put those two years of drama in high school to work.

"He attacked me. He's enraged. I don't know why. Please. I'll do anything, just get me out of here."

"Roll over," Taranus orders.

I do as he said and have to force myself to hide the joy I feel at the uncomfortable look on his face.

I'm assuming the blood Rafferty caked all over my cheek did the trick.

"What did he do to you?" Taranus questions.

"He shoved me into the wall. I can feel the blood. Is there blood?" Reaching up, I touch my fingers to the scratch he'd forced me to give myself. I wince. "Shit, that hurts." I manage to get on all fours and crawl toward the bars. "Please, I promise to do as you wish. Just don't make me stay down here anymore."

Taranus cocks his head to the side and studies Rafferty, who has played his silent part far too well. "I suppose it's time for you to get some aid, wouldn't you say, big brother?"

"Come in here and try." His words are a dare— bait—but Taranus isn't stupid. Not for all his faults.

Taranus chuckles. "I'm going to take your toy away."

"No."

The grin that spreads over his face is disturbing on so many levels. I've no doubt that if Taranus didn't think he needed me to become the true king, he'd have left me down here. Dangling me in front of a madman like a fucking carrot.

"You have no say here."

As if he were summoned like the evil being he is, Conary comes down the steps and stops beside his king. "What have we here?"

"Rafferty has enjoyed his new toy long enough. I

can't have her bruised for the wedding." He kneels beside the bars. "I am rather enjoying this outfit you've found yourself in. Tell me, Ember, are you ready to behave?"

I sniffle again, continuing to let my tears fall as I nod frantically. "Yes. I'm sorry. Please, just let me go back to my room."

"Very well." He snaps his fingers, and Conary removes his sword before unlocking the bars. "Come out, then."

I try to remind myself to keep up the ruse as I move forward toward the monsters waiting for me outside. As soon as I'm close enough, Conary grabs my hair and drags me forward then slams the bars closed behind me. When I glance back at Rafferty, he's watching me carefully, eyes never straying from my face. Taranus pulls me toward the stairs, so I force myself to look away from the man behind me and focus on tricking the one in front of me.

At least, long enough that I can get the key, free Rafferty, and get the hell out of this place for good.

We move through the castle quickly, taking hallways I didn't know existed until we're standing in front of my room. Conary steps around to open my door, and Taranus walks inside with me. Within moments, we're alone in my bedroom.

I shove my nerves down, and my stomach churns

with his promise that I'd have no choice but to go to bed with him.

"Easy, human, I have no intention of bedding you today." It's not until he says that, that I realize I was staring at the bed.

"Why are you doing this to me?"

"You needed a lesson on behaving. Was my brother not kind to you?" He moves farther into the space, walking to the window and staring out before turning back to me.

If I ran really, really fast, I bet I could push him hard enough to topple over the balcony. Problem is, if he's like the others, the bastard can fly. "Does it look like he was?"

Taranus nods. "That is a fair point. I know you view me as a monster, Ember, but I am not the villain in this story."

Not in yours, anyway. "You killed Flora and locked me in a cell."

"Flora was a rebel. Do you know what the rebels would do to you if they got their hands on you?" When I don't immediately respond, he continues. "You are the one who will make me the true king. A feared and beloved leader for this world. The Rebellion does not wish for me to be king." He takes a step toward me and reaches up to brush a strand of hair from my cheek, "Do you see the problem with that?"

"You believe they would kill me?"

"No. No, I don't think that. But they would use you to get to me. They would torture you, torment you—do things to you that would permanently alter the way you saw the world."

Kind of like the way you did the same when you had Flora slaughtered in front of me. "They sound awful," I choke out.

"They are. Rafferty is jealous of my status. He believed that, given his closeness to the first king, he has the right to my crown. But he doesn't."

"Jealous of his younger brother's success," I say dryly, hating myself for just saying the words. "I've heard that story before."

Taranus beams. "No doubt you have. Humans have their own troubles, do they not?"

"We do."

"I know it doesn't seem like it, but by killing Flora, I was saving you. I apologize for the things I said to you in that cell, for throwing you down there in the first place. The truth is, I want a happy life for us, Ember. Lots of children, laughter, and while I know you did not ask for this, I truly believe you can grow to love me."

I swallow hard, forcing bile back down my throat. "I can't promise anything."

He smiles softly. "I know you can't, my dear Ember. But mark my words, we will be happy. Centuries of joy between us." He moves past me and toward the door. "There is a bath awaiting you, and a gown will be placed on your bed. We have a ball tonight, my dear. And I want to show you off to my world."

"Can I have some food?" I ask quickly. "I'm starving."

"Absolutely." Taranus smiles. "Anything you desire shall be yours. All you have to do is follow everything I say."

Oh, I plan to do just that. "Thank you so much."

———

SNEAKING AROUND IN A STARK WHITE DRESS SHOULD have been a lot easier.

I duck behind a wall and wait for two maids to hustle past me, while also trying my best to not dump the makeshift cloth baggie full of fresh fruit I pilfered from my room. People are everywhere, rushing around, carrying large vases of flowers, platters of ribbons, and some jars full of sparkly stuff I'm not even going to pretend to understand.

Ball preparations are in full swing, which makes this both easier and harder.

"Ensure Ember is prepared for tonight." Taranus's voice echoes through the hall, and I freeze, pressing as far back against the wall as I can get. If he sees me, I can pretend that I'm out for a stroll, needing some fresh air after spending so much time locked away with the horrible brute, Rafferty. However, if he does catch me, my plan will be foiled, and I will, no doubt, be forced to follow him around, a fake smile plastered on my face.

"Yes, Your Majesty. Shall I go fetch her now?"

Shit.

"Not just yet. She spent quite a bit of time in that cell, let her freshen up for a bit longer. But be sure to fetch her at least an hour prior to our introduction. I wish to prepare her beforehand."

"Yes, Your Majesty." The feminine voice is unknown to me, but soon, their footsteps fade away, and I breathe a sigh of relief.

After peeking around the corner again, I step back out into the hall and slip into the nook that will carry me down the stone steps and into Rafferty's cell. Why they don't have a door on this, I'll never understand, but I can be grateful that it's one less barrier for me to have to make it through.

Recalling just how dirty it is, I reach down and grip my skirt, pulling it up to above my knees and tying the soft fabric in a tight knot. I'd rather have to explain why it's wrinkled than why it's dirty.

Then, with a deep breath, I make the descent.

"Back to torment me again so soon?"

Rafferty's deep voice reverberates through my body, setting my nerves ablaze and making my hair

stand on end. The awareness I feel in his presence—
it's unlike anything I've ever experienced before. And
although being down here was a hellish experience,
he'd made me feel safe.

At least, until he'd insulted me in front of the very
man who holds my future in his palms.

"Sorry to disappoint," I say softly, as I step into
the firelight.

His eyes widen, and his mouth falls partially open
as his gaze travels over the tight bodice of my dress.
I'm assuming this gown was chosen so Taranus can
show me off, and while I'd felt uncomfortable putting
it on, I'd be lying if I didn't enjoy the way it made me
feel like a woman.

A beautiful woman deserving of attention from
the man before me.

Just as quickly as his reaction flashed over his
face, it's gone, and he's glaring at me through iron
bars. "What the hell are you doing down here?"

"Bringing you fruit." I cross the distance and hold
the pouch through the bars.

"Why?"

"Because you are hungry." Opening the satchel, I
hold it out and watch his nostrils flare at the sight of
the plump grapes in my palm.

"It was stupid of you to come back down here.
Especially after what you went through to get out."

I glare at him. "Look, I don't know what crawled

up your asshole, but I need to get the hell out of here. The way I see it, you are my only way of doing that. So, I will be looking for the key, and as soon as I get it, we'll both be going. You can either accept my help or not, I really don't care. But I do know that I don't want to die in this place, Rafferty."

He stares up at me, golden eyes blazing with anger, and for a moment, I wonder if he's going to tell me to go to hell. Honestly, he might. Especially given he was not overly fond of my plan to pretend he attacked me.

But escaping rests solely on his help because I have no damn clue what awaits me beyond these stone walls. Could be more murdering bastards; could be more big snakes; could be something worse than both. But I do know that I have to try because there is no way I am going to bed with Taranus or bearing him the children he seems to think I will.

Just as I'm about to pull my hand back, Rafferty gets to his feet and stalks across the cell. I'm frozen in place, pinned beneath his gaze as he reaches through the bars and grabs the fruit from my palm. The way his fingers sear my skin, the tendrils of desire flowing up my arm and into my body, is completely unexpected, and frankly, unwanted at this point.

Whether I die here or from my disease is yet to be seen. But the fact still remains. One day, very soon, I will cease to exist.

The last thing I want is to be given a reason to live when I already have one foot out the door.

"You look very—royal," he finishes as he pops a grape into his mouth.

Heat rushes to my cheeks, even as I know that was not a compliment. "Apparently, there's some ball tonight. Taranus wants to show me off."

"How nice for you both." His tone is dry, his expression blanketed with a complete lack of emotion. It's such a stark contrast from the man I came to know during my time down here. Even as short as it was, he'd been tender, kind.

Which begs the question: Which version of him is real? The kind man who grieved the loss of Flora or the brute his younger brother paints him as?

I clench both hands into fists at my sides. "What the hell is wrong with you?"

"You are being stupid. You should be running, and instead, you're acting like a foolish child."

My temper flares. "A foolish—are you freaking kidding me, Rafferty?"

"I believe the word you're looking for is fucking. As in, am I fucking kidding you."

A snarl leaves my lips moments before something crashes upstairs. I know my time is running short, but the thought of leaving him down here—even when he is acting like a miserable ass—is not appealing at all. "This was our plan, Rafferty."

"This was your plan, Ember. If you remember, I told you many times to run. To leave this place and not come back. To forget about me."

"Not happening."

"Why? Because we bonded in our misery?"

"No. Because I may be a lot of things, but a coward isn't one of them. I won't leave you to die, no matter how much of an ass you act like you are." I run my hands down the front of my dress. "Now, I'm coming back for you, and there's not a damn thing you can do to stop me."

He grips the bars and rests his forehead against them. "Please, Ember, I am begging you. Do us both a favor and slip out tonight while Taranus is drinking his weight in whiskey and likely sharing his bed with half a dozen willing fae women."

He's telling me to run, but all I'm hearing is what a perfect opportunity tonight will give me to get my hands on the one thing that will earn me my freedom.

"I'm going to go after that key tonight, Rafferty. You will have to decide whether you want to rot down here or help me escape."

"I can't suffer your death. Not when I'm destined to protect you."

"You'll get your chance. Once I get that key and free you." *Hopefully.*

CHAPTER 17
EMBER

"**M**istress Ember, I am here to fetch you!" a woman calls through the door less than five minutes after I managed to sneak back upstairs. Quickly, I finish fixing my hair then stare at the woman in the reflection.

Whether it's due to all the running for my life or my increase in appetite, I look—fuller. My cheekbones no longer jut out of my face, and there's a healthy glow to my cheeks. My body is even returning to its pre-sickness, curvy self after only a matter of a few days, three of which were spent in a dungeon.

So crazy it took being imprisoned to make me look healthy.

"Just a moment!" I call out as I adjust my dress, and using what little cleavage I have to my advantage,

I try to appear even plumper than I am. Then, with a deep breath, I turn toward the door, letting my gaze catch the fabric I'd used to take fruit to Rafferty.

Why is the very idea of releasing him thrilling for more reasons than just my own freedom?

Focus, Ember. Eye on the prize. Since the very man holding the key is the same one who hates me, tonight is going to require me dusting off my very rusty—and truthfully not all that great—flirting skills.

And if that doesn't work? I suppose I'll be attempting something else, entirely. What? I have no damn clue, but something has to work, right? It has to because the alternative is far too terrifying.

So, after plastering a fake smile on my face, I pull open the door and meet the sharp gaze of the tall woman standing on the other side. Wearing a pristine white dress, she's woven daisies into brown hair that is secured on top of her head in a tight bun. Not a single strand out of place, she's a visual representation of the perfection I'm assuming Taranus requires.

Which makes his interest in me all the more peculiar given that I am probably the furthest thing from feminine perfection there is. Guess there is something to be said about power being sexy. And according to his prophecy, I will give him a lot of power.

"You look lovely, Mistress." She bows. "I am Bea, your new handmaiden."

"You don't need to bow," I tell her. "And my

name is Ember. Please don't call me Mistress."

Her eyes, one golden and one green, widen. She's beautiful, this young woman, and it hurts my heart to think she's trapped here, just as I am. "I truly cannot call you by first name, Mistress."

"Why not?"

"King—"

"Then how about this: In his presence, you can call me Mistress. But in private, I am Ember."

"Ember. I can do that." She smiles softly, her lips turning up ever so slightly.

"Good. Then, shall we?"

She moves to the side, and I shut the door behind me. "Where are we headed?"

"The King wishes to speak to you privately within his chambers before the celebration tonight."

Icy fear climbs my spine, but I do not cower beneath the weight of her words. The butter knife tucked tightly in the makeshift garter around my thigh may not do much, but I will definitely not go down without a fight if it comes to one. "Do you know why he wants to talk to me?"

"No, Mistress. But I imagine it is to prepare you for tonight."

"What's tonight?"

She stops and turns to me, wearing a curious expression on her face. "Your wedding, Mistress. You are to marry King Taranus before the Elder Council."

"Tonight?" All heat rushes from my body in one wave, leaving me feeling icy to the very core of myself. "That's not supposed to be tonight."

"The King wished to be married quickly, my lady."

"I cannot marry him tonight. I'm not ready."

The woman's expression softens, and she steps forward to gently take my hand. "I understand wifely duties might be overwhelming, but it will be over before you know it."

"I'm not having sex with him," I shoot back as bile rises in my throat.

Heat rushes to her cheeks, and she lifts a finger to her lips. "Shh, you mustn't speak so candidly about that which must remain private. All you must do is lie there, mistress. Let him find his pleasure within your body so you may bear him an heir. It really won't be so bad."

I swallow hard. Horrified doesn't even begin to cover my feelings on this subject. Sleep with Taranus? No freaking thank you. Not a chance in hell.

I'll die first.

But I still need that key, and if the fact that he hasn't touched me yet is any indication, he will not want to sleep with me until after we're married. Here's hoping he doesn't want a preamble. "Take me to my future husband."

Bea smiles. "With haste, Mistress."

Our soft leather shoes move soundlessly across the floor as I follow Bea up a set of stairs and down a long hallway boasting a hunter-green runner. Every step I take brings more and more nerves to the surface, and I wonder if perhaps that's not why he wants to meet beforehand.

Because he's trying to rattle me.

So, instead of allowing my fear to show, I take a steady breath, then another, and remind myself that I am a woman who has faced down death every day for the last five years. I have fought against an unseen enemy who has been trying to claim my life every moment, and I am still standing.

Bea knocks, and a muffled, "You may enter," reaches us through the door. She shoves it open and moves inside with me right behind her.

"Mistress Ember, My King."

"Good. You may both come in."

Taranus's room is humongous, boasting a desk in one corner, two high-backed leather chairs in another, an enormous copper sunken bathtub, and—to my dismay—a perfectly made bed with four large posts and a crimson quilt.

Lloren stands beside where he's seated behind the desk, holding what looks to be a quill in his hand.

I relax slightly. Surely he is not going to want to have sex with an audience. "You wished to see me?"

"Yes." He slides the paper across the desk and

leans back in his seat to study me. "You dressed well."

"This is the outfit that was left out for me today."

"Indeed, it is." His gaze shifts from me to the woman beside him. She offers a curt nod, and he turns back to me. "Take it off."

All air whooshes from my lungs like I've been sucker-punched. "Excuse me?"

"I said, take it off."

"No."

He shoves to his feet. "You are to be my wife. Tonight. Which means I will see you without that dress sooner or later."

"Then it can be later."

"No. I will see you before the marriage contract is signed."

"I'm not undressing."

"Bea."

"Yes, My King." Fingers brush the laces at the back, and I try to move forward, only to find my feet frozen in place.

"Let me go. Please."

"Remove her dress."

"Bea, please."

But Bea does not listen to me, so I shift my attention to the woman beside him as I clutch my hands to the front of the dress. Her eyes shine brightly, and she grins at me.

"You will not earn my pity, woman. The king gave you an order, and you will obey."

"Let me go!" I scream, fighting against the invisible hold. Both hands fly from my dress, and with it, the fabric flutters to the floor, leaving me nearly bare. And when Bea's slender fingers slip beneath the straps on my shoulders, the chemise falls, and I am exactly that—bare. Completely and totally at the mercy of a man I hate more than the disease ravaging through my body.

He pushes to his feet, and I clamp my eyes shut against tears as my body shivers uncontrollably.

"She's not overly impressive," Taranus says, as though I'm not here.

I choke on a sob, trying not to let show how much his words hurt.

"She will do, though. After all, you need her for nothing more than what is inside her body."

"You believe she will bear me a son?"

"She will bear the rightful king sons aplenty."

"Good."

Fingers touch my thigh, and I clamp my teeth together to keep from screaming when my hidden weapon is relieved from my body. "What's this, then?" Taranus's voice is colder than the chill of the blade against my cheek.

"The king asked you a question," the woman snaps.

"He's not my king." Pain flares in my shoulder, and I scream now as warmth trickles down my back. Eyes open now, I am greeted with the sadistic smile of the man before me as he holds a blade with my blood staining the silver.

"I am your king. Your owner. I will do with you what I wish, and you will not ever again say a word against me. Do I make myself clear?"

Without response, I glare back at him. "I will never love you."

He snorts. "I'm going to fuck you, not love you." He turns away. "As if I could ever love a human. All you need to do is spread your legs and give me access to your pussy. After that, I don't give a shit what you do."

I'm not sure what caused this change, what took him from the man who was trying to feign romance to this monster willing to force it, but I imagine it has something to do with the rushed wedding and the woman currently forcing me to remain completely still.

The door opens behind me, and boots thud against the floor as his guard comes to stand beside me. He offers me a once-over then sneers and looks away.

But I don't.

No, my gaze remains firmly on his face because hanging from his belt loop is the very key I need. And if ever I wanted to get my hands on it, it's right the hell now.

"I will not run. Please release me."

The witch does so as soon as Taranus nods to her. I let myself stumble right into the guard, and my fingers quickly relieve him of the key. Risky? Absolutely, given I'm surrounded by enemies, but I have no choice. And years of stealing food to survive have finally paid off when no one pays me any attention.

"I'm so sorry."

The guard sneers at me but gently sets me back on my feet. "My King, the Elders have arrived."

"Thank you, Conary. You may go."

With a nod and another angry glare in my direction, he leaves.

"Dress her and escort her to her room. Be sure to cover that wound. I won't have anyone gossiping on my wedding day."

"Yes, My King."

Taranus grips my arm tightly. "You will obey me," he reminds me. "Every word. And tonight, you will lie there, silent, as I fuck you."

"Yes. My. King," I spit out. If he noticed my angry tone, he paid it no mind because he smiles.

"Good, woman." He looks me over again and shakes his head. "Facedown. That's how I want you in my chamber when I get there."

Then he and the woman with a power I can't even

begin to understand shove past me and out the door. Bea scrambles for my dress and hands it to me quickly. "May I speak freely?" she asks.

"Sure. You already undressed me against my will." I sniffle, trying like hell not to cry in front of this woman. But with the lump steadily growing in my throat and the burn each time I try to breathe, that effort will be futile.

She secures the dress and turns me to face her. "He would have killed me had I not, and I have a family to think about."

Her words are a reminder of my earlier thought about her being a prisoner here. If it came down to saving my pride or her family, I certainly would have chosen her family, as well. "Fine. Speak."

"Do you know what that key opens?"

"What key?"

Her eyes narrow. "I may look young, but I am nearly seven-thousand-one-hundred-and-fifty years old. I saw you. I'm honestly surprised no one else did. Then again, I assume no one else believes you to be capable of much—certainly not deceit."

Yet, she didn't out me. "If you saw me steal the key, why didn't you tell them? You obviously enjoy obeying them."

She doesn't answer. Instead, she turns to me. "We need to move. Now."

"Where are we going?"

"To open that lock." She grips my hand and pulls me toward the door. "I no sooner want you to marry Taranus than I wish for him to be king. And you are certainly not meant to be his."

"What the hell are you talking about?"

We creep into the hall. "Behave normally, Ember, or you will surely draw attention to us."

I do as she says even as I am hammered with a million questions I want to ask. At the top of them: why the hell is she helping me? She doesn't know me, and less than two minutes ago, she was more than loyal to the bastard she's now rebelling against.

We stop in front of my room, and she quickly opens the door and ushers me inside. "What are you doing? I need to get down—"

"Give it to me." Holding out her hand, she stares at me expectantly.

"No. Why would I do that?"

"Because out of the two of us, I am the only one who can move through this castle without being seen. I can get down and rescue him, and no one will be the wiser."

"You can't expect me to trust you. Not after what just happened." I cling to the key like it's my lifeline. Hell, it kind of is.

Her expression hardens. "Getting naked in front of Taranus is a hell of a lot less painful than what most of us have had to endure since he took over this castle," she snaps. "Either you give me that key, or I am taking it and leaving you here to suffer the consequences of whatever Taranus has in store for you. Especially, once he discovers what you've done."

I consider her threat, not at all under the illusion that she wouldn't follow through. Truth is, she could have told them the moment she saw me steal the key. I can't see any reason why she would have hidden it from them, only to return it now.

"Fine." I hold out my hand, and she snatches the large golden key before I can argue.

"Remain in this room. If they come to collect you, find a way to stall."

"Okay."

She slips out through the door, and I quickly click the lock in place then turn toward the fresh wedding dress on my bed. More than likely to replace the blood-stained one I'm wearing now.

"Please come back," I whisper as the adrenaline from the past thirty minutes wears off, and I collapse to the floor as my body shakes uncontrollably. Hot tears stream down my cheeks as I tuck my knees up to my chest.

If Bea doesn't come back, I will have just handed over my only chance at surviving this nightmare.

And if she does? I'm not entirely sure what will come next, but I do know one thing. My fight has only just begun.

CHAPTER 18
RAFFERTY

"*You'll get your chance as soon as I get that key and free you.*" The fire in her eyes when she muttered those words re-ignited my own quest for freedom.

Perhaps, if I'm lucky, I won't die down here. I'll have the chance to seek out the rightful king and turn Ember over to him so she can spend her life happy, loved by a man who will also be a kind and fair ruler.

The mental image of her happy on some faceless fae's arm makes my gut clench with disgust, even as I know it's the only outcome for her. Unless—

"Get to the gate!" a woman whispers loudly as she rushes down the last half of the stairs.

Features illuminated by the soft firelight of the torches on the wall, I recognize her instantly. "Bea? What the bloody hell are you doing here?"

She whips out a golden key and yanks the door open. "We need to get upstairs and get the human woman."

"Ember?"

"Yes. She managed to retrieve the key, but the king is hell-bent on wedding her. *Tonight.*"

Fear shoots up my spine as I flex muscles I haven't had to use in quite some time. "He's not going to lay a fucking finger on her."

"He already has," she says sadly, and rage unlike anything I've ever felt overcomes me.

My vision turns red, and I rush toward the stairs. Bea grabs my arm, and I whirl on her. "I'm going to murder him."

"It took me far too long to sneak down here. We need to get back upstairs before they take her to the wedding hall. By then, it will be too late."

I nod and swallow hard, trying to choke back the rage. It won't be helpful now, not when I need to keep my head long enough to rescue Ember. We're just reaching the bottom of the steps when soft boots thud against the stone. I grab Bea and spin, plunging us both into the shadows and tucking her behind me as the guard comes into view.

"Rafferty, have some great news for you—" The fae skids to a stop at the bottom, eyes narrowing on the empty cell. He turns, ready to alert the others, but

I rush forward and grab him, covering his mouth with my hand as I snap his neck like a fucking twig.

Without hesitation, I retrieve his sword and bound up the stairs right behind Bea. The hall is empty, and I know it's because they've more than likely all already gathered in the wedding hall. Which means next up is them retrieving Ember.

"Bea!"

I step back into the stairs as Bea continues walking. "Yes, Joaquin?"

"Where the hell is the human?"

"I'm heading to get her now." Bea winces, and my hand tightens on the blade. "Release me, Joaquin."

"You should have already brought her to the preparation room."

"I am headed to get her now. In case you forgot, I had a wound to clean and dress on the future queen's back."

A deep breath keeps me from audibly growling and removing Joaquin's head from his body. If I still possessed the ability to dematerialize, I would have done it already and killed the fucker right where he stands.

But the likelihood of me being successful in remaining unnoticed while killing him is far too slim a risk to take.

"Go get her and get back down. Now. If I have to

come find you, neither one of you will appreciate what happens next."

"Are you seriously threatening me?"

"Was I not clear enough?"

"Crystal," Bea shoots back. "Be down in a moment."

"See that you are." I press all the way into the corner as he walks past me and disappears down the hall. As soon as he's out of view, I rush out, and together, Bea and I race for the stairs.

Two flights up, she's knocking on Ember's door.

No answer.

My heart hammers within my chest…fear for Ember, for what will be done to her should Taranus manage to consummate their marriage—she will beg for death. Anything to release her from the hell a life-time with him will rain down upon her.

"We may be too late, My King. You need to go. Now. The Rebellion—"

"Will survive without me, and I am not your king."

Bea's cheeks flush with frustration, though she doesn't argue. Likely because she knew my mother and knows how stubborn my family can be. "They must be in the wedding hall already."

"Even if he exchanges the vows, it's not too late." Together, we rush back down the hall.

A group of fae waits at the bottom of the stairs. Waitstaff, maids, those Taranus has deemed unworthy.

I freeze. All it would take is for one of them to out me, and this rescue mission would be over.

A man steps forward, one I don't recognize. "They took her to the wedding hall," he says. "It has begun. The fight is over."

I move toward him and press a fist to my heart. "It will never be over," I tell him. "Not until Taranus's blood soaks the ground he tried to rule."

Relief echoes over the faces of every single fae in front of me. A near dozen men and women who have been tormented by my youngest brother.

I cannot help but feel partially responsible. And that makes me even angrier.

"He killed Flora," a woman chokes out.

"There will be time to grieve," I assure them. "Time to reflect on those lost and time spent fighting, but now we need to get the future queen out of here so she may find the one true king. Otherwise, there may be no stopping him."

A man clears his throat. His hair is cut short, his face scarred with jagged lines climbing down both sides of it. "The guards are all standing outside of the wedding hall. You'll never make it inside."

I consider his words, thinking through all the

possible scenarios. Taking into consideration Taranus's arrogance, he will likely have her escorted to his chamber immediately following the ceremony even as he continues to bask in the faux approval of those he allows to attend the wedding.

And it's his arrogance that will give us the opportunity we need. "We don't need to get inside."

"But the blood exchange, it happens during the ceremony!" Bea exclaims.

"Candice can help us break that," I remind her. "She's been studying our kind long enough that she should be able to come up with something."

"And if she can't? If this ceremony binds them together—"

"One problem at a time," I tell her, placing a hand on her shoulder. "We need to focus on getting Ember out. Then, we can tackle everything else."

"What do you need us to do?"

I turn back to the fae who spoke, the scarred man. "Do your jobs until I have Ember. Then, we all leave together."

"I'll be staying," Bea says, softly.

"You can't, they'll know—"

"My family is here, dear. We've been serving this kingdom for generations, and I won't turn my back on it now. Not even for Taranus." She reaches up and pats my cheek. "I'll be here when you don that crown you were born to wear."

Swallowing hard, I accept her praise even as I feel like a fraud. The truth is, I've known for a long time that I was not meant to wear a crown.

I am not the one true king.

And I never will be.

CHAPTER 19
EMBER

"No!" I scream as loud as I can while Conary drags me down a hallway. His hand has a vice grip around my arm, though, so every attempt to pull away from him is useless. "I will not marry him! Let me go!"

"You were so amiable earlier, little bitch. What has changed?"

"I-I changed my mind." The last thing I need is him suspecting I have another plan. One that will lead to him checking his now-empty pocket and discovering a certain key is missing.

"You don't get to change your mind." The double doors ahead are being guarded by two men in white armor, neither of which spare me a glance as they open them.

"Please," I beg them, my eyes full of tears. "Please don't let them do this to me."

Neither spares me a pitied glance nor words of encouragement. My stomach twists with panic, the realization setting in. This is happening. In mere minutes, I will be married to the evilest man I've ever met.

The aisle is covered in white rose petals, and the bench seats are full of fae who stare at me. Some look genuinely uncomfortable with my clear-panic; others simply stare forward, stone-faced. Taranus stands at the end of the aisle, wearing white armor with golden plates, a shimmering crown atop his hair.

"No! I'm not doing this!" I scream again, kicking my feet out and yanking as hard as I can. Pain stings my arm where Conary still holds it; it burns my shoulder as I all but rip it free of the socket. "No! I don't want this! I refuse!"

"Shut her up," Taranus orders.

I'm expecting Conary to slap me, but when he simply delivers me to the aisle and leaves, I try to run —only to find myself frozen in place. Lloren glares at me while magic swirls around her fingertips from where she stands directly behind Taranus.

I open my mouth to scream. Nothing comes out. Not a sound, a single uttered plea. Nothing. He's silenced me and taken away any chance I have at protesting.

Tears slip down my cheeks, flowing freely as a man wearing white robes steps forward. "It is my pleasure today to join together Taranus, King of the Fae, and Ember of Austin. She is a human, yes, but a human of prophecy. This union will bring about a new era beneath the one true king."

Silence.

"Do you, King Taranus, vow to keep faithful to your mate?"

Taranus reaches forward and takes my hands into his. The contact is cold. "Always," he replies, golden eyes glittering with delight as he stares at me.

"Do you vow to shield her with your body, spill the blood of her enemies with your blade?"

"I do on both counts."

"Ember of Austin, do you vow to keep faithful to your mate?"

Never. "I do." My eyes widen in shock at the words that sound so much like my own. Until I glance at Lloren and see her open her mouth in preparation for the next answer.

"Do you vow to do all you can to bring heirs into this world so your reign may live on once you've both passed into the Veil?"

No! "I do."

The man in the robes reaches forward and takes Taranus's right hand, along with my left one. My throat burns with emotion I cannot share even as my tears soak my cheeks and fall to the ground of the altar beneath my feet.

No. This is all wrong. Please, anyone, please save me.

"Hold out your hands," he orders.

Mine raises without my consent, leveling right beside Taranus's. A tear slips down my cheek as the man raises a dagger.

Taranus covers my hand with his own, and the man holds the blade up, inches from his.

"It is with great pleasure that I announce this union! May this be the only pain you feel." He drives it down into Taranus's—and then my hand.

I want to scream at the agony of having my hand opened by a sharp blade, something I was not prepared for. But no sound comes out.

He rips the blade free, and Taranus moves his hand. The top of mine is wide open, and warm blood pours from the wound, dripping down to the ground.

"You may kiss your bride."

My hand falls as Taranus snakes his own behind my head. I try to move, to pull away, to do anything that might break Lloren's hold over me—but I'm helpless even as his mouth takes mine. Cold, wet lips move against mine.

Bile burns hot in my throat as he pulls away and faces the crowd. They clap. Some smile, but most look just as horrified as I feel.

He turns to Lloren. "Take my bride upstairs and see to it she's prepared for the final step in forging our union." Then, he leans in. "I'm going to enjoy breaking you, Ember. I'm almost joyful you are resistant. Owning you will be far more pleasant now. And once I do, we will be one, and I will be King."

Vomit fills my mouth, but I'm unable to even spit it out as Lloren moves her hands, and I begin walking, a puppet on her twisted fucking string.

All the way upstairs to the very room she forced me to undress in, she walks me. The moment we're inside and the door is locked, she releases my mouth.

"You fucking bitch," I growl as the sobs break free.

"You will thank me when you rule."

"What are you going to do? Sit in here and watch while he rapes me?"

"If that's what it takes to produce an heir and form the union, yes." She moves behind me and rips my dress down. It falls to the floor, leaving me in nothing but a cap-sleeved chemise. Then, she forces me to walk toward the bed where she shoves me face-down onto the mattress. The comforter scrapes my face as she grips the bottom of the chemise and lifts it, exposing me.

Tears burn my eyes, and I begin to sob uncontrollably.

This is it.

The moment my life is over.

I'll jump out that fucking window as soon as she releases me. There's no world where I will provide anything to this bastard.

The door opens, and I close my eyes, preparing for some smartass comment or his hands to touch my body.

"What are—" Lloren's words are cut short a breath before something hits the ground with a thud.

I'm released, and every muscle in my body begins to quiver. I roll to the side and throw up both fists as I scoot back toward the corner with eyes so full of tears I can't see a damned thing.

"Ember. I'm so sorry, Ember."

That voice. I stop and sniffle. "Rafferty?" I blink rapidly, trying to clear my vision.

"Yes, it's me."

"Get her out of here. The king is coming," a woman orders.

"May I lift you?"

I nod, and a strong arm loops around my back, another beneath my knees.

"Cover the poor dear," Bea whispers, and something warm covers my body.

"You're sure you won't come?"

"I am sure. Who else will scream about how the horrible brute, Rafferty, killed Lloren and abducted the new queen?"

"Thank you," he says. "Find Heelean; keep an eye on her. The ward may be broken now that Lloren is dead. If she can escape, help her."

"You have my word. Now, go."

We begin to move, and Rafferty cradles me to his chest. I cannot see since tears still make my vision little more than blurs of shapes.

"I need to jump. You're going to feel some jostling."

"Okay." My voice sounds pathetic even to me.

Air whooshes past me, and we hit the ground with a heavy thud. Rafferty runs with me in his arms, and my vision finally begins to clear enough, the air drying my tears as we reach the tree line. I cradle my injured hand to my chest as pain shoots up my arm with each jostled movement.

Rafferty doesn't speak, something I am beyond grateful for. It gives me time to process, and besides, what can be said? I'm married. Forced into a union with Taranus, and neither of us can change that.

My only hope is to return to my own world where I can die a miserably slow death, thanks to an illness no one understands.

I DON'T KNOW HOW LONG HE RUNS, BUT IT'S NOT until his body is slick with sweat, his breathing ragged, that he finally slows to a stop. "May I set you down?"

"Yes. Please."

He sets me down, and my bare feet meet cool grass. The sun is not quite all the way overhead, though it has risen enough to bathe the world in a soft golden glow. At some point while we ran, I dozed off, only to be woken the second nightmares took form.

I'm married.

Vomit burns in my throat, and I fall to my knees as it splatters all over the ground. Rafferty is right there, gripping my hair and holding it back out of my face. His hand rubs small circles on my back, something that aids in calming the panic.

I heave for what feels like hours until, finally, there's nothing left. Sitting back on my legs, I cover my face with both hands. "I'm sorry."

"You've nothing to apologize for, Ember." He reaches down and lifts my hand then presses his fingers to the wound.

It stings—for a moment—then, the pain vanishes.

I gape down at my injury, shocked to see the wound closed.

"How did you—"

"Magic," he whispers, then lifts my hand and presses his lips to the top, right where the skin is freshly sealed.

It steals my breath even as my own internal pain consumes me.

"I—I tried to stop him. Conary showed up right after Bea left. He wouldn't let me go."

Rafferty raises his head but doesn't release me. "You did nothing wrong. You hear me?"

When I look away, he lifts me and pulls me into his arms then reaches down to tilt my face so I can look up at him. His golden eyes swirl with pain—with regret. "You did nothing wrong, Ember. You're a victim here."

"We're mated. He mated me." Then, it hits me what that means. I shove away from Rafferty. "Kill me."

His eyes widen in complete horror. "What?"

"Kill me. If you kill me, he will die, too. Please." In demonstration, I grab the dagger tucked into his waist and pull it out, pointing it at myself.

"No."

"You have to. He's going to kill people as he looks for me. Kill me now, and he dies, too. That's what you said, right? If a fae's truemate dies, the other one does, too. Wait, does that mean that I'm his —" My stomach rolls. Never finding love is one thing, but being the soulmate to a murdering psychopath?

Rafferty steps forward and grips the hilt of the blade, wrapping his hand over mine. "I'm not going to kill you, lass." His tone is soft, understanding, and full of pity.

"Please, Rafferty. Please just do it." The quivering takes over again, and I fall to my knees, covering both eyes with shaking hands. "I don't want any of this. Please, just end it. End us both."

"I do not believe you are his true mate," he says softly. "Though, you are human which changes the rules. The wedding vows were the first spoken to turn you into one of my kind. That's what the blood exchange was for." He sighs. "And even if killing you would work, there is no force on this earth that would drive me to put a blade through your heart."

I look up, but through my tear-filled eyes, he's little more than a blur. "Why won't it work?"

"You're not magically bound to him until the marriage is consummated. Right now, the union is incomplete. We don't even know if it fully took."

"What does that mean? Can I get out of it?"

"I believe so. We need to get to my camp, see if Candice can free you."

"Candice. Who is that?"

"She's a witch who's been studying my people."

"Like Lloren? I don't want—"

"She is nothing like Lloren," he assures me. "She is kind, and if there is a way to break the connection, she'll find it." He reaches down and pulls me to my feet. "Right now, we need to focus on getting as far away from the kingdom as we can. As soon as we do, I'll begin the search for my camp."

"You don't know where it is?"

He shakes his head. "They move and reform every few weeks to keep from becoming complacent. We'll find them, though. I know we will."

"And what if we don't?"

"Then I will get you to that portal, and you can leave this world behind. One way or another, Ember, I'll protect you with the last breath in my chest."

I don't dare consider him dying and leaving me out here alone, and since I can't trust my voice right now, I simply nod.

Here's hoping our survival doesn't come to losing his life—or mine.

CHAPTER 20
EMBER

Owls hoot somewhere overhead, and if I'm not mistaken, a coyote calls in the distance. We've been walking solidly since this morning, and while I'm exhausted, hungry, and thirsty, I don't complain.

I'd much rather get as far away as possible than stop for a midday—or, in this case, midnight—snack.

"We need to get somewhere safe for the night."

"Where?"

He turns in a slow circle, studying the surroundings. I try to mimic him, to see and hear what he's seeing and hearing, but all I get are the owls and the sound of a light breeze flitting through the leaves of the trees around us.

"We need to go up."

"Up? What—"

He points to a tree above us. I glance up then back at him.

"I don't want to be a pain, Rafferty, but there's no way I'm making it up that tree."

"I'll help you. We can't stay on the ground—not unless we want to risk being discovered by creatures."

Before I can even ask what creatures he's referring to, he's moving toward the tree and reaching out a hand for me. Fact is, this isn't my world, so if he says we need to go into a tree, then into a tree I go.

Accepting his hand, I let him pull me toward the tree. Then, he kneels. "Get on my back."

I do as he asks, wrapping my arms around his neck, my legs around his waist. He stands as though I weigh nothing more than a light backpack, crouches, then jumps up. I tighten my hold and close my eyes, expecting to fall. No man can make that jump!

Then, I remember: Rafferty is no mere mortal, is he?

I crack open one eye, then another, and stare forward as he pulls us up using tree branches. A few more branches up, and he's crawling up onto the trunk of the giant tree where it splits into different, smaller branches.

The space is small, about the surface size of a medium beanbag chair, but it's clean save for some leaves. Not that cleanliness matters at this point.

"We can sleep here."

Don't look down. I look down. The ground is yards below us. My stomach flips, and I force myself to retrain my attention to my feet. "And if I fall?"

"I won't allow you to fall," he says.

"How will you not fall?"

Rafferty grins at me. "I do not fall. My sleep is light enough that, if a leaf lands on your face, I'll know about it." He removes the blanket from his shoulder and lays the crimson cover out as best he can before gesturing for me to climb on top of it. I do so, and he folds the other half over me like a makeshift sleeping bag, the seam facing the side I'd likely roll out.

"What about you?"

"I will be fine," he replies and takes a seat on my other side, likely to keep me from rolling out.

"You really should get under it with me. There's plenty of space." To demonstrate, I try to move and roll—directly out of the tree. Before I can scream, Rafferty is ripping me back to safety. My adrenaline didn't get the message, though. With my pulse pounding, I bring my knees up and put my face between them, taking deep, steady breaths to calm myself.

"You should get settled," he tells me. "I will take part of the blanket and keep you from rolling out."

"This is all so insane. We're in a tree."

"Better than being down there, I assure you."

"I suppose death by falling is much easier to

stomach than death by murderous creature ripping me apart."

Rafferty cringes. "And they would."

"Thanks for the confidence." I lie back down.

He shrugs and settles down beside me, pulling the blanket over the both of us. My back is still tucked on the one side at least, so if I do roll, it will be into the wall of muscle. As long as he stays in this tree, I will, too—or, at least, that's what I tell myself.

Not like my luck has been overly great these days.

We settle down in the tree, and I listen to the soft chirping of insects nearby. "Rafferty?"

"Yes?"

"What if she can't break the union?"

"I told you. I will escort you home and keep you safe."

"You do know if I go back there, I'll die, right?"

Rafferty is silent, his breathing level. "Then I will remain at your side until your final breaths. You will not die alone, Ember. That is my vow to you should we need to return to your world."

Tears spring into my eyes, and I reach down to grip his hand. "Thank you." Dying alone was always what I'd planned on doing—not because I wanted to —but because there'd never been any choice.

But if Rafferty is there, if I'm not alone, then maybe it won't be so bad.

I'M WOKEN BY RAFFERTY LIGHTLY SHAKING ME. "Shhh," he whispers, pressing his finger to his lips. In the dark, I can barely make out his face, but I do as he asks, remaining silent as I stare up at him, and fear ices my veins.

He drops his head down and whispers directly into my ear, "Remain still, but if I say run, you get on my back, and we will jump."

I swallow hard and shut my eyes tightly, trying to focus on what's around us. Is it Taranus? Conary? The guards? A creature?

My answer comes on the heels of an animal's deafening screams.

Rafferty grips my hand and holds on, running his thumb over the top in an attempt to calm me, but it does nothing.

Tears burn the corners of my eyes as I lie there, listening to whatever is below die. Animal or not— how much death must I endure in this damned place?

Another creature clicks, an alien sound I can't instantly tie back to anything I've ever seen on *Animal Planet*. Then, another clicks and another, and I realize with sick fear that we might be surrounded.

The cries stop.

The clicking stops.

And then there's nothing but dead silence.

No owls, no crickets. Just the breeze.

"Roll toward me," Rafferty whispers, "And hold on."

I don't even hesitate, trusting the man with every single fiber of my being. Clinging to him, I wait. Something shoots up in front of us, straight into the trees, and he jumps, hitting the ground with a grunt.

I don't even know how to process the leap he made or the fact that he's running.

Mainly because the clicking behind us is deafening. He runs, arms pumping, as quickly as he can through the trees, but it's not enough. They're gaining on us.

"When I put you down, run!" he bellows.

There's not even time to argue before he sets me down. The moment my feet hit the cool grass, I take off at a run. Within minutes, my lungs are burning, but I keep going, knowing he must be behind me.

By the time I realize he's not, I'm lost.

In a forest. In the middle of a hostile world I can't even begin to understand.

CHAPTER 21

EMBER

"Rafferty?" I whisper loudly as I spin in a circle. The owls are back, as are the chirping crickets, but there's no clicking, no Rafferty. My heart pounds with fear, turning me into little more than a shaking corpse. Do I go back? See if he's alive? Stay the course?

Is it possible he passed me somehow? That we outran the creatures? But even as I think it, I know there's no way that's the truth. He wouldn't have left me—right?

"What are ye' doin' out 'ere, you blitherin' fool?"

I spin, fists raised, which is ridiculous because—you know—what good am I up against the creatures out here? A man stands behind me wearing dark brown pants and an off-white shirt that is tucked into the top. He's carrying a satchel full of what looks like twigs and has a dark brown hat pulled over his hair. "Who are you?"

"Not lookin' to be eaten with the likes of ye'!" His accent is so thick I can barely follow along. "And ye' might as well be nekkid!"

Glancing down at my shift, I realize he's one hundred percent right. Add to that my bloodied feet and the twigs in my hair, I'm sure I look like a complete psycho. "I'm sorry. I got separated from my —friend. Something attacked us, and I don't know where I am."

The man narrows his eyes at me and takes a step closer. "Ye' weren't attacked, were ye'?"

I shake my head. *Not tonight, anyway.* "But I'm afraid I don't know where I am or where to even begin looking for him."

He purses his lips. "Come on, then. The wife'll have a fit at me if I leave ye' out here in the cold." Without waiting for my response, he simply continues walking leaving me with a choice.

Follow the strange man, or wait here for one who may or may never show back up. I choose the former, assuming that he must live close by, and Rafferty will likely find me—hopefully. I follow him as he moves near-silently through the trees.

He stops just before a massive tree—much larger than the one Rafferty and I napped in—and knocks three times on the door. Then, after a brief pause, two more times. I'm prepared to turn and run, but then a young girl answers the door. With golden eyes, she peers out at the man and smiles. "Papa has returned!"

"Keep yer' voice down, or you'll attract the monsters," he scolds, but then smiles in return. Her eyes find me.

"Who is that?"

He glances back at me. "Not sure."

She opens the door for him, and he gestures for me to follow. "Come on, we'll get ye' cleaned right up."

I follow, not sure what to make of this man who invited a complete stranger into a home with what appears to be his family. Doesn't he know there are crazy people in this world? The ground makes way to stairs that are illuminated only with a soft light carrying from upstairs. Behind me, the door shuts, and I turn just in time to see the little girl slide a huge lock into place.

I swallow hard. *If they kill me, Rafferty is going to kill me.* That is, if he's still alive. My heart tightens with that thought, so I shrug it off. He's strong enough to handle himself, right?

So many questions and not nearly enough answers over here.

We continue down the steps, my feet aching with each move, until the stairs end, and we move into a brightly lit room. It's huge, about the size of my apartment, minus the privacy of separate room. Three beds line one wall with a much larger one on the opposite side, partially hidden by a partition.

A woman groans, and the man drops his backpack with a younger boy who is stoking a fire. Which makes absolutely no sense. Where the hell is the smoke going? I look up, only to see nothing but more tree.

"It's an illusion," a second little girl tells me as she carries a wicker basket toward the partition.

"Easy, love," the man coos.

"Is everything okay?" I call out.

"Who the blitherin' hell is that?" A woman calls out.

"I found her in the woods, love. Near nekkid."

"Ye' brought a nekkid woman into our home! Owww!" she cries.

"Not naked!" I call out as I move into view.

The *very* pregnant woman stares back at me, and her eyes widen in wonder. "She's not fae."

"Human," I offer.

"What the hell are ye' doin' here?" the young boy asks.

"Watch yer' mouth, Fischer."

"Sorry, Papa." He dips his head in shame and continues stoking the fire.

The woman turns to her husband. "What are ye' waiting on! Get the lass some clothes, ye' fool!"

"Yes, love," he chuckles then turns to a wooden chest against the wall. Reaching inside, he withdraws a brown dress with a green bodice. When he hands it to me, I stare down at it.

The fabric is soft beneath my fingers, far too soft to be wool—cotton maybe?

"What are ye' waitin' on? Not a fan of green?"

I meet his gaze, and knowing what green means to some people here, I shake my head. "I love the color green."

He relaxes slightly. "Then get dressed. I've got a babe to deliver."

"Shouldn't you get her to a hospital?"

He tilts his head to the side. "What the bloody hell is that?"

"Nothing. Sorry. I'll just get dressed." I dip over into the corner and slide the dress over the top of the chemise. As much as I want to remove it, to burn and then bury the damned thing, I also don't see anywhere to change where I wouldn't have to get fully naked.

And I'm good on that.

The woman screams and growls, and the man cheers her on. "So close, love, babe is crowned. One more big push should do it."

"You've got this, momma," the older girl is seated at the base of the bed with her arms prepped to catch the baby.

Shit. I'm about to see a—high-pitched crying fills

the room, and I stare in awe as a baby covered in placenta and blood cries in the arms of its new sister as she wraps it in a thick blanket. Then, she stands and hands the baby to her mother. "'Tis a boy, momma."

"My little love, you will be so cherished," she coos.

I feel like a total intruder in this beautiful moment as the children all gather to meet their new sibling, so I slowly back toward the stairs and sit down on the bottom to watch. I know I shouldn't be thinking about it—shouldn't be focusing on my past when there's such a murky future in front of me—but I can't help it. What must it feel like to grow up in a house full of love? Where you are wanted from day one?

"Where is our guest?" the woman calls out.

"Here!" I reply.

"Do ye' not like children? Get over here, lass, and meet my new babe!"

Not wanting to be rude, I push to my feet and move across the room to the bed. The father cradles the child now, beaming down at him as a proud parent should.

All of the siblings gape up at it in complete awe.

"Shoo now, the lot of you."

They all giggle as they rush away, the older girl guiding them back toward the center of the room where they gather around the fire.

"Our wee son," the father says, tilting his arms so I can see the baby's plump face. "Seamus."

"He's gorgeous." I have always loved babies—wanted a bunch of my own to love and cherish one day. When I got sick, the thought of never getting to hold one was yet another blow, so when he offers his brand-new son to me, I can do nothing but stare at him. "You don't know me."

"I can read ye' like a book," the woman says. "Ye'r a kind lass, are ye' not?"

"I try." Swallowing hard, I accept the baby and stare down at the tiny pink face. Tears spring to my eyes. "Hello, little one."

"What is yer' name?" the husband questions.

"Ember," I reply without thinking. Truth be told, I probably shouldn't just be telling anyone that.

"I'm Griffin, this is my mate, Laoise."

"Nice to meet you both."

"Why were ye' out there half nekkid?" Laoise questions. "Were ye' harmed?"

"I was traveling with someone." Little Seamus begins to fuss, so I hand him to his mother. Without hesitation, she pulls out a swollen breast and offers it to the baby.

"Were they killed, then?"

"No. Or—I don't think so. I need to get back out there. I can return your dress." Truthfully, I never planned on staying, so I really shouldn't have accepted it. I was just so grateful to feel warm.

"I won't hear of it. Ye'll keep the dress. Looks right on you."

"Ye' really shouldn't be traveling alone in these woods, 'tis not safe. Royal guards patrol regularly."

"You are hiding from the king?"

Laoise snorts. "Who isn't? We need Rafferty to come back, to save us from this."

"Rafferty allowed Taranus to take over in the first place!" Griffin argues. "He should have killed the little twit the moment he began questioning orders!"

"You know Rafferty?"

Both eyes turn to me.

"Who's askin'?" Laoise questions.

"That's who I was traveling with. Rafferty. Big, muscled man, scar on the side of his face."

Laoise gasps. "He's *alive*?"

"Yes."

"We assumed he'd be dead by now. That Taranus would have killed him."

I shake my head. "He's alive." Closing my eyes, I clasp my hands together. "Or he was. We were attacked."

"Where did the two of ye' meet?"

"The castle. I helped break him out, and he rescued me from—well, from Taranus."

Griffin woots and I jump. "I knew the bastard was too hard to kill!"

I don't bother to point out to him that he was just blaming Rafferty, because he looks so genuinely pleased I wonder if his anger was perhaps grief.

"How long ago was he captured?"

"Few months," Griffin replies. "We had just left the camp to find a place to settle for the babe to be born. Got word of it days later. They swooped in, de-winged him right in front of the entire camp."

It's my turn to be shocked now. My heart breaks for the man who's risked everything to help me. Who swore to keep me safe. "They cut his wings off?"

"Not just anyone," Griffin replies. "His own brother did it."

"Taranus," I growl his name. I may not have been here long, but even I can see what a plague he is on this world. "He could be injured. I really need to find him. To make sure he's okay. He was wearing nothing but a torn pair of shorts."

"Then let's go and find him."

"No." I shake my head, and Griffin studies me. "I mean, I really appreciate your help, more than you can know, but you can't risk it. You have a family to care for, a new baby, and the entire royal guard is likely out hunting me."

Griffin looks genuinely conflicted—but one look back at Laoise, and he nods. "Fine, but let me get ye' some supplies." He moves past me and dumps the rest of the twigs out before cramming fresh bread, two leather pouches full of something, and some of what looks to be jerky into the pack. Then, he crosses the room and opens the chest, withdrawing clothes and soft-soled leather shoes. They go in next.

It all happens within minutes, giving me the impression that this is a family that has never truly known stability.

Something I relate to on so many levels.

He offers it to me. "Ye' be safe, Ember. Give Rafferty our best. If ye' find him near here and wish to return—"

"I appreciate it," I interrupt. "But I won't be coming back. You've already risked enough by helping me. I can't allow you to risk anything else."

Laoise smiles tightly at me. "I doona know much about where ye'r from, lass, but here, the roads are treacherous. Trust no one, and always watch yer' back."

"I will. Thank you."

With a grunt, I manage to get the pack on my back and head toward the stairs. Griffin walks right beside me, and the children all offer me tight smiles as I pass. "I don't suppose you know where I can find the camp, do you?"

"'Fraid not, lass. They move constantly."

"That's what Rafferty said."

"Raffe is a good man. An honorable one. Are ye' sure ye' doona want my help?"

Once I reach the top, I turn back toward him. "You helped a strange woman in the woods, Griffin. We met less than thirty minutes ago, and you've clothed me, given me food and supplies, and let me hold your baby. You've done plenty. Thank you." I offer him a smile, and he blushes.

"I'll be seeing you at that camp one of these days," Griffin offers.

"I look forward to it."

He reaches around me, slides the lock back, then peers out through a hole in the door. Once he's satisfied by what he is—or isn't seeing—he shoves the door open enough for me to slip outside.

My feet no sooner hit the ground than the door is locked, all but disappearing into the bark of the tree. Even in the morning light, I can barely make out the waves that don't match.

Hoisting the backpack higher on my back, I face out toward the forest bathed in light gold and say a silent prayer for the family behind me…and the man I'm willing to scour this world for.

CHAPTER 22
EMBER

Hours later, my stomach is growling, and I've still seen nothing. No sign that he was here looking for me. Shit, there's not even any sign of a struggle.

Which is a good thing, right? If he'd gone toe-to-toe with vicious beasts, surely there would be some sign of a fight? Blood maybe?

Just ahead, I hear the heavy hammering of water, so I follow it, wanting a place to sit for a few minutes if only to rest my legs. It's a damn good thing I'm in good shape for a dying woman because all this walking is draining.

The trees grow thinner now, making way for a huge clearing. Overhead, the sun is high, and birds chirp happily. A huge pond takes up the majority of the clearing with an enormous waterfall filling it from a cliff opposite of me.

It's stunning as though I've somehow stumbled directly into a peaceful painting. Shit, maybe I have. Wouldn't be the strangest thing I've dealt with recently.

As I'm setting my bag down, a gargantuan black horse trots into the clearing. Its mane hangs nearly to its knees, and its magnificent coat shines beneath the sun.

I stare, afraid to frighten the creature. Other than the brief riding lessons I bought for myself for my nineteenth birthday, this is the closest I've been to a horse. It raises its mighty head and turns toward me. Dark eyes study me with a human-like curiosity. Then, it drops its nose and inhales, large nostrils expanding.

Whatever it smelled, it must have liked because it takes a cautious step toward me. Seeing it fills me with a sense of peace—of comfort. If it's here, monsters can't be close, right? Animals are supposed to be fairly attuned to that kind of thing.

It moves even closer, so I hold out a hand, flattening it like I remember being taught. It presses its nose directly against my hand and inhales.

Its muzzle is soft against my palm. "How are you, girl?" I bend over. "I mean…boy. Sorry. How are you today?"

The soft whinny that comes from its mouth wraps around me like a greeting.

"I completely understand. I'm not feeling all that great myself. Rather lonely, isn't it? I'm looking for someone." I pet the other side of its face with my opposite hand. "You haven't seen him, have you? Huge man, scarred, wearing torn pants?"

I know it's crazy, but the horse shakes its head. I step back. Surely it can't understand me? Then again, here, people can fly, so who's to say what rules fall over animals? It bows down, dropping to its front knees.

"What are you doing? Taking a nap?" I pet his forehead.

He shakes his head again.

Surely I'm losing my damned mind. I study the horse kneeling before me. "Do you want me to get on your back?"

The horse raises its head then drops it as if nodding. I snort. This cannot be happening—can it? I can cover far more ground if I'm on horseback. Maybe this is a—

A man bellows, and the horse jumps to its feet. To avoid being crushed, I jump back as Rafferty bounds into the clearing, teeth bared, blade high. He charges the horse.

"No! Rafferty, stop!" I try to stop him, but at that exact moment, the horse's dark eyes turn bright red, and it snarls. Gone is the luxurious mane, replaced with tattered hair of different lengths. Patches of dark hair on its body disappear, leaving splotches of rotting skin.

I scramble backward, and it turns toward me.

Rafferty slams into it, the force of his body taking them both to the ground. I'm helpless to do anything but watch the horrific scene play out.

The creature—I won't even call it a horse now—jumps back to its feet and moves to kick him. He rolls out of the way just in time to avoid two huge—and now cloven—hooves to the chest.

Before he can retaliate, the creature jumps into the water, disappearing beneath the surface. I stare at it, expecting the thing to rise back up, but nothing happens.

Seconds tick by before Rafferty turns to me. His entire body is coated in blood. Fresh wounds are slashed across his chest. His hair is matted with red, and his eyes are wide and rimmed with black.

"What was that?" I ask.

He doesn't answer. Just crosses the ground toward me.

I start to back away as flashes of him losing his shit in the dungeon come to mind. But before I can get too far away, his arms shoot out, and he crushes me against his body. Forgetting all about my fear, I wrap both arms around him and hold on, too.

"I thought you might be dead," I told him.

"I believed you to have been captured," he replies, inhaling deeply, cheek pressed to the top of my hair. Then, he pulls away. "Where did you find those?"

"One of your old acquaintances, I presume." Turning away, I retrieve the backpack and offer it to him. "But maybe we should go before that thing comes back."

"It won't be returning."

"Why not?"

"'Twas a Kelpie, and they do not enjoy the fight. They prefer their prey to be easy."

"A Kelpie?"

"Evil creature that takes the form of a horse. It preys on the lone travelers, convincing them to climb onto its back so it can drown them in the water and feed on your life energy as it leaves your body."

I swallow hard. Holy shit. I was literally moments from death.

"Then we should go."

"It's not coming back," he says, opening the pack and peering inside. "They do not attack more than one person, and we're together now." Completely unconcerned with the fact that an evil horse just dove headfirst into the water, he kneels and sets the pack down. "You said an old acquaintance of mine?"

"His name was Griffin. His wife—I mean mate—"

"Laoise."

"Yes." I breathe a sigh of relief because, even as I didn't want to admit it, I knew there was a possibility they were only playing me.

"You saw them?"

I nod. "They just had a baby. Even let me hold it." I hold my arms out in demonstration.

"Their baby was born?"

"A little boy named Seamus."

He smiles. "I'm glad to hear it."

"Anyway, Griffin saw me wandering. They gave me all kinds of shit about being naked—"

His eyes all but bulge out of his head. "Why in the bloody hell were you naked?"

"I wasn't. I was in my chemise, but they said I might as well have been naked."

The way he relaxes, it's almost charming. "They gave you those clothes?"

"And the ones in there are for you. They also gave us some other supplies—bread and stuff."

"They are good people. Laoise would bring our camp fresh food whenever they came to visit." He withdraws the clothes and eyes the water with a yearning glance.

"If you want to risk the Kelpie, by all means."

Rafferty chuckles. "Very well. Let us go find a stream where I'm not at risk of drowning." After stuffing the clothes back into the pack, he slings it over his shoulder and stands. We walk together, him carrying a blade in his hand, back into the trees.

"What happened to you?" I finally ask, not really sure I want to know the answer. He's obviously alive, but as I've learned, there are things worse than that in this world.

"The Oillipheist is dead," he says, softly. "Though there will likely be more before this journey is over."

"What is an Oillipheist? And there was only one? I thought I heard at least three."

"One. They use that ability to confuse their victims. And as to what it is, it's a dark creature capable of taking on the form of a wyvern."

"Which is a—"

"Dragon," he replies.

I stop in place. Rafferty does the same and turns to face me. "You're telling me that this place has *dragons*? As in, swoop down from the sky and burn you to a crisp?"

"They've no fire, but essentially, yes."

"And you killed it."

"Not my first, likely won't be my last." He continues walking as though all of this is the most normal thing in the entire world. "You must be on guard, Ember. Anything less will lead to your death."

Something in the tone he uses, the weight of his words, it eats at me. "Have you ever known peace?"

Rafferty stops in his tracks and meets my gaze.

His golden eyes churn with emotion so strong it makes my knees weak. "Briefly."

"When you were a child?"

He nods. "And into adulthood. Until—"

"Your sister," I finish his thought, and he nods again.

"I failed Niahm. I will not fail you, too." He begins walking again, and I'm forced to jog for a moment in order to catch his long strides. Together, we walk in silence until just ahead, the noise of moving water overtakes it.

The small stream moves through the trees like a winding road, eating the ground away in its path. Trees are tall here, obliterating our view of the sky and shielding us from the hot sun. Rafferty turns his head to the sky and closes his eyes.

I know he's likely listening for any threat, but I am unable to tear my gaze from the shape of his jaw or the stubble coating it. For this brief moment, with nothing but the sound of the water, I feel…alive.

He drops his head and opens his eyes. A golden gaze locks with mine, and I let out a breath. We stand there, the air charged between us, until he turns his head and clears his throat. "The water looks to be about waist deep, we should be able to wash up. I will keep my back turned so you have your privacy."

When I don't reply, just eye the water nervously,

he chuckles. "Kelpies do not frequent moving water. You will be safe, I assure you."

Little does he know it has nothing to do with the Kelpie and everything to do with the fact that we'll both be naked—in cold water—yards apart.

"Great. I'll just go, then." I move past him and to the base of a tree beside the stream. Part of me wants to glance over, you know, to see if Rafferty is in the water yet, but the other part of me knows that he is likely already naked.

Not that I don't want to see it, it just feels wrong somehow.

Stripping out of my dress, I set it up on the rock so it won't get dirty. Then I remove the chemise from my body—finally. That, I toss near the base of the tree, never to touch it again. The water is cold on my feet but welcome, especially given the dirt and blood that washes away right before my eyes.

Cuts and scrapes from running barefoot burn momentarily, but soon, I'm wading in farther and farther until the water is barely covering my breasts. "Oh my gosh, yes."

"Is everything all right?" Rafferty calls back to me.

"Fine. The water feels good." Only, I choose that exact moment to submerge a little deeper without thinking of the fresh cut on my upper shoulder. I wince, the intake of air enough to alert the warrior behind me.

"What is it?" He's directly behind me now, though not touching me. "Ember, what is it? Tell me, or I'm turning around."

"Taranus—" I swallow hard. "Cut my back."

"He did *what*?"

"I don't know. Truthfully, I haven't seen it, and I hadn't thought about it since the chemise sleeves covered it."

"May I?"

He's asking if he can turn around—if he can look. And given how clear this water is? He'll see a good portion of my ass. However, curiosity for what Taranus left behind is greater than my need for modesty. At least, right now.

"Yes."

Water sloshes behind me as his hulking form turns. Warm fingers brush my hair aside, putting it all over my right shoulder before tracing the tender skin. "I am going to carve something much worse into him when I next see him," he snarls.

Tears burn my eyes. "What is it?"

"You needn't worry about it." His fingers touch my skin again, and the pain subsides, warming beneath his gentle pressure.

"What is it?"

"It's gone now."

"But what was it?"

He doesn't say a word, doesn't utter a single syllable. So, gathering up all the courage I can, I wrap an arm over my breasts and turn around. Pupils dilated, he stands in the water that reaches just above his abdomen, given our severe height difference.

It drips from his body, sliding over the muscled planes, and I'm helpless to not follow each droplet as it travels down, down. Before I see something I likely will never unsee, I force my gaze up—and then instantly wish I would have continued down.

My lips part, my sharp intake of breath a lust punch to my own gut. He stares at me, gaze so bright it's near-blinding. His gaze drops to my mouth then back up as his chest heaves with each labored breath.

"What was it?" I ask again, this time locking gazes with him.

"Something that never should have been put on your body."

"Rafferty?"

He closes his eyes, and his nostrils flare with a deep breath. "He branded you with the crest of our family."

My eyes widen, and I sway in the water. Rafferty reaches out and grabs my elbow quickly to keep me from toppling backward.

"I thought he'd just cut me. I didn't realize—"

"You are not his, Ember."

"He married me." My eyes fill. With the immediate threat to our lives over, the adrenaline chooses this exact moment to cease pumping through my veins, and it all crashes into me. I'm freaking married. *Married.* He'd nearly raped me—would have if Rafferty hadn't shown up when he did.

Rafferty's strong fingers trace my jaw, and I shiver, closing my eyes. His touch—it's the sweetest kind of torture. A blissful pain. Something that shouldn't feel so good because I know that there is no future where the two of us are anything more than what we are.

"You do not belong to him," he says. "Not in soul, heart, mind, or body."

"But in vows, I am. Lloren made me speak them, I don't know how but—"

"Ember." He silences me with the mere mention of my name. "I will deliver you to my camp where you may choose what to do."

"And the prophecy? I thought you were going to deliver me to the rightful king?"

His gaze hardens, eyes darkening for a brief moment. "If that is what you choose, yes."

"If he's anything like most of the men I've met— you and Griffin not included—I want nothing to do with him." Still, my plan was always to return home. This isn't my fight. Yet, if it means ripping the throne from Taranus's cold, dead fingers, I'll do damn near anything.

"I will never let you fall to anyone who will harm you," he growls. There's so much rage, so much anger in his words that it momentarily steals my breath.

"Why?"

He reaches forward and cups my cheek. Warmth spreads through my body, shoving all the recent pain aside until there's only him and me.

"You are mine to protect, Ember. Whatever future you should choose—"

"Whatever one I choose?" If it were my choice, I would give in to the lust between us, jump into his arms right now and have what I imagine to be life-changing sex, before I succumb to a disease I know is still killing me. If only to forget about everything else hanging over us.

A muscle in his jaw twitches, and he drops his hand. "I will deliver you home, or to your mate," he corrects.

The words sting, which makes little sense to me. It feels like rejection because I know he has to feel what I do. This cannot be one-sided. Not considering how my heart pounds when he's near me. How my body heats in those rare moments he lets his fingers linger on my skin. "Exactly. My future has never been mine to decide," I tell him, my tone a lot harsher than I meant. Dropping my gaze to his chest, I resign myself to the understanding that my life has never been about what I wanted.

Not really.

"I want to finish washing if that's okay."

Rafferty opens his mouth to speak, then closes it and simply turns around.

I do the same, but only after I get a glimpse at his muscled ass beneath the surface of the clear water.

CHAPTER 23

RAFFERTY

’ve never longed for the death of anyone with my blood in their veins, but Taranus is my new exception. As I sit on the bank beside a bubbling stream, building a fire that will hopefully keep the creatures away tonight, I think of all the ways I want to kill him.

Hell, I’ve already condemned myself more times than I care to count. What is one more strike against my honor?

I’m feeling things for a woman I have no business wanting. But the weight of these feelings—of these needs burning in my veins—is crushing.

Against my better judgment, I allow my gaze to drift over to where she sits, eyes closed, leaning back against the boulder. She’s fully dressed now, and a light breeze carries through the trees, lifting strands of her fire hair and delivering it behind her shoulder.

It's despicable, to want someone who is the future for someone else.

Not Taranus, but the rightful king. For all I know, he could be someone I know, someone I care for. And here I am, imagining all the ways I could make love to the woman on this embankment. In the water. Against that fucking boulder, her legs wrapped around me as I drive into her over and over again, bringing her—I shake my head and force the images from my brain.

I cannot think of such things. Doing so, especially while she's partially bonded to Taranus, is a horrible breach of the code I've spent my life serving.

Downplaying her connection with my bastard of a brother was the only way to calm her…but truthfully? If we cannot break the connection or they do not finish the unification with the second blood transfer— over my dead fucking body—she will begin to die. They will both die.

Even with all of that aside, even without consid- ering the fact that I am soul-bound to a fae steadily rotting away in the Veil, I am not the man for Ember. What she deserves is a hell of a lot more than half a man—half a fae—incapable of giving her the life she deserves.

She moans, and her lips part, head falling to the

side. When her brows draw together, I sense the shift around her. Where she'd been at peace, discomfort takes over, and anguish abounds.

And I'm helpless to save her from it. Just as I was helpless to save her from Taranus. The log in my hand snaps, and I toss it into the fire before getting to my feet to gather more. Seeing her shoulder, our family crest carved into her milky flesh, there'd been a moment there where the dark power in my blood shifted.

It surged forward, adrenaline pumping, red invading my vision.

But her words—her sweet, deadly-to-me voice—brought me back into the light.

Why in the bloody hell would destiny deliver me a woman who consumes me, even knowing I cannot have her? Have I truly offended that horribly?

Ember cries out in her sleep, so I rush forward, unsure what to do but knowing I cannot simply sit by and watch it happen. Then, she whispers, "No. Please—"

"Ember." Gripping her shoulder, I gently shake her.

Caramel eyes open slowly, and she blinks rapidly, coming out of her nightmare slowly. "Rafferty?"

Why is my name on her lips such sweet fucking torment? I'd take a thousand lashings before I allow anything to touch her. In sleep or waking moments. "You were having a nightmare."

She stares at me a moment longer, and I study the freckles dotting her cheeks, the one right at the corner of her mouth. I want to press my lips to it, want to caress her skin with my tongue, the tips of my fingers.

Maybe— I release her and get to my feet. Distance. I need distance before I fucking lose it.

Because the painful truth is that she's not mine.

She will *never* be mine.

Ember is far too pure to belong to a damned man like me.

"Thank you for waking me."

"Of course. The fire is nearly ready."

"Are you sure this is the best place for us? Taranus is probably looking for us."

"He is most definitely looking for you, but you need rest. I will keep watch to ensure you remain safe."

"What about you?"

I turn toward her—this human woman who cares for the damned likes of me. "What about me?"

"Do you not sleep?"

"I do."

"Then why don't we take turns keeping watch? I can sit beside you and wake you if anything seems out of place."

"You need your sleep."

"So do you," she argues, her jaw tightening with her stubbornness.

"Very well. After dinner, you will sleep for a few hours, and I will wake you."

"No. You will sleep first. I just took a power nap and feel great." Getting to her feet, she crosses the ground and kneels before the pack. After digging around in it a few minutes, she withdraws a loaf of bread, tears it in half, then tears that in half and hands one side to me. "We should conserve."

"I agree." It's not something most fae would have thought about, let alone a human woman, yet she has the mind of a fighter.

Her disease, I suppose.

A life alone, maybe.

After reaching into the pack again, she withdraws a small pouch and offers it to me. "I saw him add some jerky—or what looked like jerky—in here."

Opening the pouch, I peer inside then withdraw a few pieces. "Eat what you need, we can always hunt more."

"Hunt? As in—"

"There are plenty of animals out here we can eat," I tell her, enjoying the way her eyes widen far too much than is surely allowed.

"I once ate a rat," she tells me, nose scrunching. "A homeless man cooked it for me one night when I was shivering under a bridge."

The visual image of her alone—cold—it angers me. What kind of parents would abandon their baby to such a horrible fate? "No rats," I promise. "Though I do prepare a delicious rabbit if my men's approval was any indication."

She smiles softly. "You miss them. Your people."

"More than I can say."

"What about the others still in the castle?"

My mind drifts to Heelean, to Bea and the others forced to remain in such a horrible position. "I will rescue them once I have my men and weapons."

The sun begins to dip, casting us in shadows, so I lean forward and lift the piece of flint I managed to find buried in the dirt. After lifting a rock, I begin to slam them together until sparks fly against the kindling.

Flames burn to life, devouring the smaller twigs and spreading to the larger ones.

Soon, we're both sitting in the amber glow of the firelight.

"Can I ask you something?" Ember is not looking at me but rather at the skirt of her dress as she smooths it out.

"Of course." *Anything to hear your voice, my tormenter.*

"Griffin told me what Taranus did to you."

I swallow hard as my wounded soul cracks, yet again. "He told you of my wings, then?"

She nods.

"Taranus meant to humiliate me, to stifle the strength of the Rebellion. He knelt me before my men and removed my wings. He shaved my head, cutting my hair to the scalp, but he did not douse the spark," I assure her. "The Rebellion was never built on one man but on the strength of many. I've no doubt that, in my absence, another rose to take over."

Even as I speak the words, I pray they are true. Otherwise, I'm leading Ember on a wild chase for something extinct. And if there is no Rebellion—no true king—I cannot even begin to think of what will happen to the woman in front of me. Not if she chooses to return home.

Part of me, a twisted, damned part to be sure, almost yearns for there to be nothing left. Because if there's no one to deliver her to, then there's only me. And I will deliver her everything I have.

Ember stands, and leaves crunch as she makes her way over to sit beside me. "You're the strongest person I've ever met," she says. "I just wanted to tell you that."

"I feel the same about you, Ember of Austin."

Ember's answering smile is half-hearted at best, but it stills the burning battle within me.

For now.

"Raffe!" Ember whispers directly into my ear. I roll over, not at all surprised to see that the fire has died. Some moonlight sneaks past interlaced branches above, our only light in the otherwise complete darkness.

Eyes wide, she's inches from me.

There's no need to speak because I hear them. Placing a finger to my lips, I slowly get up, pulling her with me. We creep to the trunk of the tree we're sitting beside, hiding, the stream to our backs.

"We'd better find her, or Taranus will have our cocks," one man groans.

"Keep speaking so loud, and you'll alert her a mile out!" the other retorts.

"Little bitch. I'm so tired of being out here. When we find her—"

"You'll do what?"

"I don't know. Apparently, she has the power to make a king in that pussy of hers. Maybe I'll find out if that's true."

Ember audibly gasps.

I glance down, and she covers her mouth with a hand, shutting her eyes tightly.

My hand clenches into a fist around the hilt of a blade I do not remember withdrawing.

One word, the darkness within me whispers. *One word and we end it all. We can make them drive their own blades into their dark hearts.*

I shake my head. Doing that would put Ember in even more danger because it would be unleashing something far worse upon her: me.

"You hear that?" the man says.

"I did. Come out, Your Majesty," the other calls out, his tone tainted with humor.

"You cannot hide from us!" the first man says.

Ember's entire body goes rigid, and I wrap my arm around her, trying to duck further into the trees. While I only hear two, that doesn't mean there aren't more nearby. The last thing I want is for Ember to be recaptured. Without the wedding vows looming over them—Taranus won't hesitate to take what he thinks is rightfully his.

We move, steadily picking up pace.

Until someone drops directly into our path. "Well, well, well, look who it is." Joaquin's ear-to-ear grin is perfectly visible beneath a solid beam of moonlight.

"Walk away, Joaquin."

"Or what?"

"I will do what I've wanted to do since you traded your soul for a seat in the castle."

His humor is apparent in the way his grin spreads. The arrogant bastard doesn't even bother to draw his sword. "You hear that, men? Rafferty believes he is strong enough to take us all on!"

My stomach plummets when not one, not two, but

nearly a dozen more men drop down into the clearing. Ember whimpers, clutching my arm.

One. Word.

"We're going to have some fun, Your Majesty. You like fun?"

"Quiet, Pani," Joaquin scolds. "She belongs to the king."

"Does that mean we can't have fun? I doubt she's untouched. Out here with him, the king will never know."

"I will cut your tongue out myself," Joaquin scolds. Then, he turns back to me. "Rafferty, you are under arrest for treason and the kidnapping of the future Queen of Faerie."

"He did not kidnap me," Ember says, her voice wavering even as she attempts to appear unafraid. "I ran the moment I had the chance."

"You killed Lloren," Joaquin accuses.

"And I'd do it again in the beat of a heart."

His grin turns to a sneer. "Take them."

"Duck!" I order Ember as the fae charge us. She hits the ground with a thud, and I swing out with the short blade I managed to steal before leaving. Tonight, I will leave with a sword off the backs of my enemy.

Metal clashes and the heavy crunch of armor fills my ears as the hilt of my blade hits the chest plate. Knowing the blade is not sharp enough to penetrate, I immediately lunge forward and grip the chest plate of the nearest fae, yank him toward me, and drive my blade down into his throat.

He sputters and falls to the ground.

I retrieve his sword and swing out, blocking another hit.

Ember screams.

I whirl. If one of them gets his hands on her, they can be gone in an instant. She's running, sprinting through the trees while Joaquin chases, right on her heels.

Panic burns my veins.

His hand closes around her arm. "Stop!" I roar, invoking magic I swore I'd never use.

Every man in the clearing, Joaquin included, stops.

I feel it, the seductive power. I could stop now, but it feels so fucking good. Carrying the blade in my hand, I move through the clearing, passing the men who still have their blades raised. It's not until I am standing before Joaquin that I stop.

"Rafferty?" Ember whispers my name, and I turn to her. The way her eyes widen—I know she can see the change.

"It was either this or your life."

"I always knew you were a coward," Joaquin spits out, frozen in place.

"Release her."

He does as ordered.

"You will take your blade and kill every single one of the men behind you."

Joaquin's jaw tightens.

"Then, you will deliver yourself back to Taranus and tell him I am coming for him, right before you drive your blade into your own heart."

He begins to move back toward his men. "You won't get away with this!" he bellows as I grab Ember by the arm and rip her away from the carnage.

"What did you do?" she calls out as I drag her into the tree line.

Behind us, men groan, they plead, they beg for mercy, but I know that Joaquin will give them none. Because I own the fucker.

A smile toys at the corners of my lips. Given that I just traded a piece of myself, I should be concerned.

But I'm not.

Because I feel more powerful than I have since the day Taranus stole my wings.

CHAPTER 24

EMBER

Sunlight streaks through the trees, illuminating our path as it sprawls before us. The mossy ground is covered in various topiary, the trees around us so thick we can barely manage to move through them.

Rafferty hasn't spoken a word to me since we left the guards behind. I'd heard them crying out, screaming, begging Joaquin to stop as he did what Rafferty ordered—why? I still have no idea, and I haven't really had the confidence to ask.

So I follow, silently, waiting for him to confide in me—if he ever will.

It was either this or your life. He'd looked so tortured, his words so broken as he'd spoken them; I could all but feel the weight of his regret pushing down on my shoulders, and yet he'd done it.

To save me.

Me.

Why?

"Why did you do it?"

Rafferty stops in his tracks but doesn't face me. "I told you."

"You said it was either 'this' or my life. What did you do?"

He takes a deep breath and turns toward me. The gasp leaves my lips before I can stop it. My eyes instantly meet his own—a gaze that is much darker now, rimmed with black, the golden color dimmed.

"Rafferty."

"It was either them or you," he snaps. "Or would you rather I let him take you back to Taranus? Back to a future of being forced into marriage, of being raped?"

"No. I—"

"You what?" he snarls the last word, and I take a step back, honestly not sure what the hell to expect. This change in him is so drastic—and then I remember the day in the cell. When he'd nearly lost it.

"The dark magic. That's what's doing this to you, isn't it?"

He glares at me, and a muscle in his stubbled jaw twitches. "Does it matter?"

"Yes. It does." Taking a step toward him, I place a

hand on his arm. "Do you need to let some of your blood out?"

"Let some of my blood out," he repeats the words, carefully, slowly.

"Yes."

"Why the hell would I do that?"

"Because you're not acting like you."

"You don't even know me," he replies. "Therefore, what gives you the right to decide what I should be acting like?"

"Rafferty."

"You needed to be saved. I saved you. I'm not seeing the problem." He turns around.

"If it wasn't that much of a problem, why didn't you use that nifty ability to stop Taranus before he cut your wings off?"

Rafferty explodes on me, whipping around with such force I jump back. My feet slip out from under me, and I hit the ground with a heavy thud. Pain radiates up my spine from what is potentially a cracked tailbone. *Fun.*

But that pain goes mute when he bears down on me, golden gaze even darker now. "You know not of what you speak, woman," he snarls.

Fear ices my veins, and I'm helpless to do anything but stare up at him as he continues to advance. My attention is fully focused on Rafferty, so I don't feel the icy tendrils snake around my wrist.

Not until it's too late.

Something wrenches me backward, and I scream as branches and other brush rip at my skin. They tear at my clothes, slicing the skin of my back, my arms, my legs, as I'm dragged at breakneck speed through the forest.

"Ember!" Rafferty's deafening roar is the last thing I hear before pain explodes in my head and everything goes black.

MY SKIN IS WARM.

Too warm.

Sweat beads along my skin, slicking my hair to the side of my face. Slowly, I open my eyes as pain continues throbbing inside my brain. Every inch of my body hurts. Even my damned fingernails burn.

Vision clearing, I attempt to remain still, not wanting to alert whoever—or whatever—is lingering nearby.

Heat licks my body from a fire literally a foot from my face. The willpower to remain where I am is immense. Stone rises in front of and around me, telling me that I'm somewhere underground.

"You might as well sit, girl. We know you wake." The raspy voice echoes through the cavern.

My heart pounds as I sit, and my vision swims

once again. Every movement hurts; every breath aches. Lifting my shaking hands, I study the tears in my skin. Blood crusts every inch of my arms and what I can see of my ankles.

"Who—" I turn, having to twist my whole body, thanks to the stiffness in my neck, and very nearly scream when I get a look at the small creature behind me.

Wearing a black cloak, it's hunched over with a face so pale it's near translucent. Yellow eyes stare back at me from cavernous holes in its gaunt face. Teeth sharpened like knives are bared in a sinister grin.

"You were lost, girl," it rasps.

"No. I wasn't. What are you?"

"You were lost. We saved you."

"I wasn't lost. I was with someone," I argue back. I try to stand. Pain shoots up my leg, and I drop back down, wincing as tears fill my eyes. "What happened?"

"We saved you," it repeats. "We will deliver you to safety, and you will help us in return."

"What—how am I supposed to help you?"

"You will feed us."

My stomach churns. "Feed us?" I inquire, pretty damned sure I don't want to know the answer.

"Your life will feed us." It presses clawed hands to its chest. "It has been a while since we've eaten."

I glance around the cavern, looking for the others, but see none. "Who is we?"

"We." It gestures to itself again.

Swallowing hard, I scoot toward the door. The pain is so intense; every movement sends more tears to my eyes. "Please. My friend, he's looking for me," I manage through the tears.

"Your friend is bad. Very bad. We saved you."

"No. You don't understand. He's not bad."

"He *is* bad. *We* saw it," it counters. Then, it turns its back to me and begins to hum a dark tune I can't even pretend to try to listen to. I attempt to scoot more but fall backward, unable to keep going when my entire body might as well be broken. Who knows, maybe it is.

"You hurt me," I whisper. "You dragged me through the trees."

It whirls on me again, eyes narrowed. "We saved you!" it roars. "We will stop the pain—very, very soon." Turning fully toward me, it shows me a long, sharp blade. The silver glints in the firelight, and I cry out.

"Please, no. I don't need your help." I try to scoot some more, biting down on the inside of my cheek, trying to swallow down the pained screams threatening to rip from my chest.

"You do need our help," it says. Then, it takes a

step toward me. "We will help you, and you will help us in return."

"How is killing me helping!" I scream.

"Killing you? No, we are setting you free. You are in pain." It gestures to my injuries.

"Injuries you caused by ripping me through the trees!" I scream. "Rafferty! Help m—" The thing blurs across the room and slams a clawed hand over my mouth. It shoves me to the ground and kneels on my chest.

"You will be quiet or else you will offend us," it snarls. Saliva drips out of its mouth and onto my face. I close my eyes and whimper, turning my head to the side. "Now. We will take our payment." Something sharp bites into the side of my face. My hammering pulse blocks out all other sounds as I await what is coming for me.

What's been coming for me since I turned twenty-one: death.

But then the pain is gone. The weight no longer presses down on my chest.

Cautiously, I open my eyes just in time to see Rafferty rip the creature's head straight from its shoulders.

Blood splatters the wall, dousing the fire, and he drops the body. When he turns to me, I expect to see his once darkened gaze, but instead, bright golden eyes stare back at me. "Ember," he whispers, his words so soft I can't help but imagine how shitty I look right now.

"Rafferty." My voice is hoarse, shaky, and I let the violent sobbing take over now, no longer caring who —or what—sees me.

Rafferty rushes toward me and kneels, wrapping me in his arms. "I'm so sorry."

"I—it hurts."

"I need to get you to safety before I can heal you. There's always more than one *Puka* about."

Before I can ask what a pooka is, cold hits my skin. I hiss at the pain, which is stronger than anything I've ever felt in my entire life. My sobs turn into shivers; my entire body quivering with the freezing cold settling around me.

"Shit. I'll hurry." He turns back into the cavern and begins to run, moving quickly as I shut my eyes, not wanting to see the headless creature lying on the floor.

We wind, turning corner after corner until, finally, Rafferty begins to slow. He sets me down carefully and moves away, so I curl into myself as much as my injuries will allow. Whimpering, I lie there, exhausted and aching.

I'm not entirely sure how long it takes him to return, but the next time I open my eyes, he's kneeling beside me. "I need to see all your wounds," he tells me. "May I lift your dress to look at your legs?"

"Yes."

I close my eyes tightly as he pulls the fabric. It sticks, and I hiss through gritted teeth.

"Dammit. We need to clean you up, or you could get an infection. I can't heal them if I can't touch them, and your gown is sticking to the worst of them. There's a spring here. I'm going to carry you inside, okay?"

Nodding, I wait for him to lift me. Strong arms wrap around my body, and he lifts me, moving slowly toward the water. It's nearly silent, a steady trickling until he steps into it.

I fade in and out of consciousness as he submerges us both, coming to when the warm water hits my skin. A fresh wave of pain overtakes me, and I cringe, tightening my hold on Rafferty.

"I'm sorry, Ember."

"It hurts."

"I know. I'm going to set you down, but I'll keep a hold on you. I want to look at your back."

I begin to shiver so violently speaking is of no use, so I nod, instead. He releases me into the water enough to wrap an arm around my waist. Warm fingers start at the top of my dress. Then I can feel him tugging at laces until they come free.

"Bloody hell."

"Bad?" Even as I say it, I look down at the water. Blood turns it cloudy, and I'm pretty damned sure it's not from the pooka.

"I'm going to do the best I can, but this will take days to fully heal without draining myself."

"Okay."

His hand touches my back. It stings where he touches me, but even as it does, the pain begins to fade as my body warms where he touches it.

A golden glow surrounds us, flittering about like mist.

He moves his hands down, then down again, until it's at the very base of my spine. Moments pass, minutes turning into what feels like hours as we remain mostly submerged in the water.

All the while, Rafferty doesn't speak above a whisper, and even those words are in a language I can't understand.

He slips the dress down my arms, letting his fingers trail over the broken skin as he goes. Then, he stops and tugs the tattered remains back up.

"I need you to face me," he says, tone barely above a growl.

I do, more than ready to feel the same relief on my abdomen.

Rafferty's gaze drops to my face. His expression is strained, jaw set. "I need you to remove your dress.

I will close my eyes and not open them until you've covered your breasts."

My heart hammers. Though I know it's foolish, Taranus's words run through my brain. *She is nothing impressive.*

Tears spring to my eyes as I nod and avert my gaze. Reaching over, I tug my dress down until the fabric pools at the top of the water. Then, I reach out and grip his arm as I float up and shove the dress down. It takes quite a bit of effort, especially with the pain, but I manage to get free of the fabric before wrapping both arms around to hide my breasts. "Okay," I whisper, shutting my eyes so tightly it intensifies the pounding that's been in my head since I woke in that cave.

Rafferty sucks in a breath. "Ember—"

"I know. Not impressive. Please, just fix me. I want to get dressed."

He doesn't say another word. Nothing to counter what I'd said—nothing to confirm it—so I remain perfectly still, listening to the water sloshing over my body as he presses his hands to my waist, my stomach, my thighs. Healing my body when I fear the greatest injury I have—is something not even he can fix.

CHAPTER 25
EMBER

What must have been hours after we entered the water, Rafferty is carrying me back out and setting me down gently on the ground. No longer bathed in warmth, it doesn't take long for my body to cool.

Goosebumps cover every inch of my exposed skin. He steps back, so I open my eyes as he strips out of his shirt and offers it to me. "It's wet but will shield you."

I reach for it and quickly pull it over my head. My body no longer feels like it's on fire—so that's something—but the aches are still there, likely from what I now see are long, deep gashes on the tops of both of my thighs.

Rafferty kneels beside me and presses his fingers to the torn flesh. I watch, breath held, as he whispers something. Golden threads wrap over my injury, pulling the skin back together as he whispers.

Soon, I'm staring at nothing but a jagged pink line. Then, he moves to the other side, repeating it and leaving me with a matching set.

"I can do more tomorrow," he says as he stands. As soon as he's on his feet, though, he sways, catching himself on the wall.

"Maybe you should sit, too."

"I will once I've retrieved your gown from the water." He turns, and my gaze falls to the two scars on his shoulder blades. They are huge and still red. The fact that I know where those came from brings a fresh wave of anger washing over me.

To lose such an intricate part of oneself—something that might as well have been a limb—I can't even imagine.

He splashes into the water and grabs the dress still floating. When he turns to me, I drop my gaze then close my eyes as I track his movement with my hearing.

A few moments later, he drops to the ground beside me. "I'm sorry, Ember."

"You saved me."

"I should have heard it coming."

"You would have if you'd just talked to me instead of getting pissed."

He grunts. "When I get like that, I don't know

how to explain what comes over me. It's like I'm not myself."

"You seem fine now."

"I seem that way, but I assure you, I am not. Something was lost in that clearing…and I'm afraid I'll never get it back."

I crack open an eye now and look over at the massive man sitting beside me. With his knees pulled up, he's resting both arms on top of them and staring out over the water. "You forced him to kill those men."

"I manipulated his mind, yes. Something that can only be done to a light fae by a dark one."

"You're a dark fae?" I whisper the words, only partially understanding the implication behind them.

"I don't know what I am," he admits. "I was born a light fae, but when I claimed vengeance for my sister and absorbed that dark magic…" He trails off, sighing. "I'm no longer sure what I am. For centuries, I've kept it at bay, refusing to use that ability because I knew what it would mean, and now I can feel it, Ember." He turns toward me. "I can feel the darkness closing around me like a vice. It's suffocating."

He'd already explained as much to me, which has me even more concerned that he'd given in. Does that mean he'll change now? Or does he have to fully embrace it? "You traded a piece of yourself for my safety. Why?"

His golden eyes, still rimmed with black, focus on me. "How could I not?"

Taking a page out of his book, I clear my throat. "I keep giving you the reason you shouldn't: You don't know me."

"While that may be true, I know that you do not deserve the fate Taranus has in store for you." He turns away from me, shoulders slumping.

"What he's done is not your fault."

"It is absolutely my fault," he replies. "I was warned, over and over again, and ignored it. All the deaths of my people—they are mine to carry. You will not be another added to that list."

"Rafferty, Taranus is his own person."

"Taranus is a monster," he interrupts. "A monster that should have been put down years ago."

"He's your brother," I argue back. "Had you killed him before this, you would have been the monster."

Rafferty hangs his head down.

Sensing him closing up, I look back to the water. "Are we safe in here?"

"I warded the entrances. It is not as strong as witch magic, but it will hold the *Puka* out."

"What is a pooka?"

"A shapeshifting creature. Vile. They feed on flesh and will kill anything that draws breath."

"Shapeshifting?"

"Yes. Which is likely how it was able to sneak up

on us. Even had I sensed something approaching, it was more than likely an animal of some kind until it grabbed you."

I wrap both arms around my legs and shiver. "It moved so fast."

"They do. I am sorry it got to you. I lost my head."

"You were being an ass," I reply with a smile, hoping to ease some of his internal turmoil. He'd accessed that dark magic to save me, and it backfired on us both. Still, I'd rather go through what I did than end up trapped with Taranus again.

Hell, I'd rather die.

And it's that thought that has me laughing. It starts off small, a slight giggle, but soon, I'm laughing like a crazy person, which makes my sides hurt from more than just a bone-deep ache.

Rafferty stares at me as though I've lost my mind —who knows, maybe I have. "What in the bloody hell are you laughing about?"

"I've been dying slowly since I was twenty-one," I tell him. "Do you know how many times I wished they would either find out what was wrong or it would speed up and take me quickly? Then, I arrive here. My sickness subsides enough to where I can enjoy living again, and I've nearly died more times than I can count." I snort. "It's all insanely ridiculous, isn't it?"

He continues to stare at me. "You are the most interesting person I've ever met," he finally says, shutting me right up.

The intensity of his stare—it heats my blood in a way that I shouldn't even be considering. After all, ridiculous irony aside, I did literally nearly die only a few hours ago. "*I'm* interesting? You just healed me with a touch of your hands."

"That is not interesting in my world," he replies. "Simply ordinary."

"There is nothing about you that is ordinary, fae or not." Our gazes lock again, and a warmth spreads through my body, igniting passion I long thought dead.

"We should probably get some rest."

"I suppose you're right."

He gets to his feet, so I curl on my side, resting my head on the crook of my arm. "I will get a fire going."

A BREEZE RUFFLES MY HAIR, SO *I* SIT, CONFUSED.

The forest around me is dark, though an orange glow on the horizon catches my attention. Standing, I move toward it, drawn like a moth to light. For some reason, seeing it brings me an overwhelming feeling of peace.

Belonging.

Ahead, someone roars, and that peace vanishes. I begin to run, sprinting toward the orange as my lungs burn. "Hello!" I call out.

No one answers.

Just ahead, the ground rises to form a peak. My thighs ache, but I push on, reaching the top within moments.

And then I wish I would have remained where I was—curled in the forest.

Fire scorches the earth before me, eating away at the trees, the brush. Gasping, I take a step back, but then I see him.

Standing in the midst of the flames.

My warrior.

My love.

I run toward him, but just before I reach the edge of the fire, it envelops him.

I OPEN MY EYES. THE FIRE A FEW FEET AWAY IS smoldering, but it's what's at my back I find most interesting.

He's wrapped around me, pressed against me like a second skin, and before I can help myself, I'm arching back into him.

Rafferty groans and tightens his grip on my body.

"You were cold," he whispers, his hot breath fanning over my neck. "I meant to keep you warm."

"I am warm." *Blistering hot, even*, I think silently as I clench my thighs together in an attempt to ease the ache.

"I can move—"

"No. Stay." I grip his arm and hold it in place.

"This is not a good idea."

"Why?"

"Because I am unable to think honorably when your body is formed to mine."

Please, for the love of everything, just make a move. "Why is that?" I clear my throat.

In demonstration, he tightens his hold, and my ass presses against his hard length.

"Oh," the word leaves my lips on a plea. "Maybe I don't want you to think honorably," I whisper.

Rafferty's answering growl burns a hole in my soul. "You've no idea what you're asking. I'm a damned man."

"I may not know much, but that's a lie, and you promised never to lie to me."

His lips caress my neck, and goosebumps flare to life on my skin. "You make it impossible to control myself."

I know it's wrong to sense a weakness and purposely seek out to exploit it, but I want him. *Badly.* Is it really a crime to enjoy myself before I die?

Swallowing hard, I roll over. His hand remains on my body, stopping on my belly. The shirt I'm wearing comes up to just barely cover the area of my body currently demanding his attention.

His eyes are closed, his breathing ragged.

"Rafferty?"

He shakes his head.

"Please, look at me."

Finally, he opens his eyes, and the lust drains right out of me.

"Not what you wanted to see?" he sneers.

Eyes nearly completely black, he's nothing like the man I've known. "Rafferty?" I reach up and press my hand to his chest. He doesn't move, though his eyes close once more, and he takes a deep breath. "You are strong," I say, though my voice is anything but.

If this is what he's so worried about, I get it now.

He releases me and pulls back, rolling away from me before pushing up to his feet. I do the same, and when he faces me again, his eyes are golden once more.

"I'm sorry. I—I knew it was a mistake."

"You said I was cold."

He nods. "You were shivering, but I should have stayed away."

"Why?"

"You are the greatest threat to me right now, Ember."

"What? Why?" I demand, taking a step back from him.

"My honor is the only thing keeping me in the light," he replies, softly. "And wanting you the way I do, even as I know I would ruin you, it's making me want to embrace the darkness."

CHAPTER 26

EMBER

A storm rages just outside the cavern where we've sought shelter. It offers just enough protection from the bitter wind and is deep enough that if we need to venture farther inside, we can do just that.

Ever since the moment two days ago where Rafferty confessed his pain to me, I've kept my distance. Even now, I sit at least two yards away from him, on the opposite side of the fire. I hate it, being so far away, but if being near him is actually causing discomfort, I'll keep to myself.

"Tell me of your home."

I glance up at him. "What about it?"

"Your work, home, friends. I know near nothing about that world."

"Um, I can't imagine I'm the best person to ask. I

never really had much of a life," I reply, honestly. "You already know that I was an orphan. When I turned sixteen, I filed for emancipation, it was granted, so I floated from shelter to shelter until I was able to save up for an apartment."

"Emancipation?"

"Basically, I had to go before a judge and ask to be considered an adult."

"At the age of sixteen?"

I nod.

"That's so young."

"For you immortals, maybe. But for a girl who'd been on her own pretty much since she could walk, it felt like forever before I was finally allowed to make my own decisions."

Rafferty grunts. "What happened after that?"

I study his features in the firelight. "Are you sure you want to hear all of this? It's not the best story."

"I want to know all there is about you."

How the hell am I supposed to stay away when your words make me want to curl into your lap? "Okay. Uh, well, I worked as a waitress, went to school to get my GED—basically a piece of paper that said I was okay to graduate high school—and after that, I started working full time. I took on more jobs; started teaching self-defense. Then, I started ghostwriting."

"You wrote for ghosts?"

I snort. "No. I wrote material for authors to use as their own. It helps when they have a lot on their schedule or need someone else to nail a scene they're struggling with."

"So you help them lie."

"I mean…I guess in a way, but it's not unusual. Especially not these days."

"Why did you never write for yourself?"

"Fear, mostly."

"What is there to be afraid of?"

"Rejection? Not being good enough?" I laugh as I lift a twig and drag it around in the dirt below me. "There were plenty of reasons that seemed valid at the time."

"Fear seems a strange reason not to do what you want."

"I've been driven by fear my entire life. Though, all of it seems silly now, given what I've faced the last few weeks." Dropping the stick, I draw my knees up to my chest.

"You've certainly had a lot to deal with."

"What's crazy, though, is that it wasn't until I actually believed I was going to die that I got the courage to live."

"I can relate to that," he says, sadly. "After Niahm was killed—after what my mate did—I lost my head. You once asked me if I had ever known peace. I did when Niahm was a child. Before I met—" he swallows hard. "Before I was pushed into a mating ceremony I never really wanted."

The confession on his lips pains him, that much is clear, and it catches me off guard. "But she was your mate."

"I didn't love her," he replies. "My magic wanted her, it sensed a match, but she was always so—entitled. And never satisfied."

The idea that the man before me couldn't satisfy someone seems impossible. "She always wanted more?"

"She did. More power, more attention, more of everything, and I was honor-bound to the king, to my family." He closes his eyes and turns his face up. "She asked me to take the throne, tried to convince me that the king was weak, that he was not as good a man as everyone believed."

"Did you try?"

"Of course, not. The king was a good, fair man. Everyone loved him. By then, I'd seen enough to know she was never going to be happy. I told her to leave, to go where she wanted, that she was free of me, but that was not enough. She trapped Niahm, convinced her that I was injured, and then…" He trails off and lowers his face again, eyes shut tightly.

I'm hanging on every word; every moment of this horrible turn of events that led to the man before me.

"She sold her to a dark fae who murdered her. I'd

been too late—missed rescuing her by minutes because Taranus had managed to get himself into a bind with one of the other guards. I'd lost my sister, protecting the brother who ended up turning on me."

Rubbing the heel of my palm against my chest, I attempt to ease the ache. The burdens Rafferty carries, they are so damned heavy, and none of it is his fault.

"I found my mate in bed with the dark fae. I killed him, absorbed the magic, and then turned on her. When she tried to get onto her knees and 'make up' for what she'd done, I ripped her up and delivered her to the king."

"She honestly thought giving you a blow-job was going to fix the fact that she'd had your sister murdered?"

He nods.

"What a psychotic bitch."

A muscle in his jaw twitches, and he turns his head to the side. "I'd been so consumed by the dark magic; I'd very nearly considered doing as she'd asked. Taking the throne, it was Heelean who saved me. And then, when I was out on a mission, they were attacked." He gets to his feet and leans back against the cavern wall. "My life is riddled with failure, Ember. I cannot fail with you."

I get up and cross the cavern to him, stopping when I'm a few feet away. "You won't fail with me."

"I nearly have," he whispers. "So many times.

Every single moment I am in your presence, I fight the urge to simply take you somewhere none of this will touch us. Faerie is vast. We could run. Hide."

"The bond with Taranus?"

"We can find someone to break it. Then live out our days happy."

"Except you wouldn't be," I say as I cross toward him. "And neither would I. Not knowing what we sacrificed."

"Therein lies my dilemma. I believe that I am honor-bound to help you find your other half. That whatever is between us is merely lust—a craving."

I let him cheapen what I feel because it seems the only thing keeping him grounded, but it pisses me off. "I—"

"Did you hear that?" He cuts me off and tilts his head to the side.

"Hear what?" I listen, but all I can hear is the sound of rain hammering the ground outside.

"That!" he rushes out into the storm.

"Rafferty!" I follow, gathering the skirt of my dress as I race out after him.

"Call to me!" he yells.

Still, I hear nothing. "What is happening?"

"Someone is hurt!" He runs so quickly that I lose sight of him in the trees.

Panic races through my veins as I scan, barely able to see a few feet in front of me. "Rafferty!"

Nothing.

I run, sprinting now, in the direction I last saw him. Leaping over a log, I stumble, cracking my ankle beneath the weight of my body. "Rafferty!"

A gust of wind blows over me, and lightning splits the sky. Then, I see him.

On his knees.

A woman stands over him. Her obsidian hair is nearly to her knees, and it shields her face from my view. But the claws where her hands should have been get me onto my feet. I grasp a fallen tree branch and limp, barely managing to make it to the clearing.

She throws her head back, opening her mouth wide, but nothing comes out.

Rafferty continues to kneel, his eyes wide, mouth slack.

"Move, Rafferty!" I scream.

He doesn't look at me, but she does with eyes as black as her hair, sneering at me. Wrapping my fingers around the branch, I lunge forward and swing.

She catches it with a clawed hand, though, and snaps it like a twig. Shards of wood fall to the ground, and she stalks toward me. I throw myself in front of Rafferty. "Back the hell off!" Keeping my eyes on the creature, I pat down the side where he stashed the dagger.

My hand closes around the hilt, and I hold it out

in front of me as rain continues to hammer the world around me.

"You are not getting him!"

The thing glares at me. *You will be dead, soon enough.* The voice in my head is so loud its deafening. Pain splits my brain, and the dagger falls to the ground as I cover both of my ears.

Visions of me, pale and lying in a satin coffin fill my brain.

No one is there.

No one cares.

I'm alone.

Dead and alone.

Orange eats up the vision, and soon, I'm watching the coffin shoved into an enormous concrete box. Fire eats away at it, reducing all that is left of me to ash.

A man roars.

Then, Rafferty is in front of me, shaking my shoulders. "Ember, get to your feet!" he yells.

I try, but my body is frozen in place. He mutters something then lifts me and runs back through the trees.

My gaze falls on a body lying in the clearing, a dagger sticking out of her chest.

"Are you all right? Injured?" He sets me down inside the cavern and falls to his knees in front of me.

"Wha-wha-what was th-th-that?" I stammer as the cold settles into my bones.

"A bloody banshee," he snaps as he rubs my arms with his hands. "They seek out those who are dying or those who will be dead soon."

"It told me I was going to be dead, soon enough," I manage through chattering teeth.

His eyes darken. "It wasn't even here for you," he says.

The implication of what he'd just told me—it clears the rest of my fog. "What?"

"It appears I am also not long for this world."

"No. No. No. You can't die. The people…they need you—" He presses a finger to my lips, silencing me.

"I'm not going anywhere just yet, and there's no sense in worrying about what may or may not happen."

"She could be wrong?"

He doesn't answer me. "Let's get some sleep, Ember. The storm will pass, and we are about a day from the nearest village. There, we should be able to get some help." He moves back and sits against the cavern wall.

Shoulders slumped, he stares out at the storm.

"What did she show you?" I ask, needing to know.

He swallows hard. "My body being eaten by flames."

CHAPTER 27
EMBER

The village is small, consisting only of a handful of wooden buildings lined on a dirt street. It's tucked away in the middle of the forest, and those out and about as rain drizzles down on top of us keep their eyes focused on the ground as they walk.

The mood is somber, though I'm not sure if that's due to the still drizzling rain or normal for this place. Based on the fact that they have Taranus as their king, I'd say it's a combination.

Rafferty guides me down an alley and up to a door set in the back of the largest building. There, he raises his fist and knocks once, twice, then pauses before knocking three more times in rapid succession.

A secret knock…*interesting*.

Hope burns in my chest. Is it possible we found the Rebellion? Is this it?

The door opens, and a short, round woman peeks her head out. Golden eyes narrow on Rafferty, then she gasps and jumps back. "As I live and breathe, Rafferty, is that you?"

"Hello, Marie," he greets.

Tears spring to her eyes, and she rushes forward to wrap her arms around his waist. "We thought ye' dead, boy! Dead!"

"Shhh, or I might still end up that way," he jokes.

She pushes back and moves to the side, ushering us inside. Warmth envelopes me, and I smile, breathing in the aroma of freshly baked... well...something.

The moment we're inside, she leads us from a dimly lit hall and into a quiet kitchen. Something boils in a pot hung over a roaring fire while some-thing else presumably bakes in a metal box directly on the coals.

"Ye' poor dears, you both look absolutely awful."

"Thank you for the warm greeting."

Marie purses her lips. "We need to get ye' to a room, quietly. The guards are here in town looking for ye'," she whispers.

"Then you shouldn't have let us in." Rafferty straightens and peers back down the hall.

"Hush yer' mouth. I won't have it. Besides,

they've already searched all the rooms, and based on the mead they're inhaling, they won't be looking again. Come." Shifting quickly, she gathers her skirts and moves past us, heading for a set of wooden stairs.

In near silence, she ascends them, one at a time, with me behind her and Rafferty directly behind me. A door opens above us, and Marie quickly steps out, closing the door in front of me.

"Marie. We were just looking for a room."

"Then take yer' pick," she replies, the sound muffled through the door. "You've already ripped them all apart."

Rafferty grabs me and yanks me through a door I hadn't even noticed. He shuts it quietly and pins me against the wall, pressing his massive body into me. Not that he could have given me much space, anyway. From the looks of it, we're standing in the world's smallest closet.

My heart pounds while I try to keep my breathing steady.

Rafferty drops his face to my neck and inhales.

Lust pounds in my ears.

Knowing I will likely regret it, I turn my head so my face is in his neck, too. I breathe in, inhaling the scent of pine and fresh rain—something that is a double sucker punch of lust to my gut.

I know we're supposed to be keeping our distance, that me being near him makes it difficult for him to control his lust—but when we're this close, nothing else matters.

Rafferty growls, tightening his hands on my waist, and it's all I can do to keep myself standing when he lifts his head and looks at me. Eyes, so golden they illuminate the closet around us, meet mine, and I lose my breath.

Forgo any rational thought.

Because Rafferty looks like he wants to *devour* me.

The door opens. "If ye' want to neck, do so on yer' own time," Marie scolds and rips Rafferty from me.

I clear my throat and follow. My legs shake the entire way through the door and down the hall. It's empty, though there is loud, live music carrying up from downstairs. Someone laughs, the boisterous sound all but shaking the wood as Marie unlocks a door and pulls it open. Rafferty and I follow, moving up another set of stairs at break-neck speed.

Once we reach the top, she pulls out a set of keys and unlocks the door, pushing it open to reveal a quaint room that looks more like a single bedroom apartment.

Rafferty moves into the room first, and I follow. "Marie, we cannot take your home."

She waves a hand in the air as if to physically bat away his words. "Hush now. I won't hear of it.

Besides, they've already checked my room, and as ye' heard, there's no telling if they're going to all want rooms. Mine is off limits, as is."

"But where will you sleep?"

Marie winks at me. "Doona worry about me, lass. I've somewhere to go." She turns back to Rafferty. "Ye' stay here. I'll bring ye' fresh clothes and food. As soon as they get to sleep, I'll bring ye' up some water for a bath. For now, there should be fresh water in the basin and some cloth on the shelf near the bed."

"Thank you," I tell her, and she turns to me, gripping my arms.

Marie's eyes mist. "I know who ye' are, dear; what ye' mean to our world. Thank ye' for being here." After one final squeeze, she releases me and gestures to a cabinet painted green on the far wall. "Ye' might be a fit for one of my sleep gowns, though I imagine it will be short."

Then, with one final look, she leaves the apartment and closes the door softly behind her. Rafferty crosses quickly and flips the lock.

It's only then that I realize where I am—and who I am now alone with. Sure, we've been alone before, but after that little preview in the closet? Now we're in a room with a bed? Yeah, this may not be the world's best idea for a dying woman and a man toying with the edge of a sharp blade.

But, shit, what a fall that would be.

He turns toward me. "You wash up first," he says, voice deeper than normal. Before I can respond, he turns away, so I head for the washbasin. Hanging above it is a small gold-rimmed mirror. The woman's reflection staring back at me should have looked familiar, but she might as well have been a stranger.

Dark circles line my eyes; eyes that are haunted by horrific things witnessed. Bruises cover the left side of my dirt-crusted face.

Reaching up, I touch the darkest purple blotch sitting on top of my cheekbone. So much has happened, and yet, here I am, running from death, yet again.

Different world, different source, same outcome.

Briefly, I see myself in that coffin again, and a shiver runs through my body.

"Are you all right?"

My gaze lifts, catching Rafferty watching me, his gaze reflected in the top right side of the mirror. "Just tired," I reply. "It's been a while since I had a nice night's sleep."

"I'm sorry."

"Not your fault," I remind him.

Reaching up, he runs a hand through his hair. "You can take the bed. I'll pull some blankets from the bureau and sleep on the floor. Marie will wake us when she brings f—"

"Don't be ridiculous," I interrupt. "We can share

the bed. It's large enough for us both." He looks to the bed, then back at me, then back to the bed. I'm not sure why, but it pisses me off. Which is ridiculous, of course. I know what's at stake. "Fine. You want to sleep on the floor? Go for it." I march over toward the bed where he's laid out an off-white chemise. Then, just because I'm angry, I reach up and tear the shredded dress from my body.

Rafferty mutters a curse in some language I don't understand and turns around. "For shit's sake, woman, warn a man."

"Why?" I demand. "Because I'm so offensive to look at?" I yank the new fabric over my body. "Your brother seemed to think so." My words make no sense, given his confessions about his attraction to me, but I'm so overwhelmed by everything we're facing I cannot understand why us being together would be such a bad thing.

Why does he have to set his honor aside just because he wants to be with me? I don't belong to anyone. I'm a consenting adult, so what the hell is the big deal?

Rafferty grips my arms and yanks me around to face him. "Taranus is a damned fool. You do not get to compare me to him."

My bottom lip quivers. The idea that this strong man before me is so offended by my nakedness makes me want to crawl into a hole. Which is ridiculous, of course, because I shouldn't fucking care.

"You are absolutely stunning in every way. But you are not for me." He swallows hard. "And no matter how badly I want you, that fact does not change."

"So you say. I'm starting to believe it's just your way of keeping me happy while you deliver me to yet another man I…don't…want."

"I told you that I would not lie to you."

"Sure. But a man who needs to keep me occupied would say that."

"What about the past few days has made you distrust me?"

He looks wounded. *Good.* Because I've taken enough emotional beatings to last a lifetime. "You claim you want me—that I drive you crazy—and yet you use the dark magic as some kind of barrier between us. And for what? I don't belong to anyone. Not Taranus. Not some king. And certainly, not you." I shove at his chest, trying to push him off of me, and he stumbles back a step.

His chest rises and falls in rapid succession, and his pupils dilate. Until he snakes a hand around the back of my neck and yanks me toward him.

Rafferty's mouth claims me, his lips scorching my own as he devours me. His tongue slides over the seam of my lips, and I open, gripping his biceps as he reaches down and grips my ass. He lifts me, stepping between my legs as he pins me to the wall.

Large hands slip up my thighs, gripping, kneading the muscles beneath his strong fingertips. I moan and tighten my legs around his waist.

The man invades my senses, overtakes my thoughts, my words. Everything about him calls to me.

I grip him as he turns and carries me across the room. The mattress is soft beneath my back and he grinds into me, his erection pressing against the fabric separating us.

"You drive me mad," he whispers against my lips. "Make me not want to fucking care about anything else."

I press my hands to his shoulders and push him up so I can see his eyes. They're rimmed with black, a band that is thicker now. Visual representation of the fight I'm giving him.

Guilt crushes me.

I've been selfish.

And Rafferty is paying the price. "Stop."

He leans down and runs his tongue along my jaw.

Torture shouldn't feel so damn good. "Stop, Rafferty."

"Why?"

"We can't do this." I shove at him, and he pulls

away, taking steps back until he's all the way across the room.

"What the hell do you want, Ember? One minute, you're begging me to forget about everything—tormenting me into setting aside the one thing I have left for you. Then I do just that, and you push me away? Do you get off by tormenting me?"

I shake my head. "You're right, though. I saw it… the magic. I'm so sorry I pushed you." I curl my legs up into my chest and stare at him.

"There is no world where I can watch you marry another," Rafferty says, his voice strained. "Not now."

"Then don't. Can't we still have everything? Can't we beat Taranus and then be together? Your honor—"

"Niahm was stolen from me. My parents before her. Ridley will never return home permanently, and Taranus has turned his back on me. He stole my wings, my life—Ember, my honor is *all* I have left. And even that is hanging on by a bloody shred!" he roars it, then gets to his feet and grips the wooden bedpost.

"I'm sorry."

He shakes his head. "It was my fault."

"No. I pushed you. I accused you of lying, of manipulating me."

"And I reacted poorly." He shakes his head and

moves toward the other side of the room. "Please, get some sleep, Ember."

"I—"

But he's already settling against the far wall.

Not wanting to make things worse, I slip beneath the blankets and pull them up to my chest. Tears stain my cheeks as I reach up and touch lips still tender from his kiss.

There is no world where I can watch you marry another. Truthfully, there's no world where I can watch him and not have him. Where I can spend every moment reminded of the first man who'd treated me like a woman.

Like I was worth something.

I'd rather die.

"I want to go home," I choke out.

He sighs. "Then I shall take you there."

CHAPTER 28
RAFFERTY

The darkness outside would seem a perfect match for my soul if not for the twinkling stars overhead.

I'd been so close to taking what I want—what we both want—and destroying what little honor I have left. Within moments of burying myself inside of her and experiencing passion for the first time in my long life.

Had she not stopped me—I would have done just that.

She may not want any part of this world, may be insisting on returning home, but it won't be because I claimed what was not rightfully mine.

I stare down at the blood dripping from my wounded arm. I'm not foolish enough to believe that giving in to her, alone, will be what turns me, but it's a start. A step in the direction of losing all sight of who I am.

And I am not a man who takes what is not his.

I am not a man who claims a woman who deserves better.

She wants me, the dark side urges. *Take her.*

The voice that I'd been able to silence with little effort before has now grown in full force. Much the same way it was when I first took in the dark magic.

It wants me to give in—to take everything it offers. What's even more twisted? That dark shadow on my soul is one hundred percent me. The dark magic didn't add to me; it enhanced parts of my personality that were already there.

I was a monster before. The power simply gave me an outlet.

Wood creaks, and I get to my feet, retrieving my blade and eyeing Ember sleeping soundly as I creep to the door.

With the same attention I take on the battlefield, I listen, extending my senses to pick up whoever is outside the door.

Kill. The word echoes through my brain, an order I will gladly follow should whoever is on the other side be here to bring harm to Ember.

I reach forward and quietly click the lock. Then I slowly move toward the handle. With one final breath, I rip it open and grab the man on the other side by the throat. In the blink of an eye, he's pinned against the wall, my blade at his throat.

"What the fuck do you want?" I snarl, leaning in close enough that I can easily make out the bright golden eyes staring back at me.

"It's me. Fin," he chokes out.

Kill.

"Fin?" I take a step back, keeping my blade at the ready as I take in the man before me. Dressed in dark brown trousers and a cloak to match, he looks nothing like the hardened warrior I'd last seen.

He reaches up and removes his cloak, revealing dark hair braided on the left side, two black beads woven into the bottom.

"What happened?"

His expression falters. "I'm so glad to see you, brother." Not answering my question, he steps forward and wraps both arms around me. It takes me a moment, but then I return the gesture. We stand, embracing for a moment, before he releases me and steps back, sniffling.

"What are you doing here, Fin?"

"Looking for you. Marie got word to me that you'd arrived."

"I can't tell you how damned glad I am to see you."

"Nor I, you," he replies, then peeks into the room.

Eyes widening, he gasps. "That's her? The woman from the prophecy?"

"Yes." I reach behind me and shut the door, not wanting Ember to be disturbed.

"You found her."

"Actually, she found me. In a cell beneath the castle. She's the only reason I'm alive."

Fin stares in wonder at the door then shakes his head. "We all thought you dead, Rafferty. Every single one of us."

"You went back to the camp? After leaving?"

Fin's eyes darken momentarily. Then he shakes his head. "The tavern is clear. Let's go down to the kitchen and get a drink."

"Soldiers?"

He shakes his head. "They all left, even the ones planning on staying. Taranus called them all to the other side of Faerie."

I glance back at the door then nod. "Let's go down, then."

We walk in silence, and by the time we reach the bottom, Marie has already filled two mugs with ale. She offers me one and Fin the other. "I'll be out there if ye' need me." She squeezes his hand gently then leaves without another word.

The two of us sit together on stools, and I try to wait for him to speak, but my gaze drops again to the two black beads in his braided hair. "Who do you grieve?"

Fin's jaw tightens, and he takes a deep drink before setting the mug down. While his eyes shimmer with tears, he turns to me. "We'd made it away from the camp," he begins. "Meena and me."

His voice cracks at the mention of his mate, and my heart plummets to my feet. She'd been pregnant last I'd seen her; a new development.

"That fucker found us and killed her."

I stand so quickly my stool clatters to the ground. "Taranus?" I choke out, my voice cracking.

He nods, and a tear slips down his face and into the stubble on his cheek. "He killed her right in front of me. Would have killed me, too, had Karver not shown up and gotten me out of there. Not that it matters. She was mine, Rafferty. My true mate. My one—" His voice cracks.

Red-hot rage burns through my body as magic pushes to the surface in desperation for it to be freed, obliterating all logical sense.

Kill. One word. One word and I can kill him. I can kill Taranus then have enough sense to end myself before the dark magic can hurt anyone.

"I still see her in my dreams," he chokes out. "I was so weak that I could not save her."

"Taranus is the one responsible for her death, not you."

"I couldn't believe him. When he'd said what they'd done to you. Your wings, Raffe…the fucker stole your wings!"

"He stole your mate," I whisper. "And that is so much worse than my bloody wings." My muscles quiver with the need for blood to be spilled—greater than anything I've ever experienced. Meena was a ray of sunlight; a bright soul who'd been so happy to move forward with her life—her family.

Guilt weighs on me for the very fact that I didn't let Fin kill him the first time he'd shown interest in the man's mate.

Joaquin was right for what he said in that cell: I was weak. But no more.

Fin nods, shutting his eyes tightly as tears stream down his cheeks. "I know Meena wouldn't wish for me to lose my head, but I've been trying to find a way to get to him ever since. I'm going to kill him, Rafferty. I'm going to kill your brother." The look on his face, the steadiness of his gaze, makes me wonder if he's worried I'll ask him not to.

But we're way past me protecting that fucker.

"There is not a force in this world or any other that will prevent me from putting Taranus in the ground. What he's done to all of us is unforgivable, so if you're here asking for my permission to claim vengeance for your wife, you never needed it." I clasp a hand on Fin's shoulder. "All I ask is that you allow me the honor of fighting alongside you."

Fin purses his lips and nods. "It is not the only reason I came," he says after a few moments of brief silence.

"Then what is it?"

"The Rebellion has scattered," he says. "There is no one to lead us, no one to keep us fighting."

"No one stepped up?"

He shakes his head. "Once the camp was decimated, the ones who survived ran. I went looking for them after—after Meena and discovered that they were all gone."

"No." I shake my head and begin to pace. "This is not good. If there's no one to fight back, no one to push against what he's done—"

"I know," Fin replies, angrily. "Fucking cowards."

"Taranus was one of us—or, at least, we all thought he was. He knew us, our faces, our families," I remind him. "To run was not cowardly. It was smart."

"The smart thing was to regroup."

He's grieving—rightfully so—which is why he can't see it from their side. Even as much as I hate that no one stepped forward, as much as it surprises me, I can understand why. Taranus's betrayal came out of left field for a lot of us—mainly me. While I knew he wasn't an honorable man, I never pegged him for a murderer, a rapist.

"Do you know where Candice is? Any word of her?"

He shakes his head. "I've looked, hoping she could help me locate you, but it seems like she's completely disappeared."

My heart aches. A steady burn in my chest reminds me that she was my only hope of severing the connection forged between Taranus and Ember. "You told me that Taranus called them all to the other side of Faerie."

"Yes."

"Do you know where?"

He shakes his head. "My guess is somewhere near the castle to prevent you from marching the Rebellion straight to his front door."

"Good. Then that makes things a bit easier for us. We need to track everyone down. We need to find Candice."

"I will carry the word myself. Though, don't hold your breath on the witch. She was already a bit dodgy, so I wouldn't count on her showing back up."

"We need her, badly," I tell him. "To prevent Taranus from tracking Ember."

"The woman?"

I nod. "Tomorrow, we can go look for a new

place, start rebuilding for the others when they do arrive."

Fin nods. "I know I've already said it, brother, but I am so damned glad you're back."

"Me, too. And I am so sorry for the part I played in Meena's death. What happened to her—had I known what he was capable of—"

My friend shakes his head. "Taranus was your brother, and until he overthrew our camp, the worst he'd done was put his hands on her arse." The ghost of a smile plays at his lips even as grief washes over his face. "She handled herself pretty damned well, don't you think?"

"Absolutely. I still remember when she broke his nose for making inappropriate comments."

Fin's choked laugh guts me. "She was quite the woman."

"She was."

The mood darkens, and Fin downs his ale. "She was my mate," he says. "You know that, right?"

"I do."

"I will see Taranus dead before the Veil takes me." He looks to me.

Losing a mate will kill the remaining fae within the year of passing. When bound, our souls are so woven together the magic becomes one in the same. "How soon?"

"A few months, maybe. I grow weaker by the

day." Setting his mug down, he pulls the cloak back over his head. "I long for the day I'm reunited with Meena, but I will be taking Taranus and his men with me." He heads for the door. "I shall come back in the morning. Then we can go find a new location for our camp."

"Our final camp," I tell him. "Because we are going to stop this before the next snow."

Fin nods once, then disappears into the night.

On heavy legs, I make my way back upstairs and into the room where Ember is sleeping. She looks so peaceful, so calm as I study her ethereal face. My lips still taste like her despite the ale I just drank.

To know love once is a gift.

But twice?

Ember rolls over onto her back and groans. It's then I notice the paleness of her complexion. As fear takes root, I kneel at her side and press my hand to her forehead. It's cool to the touch, far cooler than it should be.

"Ember." I shake her. "Ember."

Her eyes flutter open, and she groans again. "Rafferty? I feel—" She tries to sit up but falls back down. "No. It can't be happening. This is different."

"Different?"

"Usually when my disease rears its nasty head, I'm hot," she whispers as she draws the blankets up to her chest. A violent shiver overtakes her, and her teeth begin to chatter uncontrollably. "But I'm so cold."

I don't even hesitate as I rush around the other side of the bed and climb beneath the covers. Gathering her into my arms, I pull her into my lap and cradle her against my chest. She begins to relax slightly, but that does nothing to ease my own terror as I realize what's happening.

The bond with Taranus is killing her, eating away at her because the second blood exchange was not made. I'd hoped that since she'd shown no signs of fading, the bond between them was void given that she didn't speak the oaths herself.

A hope that is now dead.

"Thank you," she whispers. "If it's too hard—"

"It's not. Shh now, and get some sleep." Lust and want are the last things on my mind.

"Okay."

"You're welcome." I cling to her as she drifts to sleep again, not releasing her body even as she warms up. And then I realize that with the bond secure, the promise I made to Fin just sealed her fate, as well.

I'd been so enraged over what Taranus had done that I didn't even think before I sent him off to re-spark a Rebellion that is going to destroy the one thing that matters to me.

If I kill Taranus, I lose Ember.

If I let Taranus live to save her, I lose hundreds—

if not thousands, including the sacrifices of those who died that day in the camp—of Meena.

Save one.

Lose many.

Kill one.

Lose everything.

CHAPTER 29

EMBER

S unlight warms my face as I come awake. I stretch and then still as my arm presses against something hard—*really* hard.

I open one eye and peer at the tremendous wall of man lying on his side facing me. Our bodies are entwined, his arm over me, my legs between his. Lust pummels me from all sides, heating my body well past normal—even for me.

More so now that I know how he tastes, how he comes alive with a passion so bright it's blinding.

Rafferty's eyes are closed, though his expression is far from relaxed. Swallowing hard, I reach up and touch his shoulder, lightly tracing a huge scar that disappears behind his back.

This man has seen more violence, more pain than anyone I've ever met, and yet, he still feels so alive.

As though he's clinging to even a shred of hope despite everything.

His own brother betrayed him.

Clipped his wings.

Stole…*everything*—and he's still standing. Still fighting.

Still clinging to what he believes makes him good even if it keeps him from what he wants.

What strength that must take—to keep going even when you should want to fall. It's something I know quite well, even though I was more than prepared to roll over and give up when the time came.

I have a feeling Rafferty doesn't even know the meaning of quit.

Glancing up, I still when my gaze locks with his. This close, I can make out the thin black rings around both golden irises. They're threaded with obsidian that has grown thicker since that night in the woods.

Even thicker now than it was last night.

I open my mouth to say something, but nothing comes out. Nothing but a quiet sigh that is somehow far more sexual than intended. I take a chance and draw my bottom lip into my mouth.

Rafferty's gaze drops to it, and his nostrils flare. The strong, muscled arm draped over my side tightens, pulling me closer. Close enough that his erection presses into my lower belly.

Oh my— My breaths come quicker now as my

pulse hammers. I want to feel him, to have his body on top of mine. Even as I *know* what a bad idea that would be.

So when I look back up at him, meeting his gaze for the second time this morning, I try like hell to reflect that in my expression.

His pupils dilate as the black ring around his irises expands and contracts, a visible representation of the battle he told me he's waging with the dark magic inside of him. Is it bad I want it to win right now?

Reaching forward, I press my palm to his chest, and he growls. The sound, low and deep, vibrates against my hand, spurring on my own lust. The aching heat between my legs is near-painful now, and I know he could sate my hunger with a single touch.

One moment of contact and I'll come undone.

I lift my gaze to his again, carrying with it a silent plea to just give us this moment—this morning of passion before we head back into a world determined to see us both dead.

But a knock on the door steals even that from us both.

Rafferty gets out of bed quickly, leaving me lying alone as he rushes to the door, already holding a blade in his hand I hadn't even seen him retrieve.

"It's Fin," a man says.

Rafferty opens the door, and a dark-haired man moves into the room, wearing a brown cloak and pants of the same color. His cheeks are pink as though he's been running, and I sit up, covering myself with blankets.

"What is it?"

"We need to leave—now. Taranus's men are coming."

"How did they find out?"

"I don't know," he says quickly. "I did as you asked, spread the word with the others, and when I got back, Marie told me they've been spotted sweeping the woods just outside the city."

Outside, someone screams.

"Now." Fin rushes into the room, and Rafferty turns toward me. Eyes hard, he seems to be battling with something, though I can't be quite sure what it is. Maybe whether to stay and murder his brother? Who the hell knows at this point? But the air becomes charged between us, so much so that the man he'd called Fin clears his throat.

"Fine. One minute. Then we're out of here." He shuts the door, and Rafferty continues staring at me as I get out of bed.

"We need to go, right?"

He doesn't speak.

"Rafferty?"

Without a word, he crosses the room toward me and grips the back of my neck. I tilt my face up, heart pounding. "You cannot tell anyone of your connection to Taranus, do you understand me?"

"Why?"

"Don't do it. Please."

"But—"

"I will explain it to you later, but promise me." His hand tightens in my hair.

"Okay. I promise."

With a sigh, he releases me just as Fin comes rushing in. Heavy boots thunder on the wood outside, and he doesn't say anything as he lunges forward and grabs us. "Deep breath!"

"Wha—"

Water surrounds us. I gasp for breath, my intake stalled by liquid filling my lungs. They burn, ache, and I scramble to reach the surface. Something grips my ankle, ripping me down, and I squint, barely making out Rafferty's face in the murky liquid.

He shakes his head and points to the surface with his other hand, but I ignore it.

My lungs continue to burn as the need to breathe overtakes all rational thought. It doesn't matter why he doesn't want me to surface because, if I don't, I'm as good as dead, anyway. I kick, trying to reach it, but he pulls me farther and farther down until I'm eye-level with him.

Then, he reaches forward, yanks me to him, and covers my mouth with his.

The contact is a punch to the gut as he breathes into me. A right hook that knocks me senseless even as I should be worried about what's happening around us.

Then, we slam into the ground. I cough and sputter, rolling onto my back as Rafferty falls to his side beside me.

"What the bloody hell, Fin!" he roars as he reaches for me. I gasp for air, still unable to get nearly enough.

"I needed them to think we'd tried to lose them."

Rafferty grips my arm and rolls me to my side. "By drowning us? Breathe, Ember," he rubs my back.

"We need to go again, they'll be here in a matter of time." He reaches for us, and I groan, but before I can protest, we're shooting toward the sky.

My stomach lurches, what little contents are in there threatening to come right the hell on up. Rafferty grips my arm as Fin holds my other one and Rafferty with the other.

"Fuck you're heavy," he groans. "Raffe, not you, Your Majesty."

My eyes shut tightly. I don't dare look anywhere. I'm terrified of heights already, and, well, we all know how my first flight went.

"Put us down," Rafferty orders.

"Almost."

My stomach drops with our descent, and then

finally, the ground comes up. I fall to my knees, digging my fingers into the soft grass as I heave, bile the only thing coming out. "Just kill me already," I groan.

Someone touches my back gently. "Not a chance of that, dear."

I know that voice. "Heelean?" Hopeful, I look up and into the kindest golden eyes I've ever seen.

"Good to see you, lass." She gently rubs circles on my back with one hand then offers me a green leaf with her other. "Eat this. It will help ease the nausea."

I don't question, just take the thing and put it in my mouth. The minty leaf immediately begins to work, and the muscles in my stomach finally stop spasming.

"How did you escape?" Rafferty asks.

"Not happy to see me, then?"

He sighs. "Of course, you know that's not true."

Heelean smiles. "I know, dear. It appears that when you killed Lloren, the spell work binding me to my tower collapsed as well. I left shortly after I imagine you did, been looking for the two of you everywhere. Wasn't until Fin here put out the word that I hoped to find you."

"We cannot stay here long," Fin says. "We need to get moving."

"Why do we keep going everywhere? Surely they

aren't tracking us." My words are barely above a whisper, and all three fae turn toward me.

"They can track our magic," Fin explains. "Which is why I left you both in the water. In doing so, I was able to trick them into thinking we'd, left then looped back to get you again."

"Ember nearly died. She is not fae."

"I got that after I pulled you back out," he retorts, then turns to me. "I truly am sorry, Your Majesty." He bows, and I want to hurl all over again.

Especially when I note the darkness in Rafferty's gaze. Something Heelean seems to pick up on, too, if her expression is any indication.

"Please, just Ember. Not Your Majesty, or Queen. I'm neither of those things."

"Yet," Fin replies with a hopeful smile. "Meena believed we'd find you. That you and Raffe—"

"Hush, Fin. Can't you see the girl has been through enough?"

"Yes, mother."

"Mother? This is your son?"

"Oh, no," she chuckles. "Not in blood, at least. Finley was very close friends with my Fearghas, though, weren't you?"

"Thick as thieves," he replies. "Now, can we get moving?"

"Yes." Rafferty looks to the sky then to the tree line. "Why in the bloody hell did you bring us here?"

"Where are we?" I ask, turning in a slow circle. To be honest, it looks exactly the same as everywhere else we've been.

"We are standing in front of the Cursed Forest."

Snorting, I turn to Heelean. "You guys literally have a forest that is called Cursed?"

"That we do," she says, darkly. "And it is exactly as it claims to be."

"Then why the hell would we go in there?"

"Because it's the last place Taranus will look for us," Rafferty explains, even as he glares at Fin. "It's rather brilliant, really."

"We need somewhere to hide, at least, until Taranus loses our trail."

"He's with them?" Rafferty asks, stepping forward.

"Oh, yes." Fin's sadistic grin bears no joy. "He is tracking us with them. Should we finish them off? From what I hear, you could do it with a word."

Rafferty goes completely still. I don't know how, but even from where I'm standing, I can feel his nerves, the turmoil rushing through him. Which, of course, makes no sense. Why the hell can I *feel* him? "I cannot do that."

"I heard the rumors of what you made Joaquin do in that forest. They spread through Faerie like wild-fire. You could take him out with a single word, Rafferty. One word and this whole thing is over."

"No."

"Why the bloody hell not?"

"Because I will create something much worse than Taranus if I continue accessing that magic."

"What?"

Rafferty steps forward, his hands clenched into fists. "Me."

"Time to go, boys," Heelean says, stepping between them. She gestures for me, so I move toward them as well, and she touches both Fin and Rafferty. "Put your hands on them."

I do, and the world falls away.

Fourteen more times we move that way. No one speaks a word as we land, walk for at least a mile, then leave again. Over and over again.

Whatever herb she'd given me managed to last for most of it, but as the ground returns beneath my feet once more, my stomach heaves.

"We must walk now. The Cursed Forest does not allow any magic to be used within its boundaries."

"Cursed Forest? We're back here?"

"We are." She loops her arm through mine and guides me into the tree line. The moment we step into it, she shivers.

"What is it?"

"The trees and ground here are full of iron. It is why we tend to avoid it."

"Iron."

"Fae cannot tolerate it. The iron blocks our magic."

"So why are we here? Isn't it dangerous?" I glance back at Rafferty, who is lingering a few yards behind me.

"It would be far more dangerous to not be in here right now."

"Will it help him?" I ask, hoping she understood.

"For a time. Though the dark magic will eventually eat away at the last of his soul."

I gasp, recalling the few times I witnessed Rafferty losing control. If he were to be permanently out of reach, he would be unstoppable. Especially since he can force anyone to do whatever the hell they want with little more than an uttered order.

"Do you fear him?" she asks. When I don't respond, she taps my hand. "He cannot hear you in here, lass. The iron blocks our enhanced senses, as well."

"I'm not scared of him because I've seen so much worse." The truth behind those words surprises even me. If I'd met Rafferty before Taranus, I can't say for sure that he wouldn't have terrified me. A man, who is basically solid muscle, running around with the ability to force others to follow his every order? Absolutely terrifying.

No matter how sexy he is.

But compare the above to a man who will kill just

as soon as smile, who forces a woman into marriage, only to rape her because he thinks she will make him king?

Very few monsters scare me worse than Taranus.

"Taranus was always a bastard," she says. "Even when Rafferty came and worked with us."

"Worked with you?"

"My late husband was king once upon a time," she says, and I whip my head toward her so quickly it nearly gives me whiplash.

"You were queen?"

"I was."

"What happened?"

"A man came and—" she shuts her eyes tightly, leading me to believe whatever was done is not something she wants to talk about.

"You don't need to say anything."

"The crown was stolen from us," she says. "My husband cast aside, my daughter lost, my son—he never fully recovered."

"Do you want it back? The crown."

"No. Not even a little bit. I want Rafferty to wear it, though I sense he believes the honorable thing to do is pass it off to someone else."

We fall into companionable silence, and despite being in a place with the word 'Cursed' in the name, I'm calmer than I've been since arriving in this damned world.

"Do you believe the prophecy is true?" I ask curiously.

She glances at me. "That you are meant to make the next king?"

I nod.

"No, I do not."

My relief is instantaneous. "I cannot tell you how grateful I am to hear that."

Heelean smiles at me. "The pressure you must have felt when that was laid on you."

Chuckling, I nod. Then, pain pummels my gut like a fist. I fall to my knees.

"What is it?" Heelean is there in an instant, touching my arm as the cold overtakes me. My entire body goes rigid, my muscles seizing.

"What happened?" Rafferty is at my side, pulling me into his lap and checking me for injury.

"I'm not sure. She collapsed."

"So. Cold." I begin to shake violently, uncontrollably. My limbs go numb, my mind reeling. What the hell is happening to me? Tears burn my eyes.

"I'll get a fire going," Fin says, right before he disappears.

Heelean reaches into her satchel and withdraws a small pouch of water. A few muttered words and she's offering it to me. "It's warm, lass, open." The spout presses against my lips, and I open as warmth slides down my throat.

It soothes me just enough to stop the violent tremors, but seconds later, they're back. "What. Is. Happening. To. Me?" I choke out as I tip my face up to Rafferty.

He doesn't speak.

But his eyes tell me that he knows exactly what is happening to me.

Why is that more terrifying than the unknown?

CHAPTER 30

EMBER

The world around us is quiet save for the cracking fire between us. Heelean and Fin left hours ago in search of food, something they told us would take quite a while since they had to re-route multiple times like we did to keep from being followed.

Rafferty hasn't spoken a single word since they left, not that I've been overly chatty. Mainly because I fear what he will say when he does finally speak. Is it possible that my disease is back? That it's simply chosen a different way to kill me?

Or something else entirely?

"Why didn't you tell them about the ceremony?"

His gaze rapidly meets mine. "You cannot mention that."

"Why?"

Rafferty doesn't reply, just stares back down at the twig in his hands.

"Rafferty. Raffe."

He looks at me now. "You are dying."

"No shit, Sherlock. Tell me something I don't know."

My Sherlock joke doesn't land, and his expression darkens. "You cannot talk about yourself so callously. I'm not speaking of your disease, Ember."

"Then what?"

Rafferty stands and crosses the space between us. He reaches down. "Come with me."

I do without hesitation, letting him lead me farther into the trees and farther away from the fire. "Are you planning on killing me? Is that what this is about?"

"Never."

"Then what the hell are you doing?" I stop and rip my arm from his grasp. "Tell me what's going on."

His gaze drops down. Then he swallows hard before meeting my gaze again. "That ceremony with Taranus bound you to him."

"What?" I choke out the word, really hoping like hell it's not as bad as it sounds.

Because it sounds pretty fucking terrible.

"I had hoped that since you weren't speaking the words yourself—that Lloren had forced you—it meant the binding didn't work."

"What the hell do you mean, Raffe!" I yell, rushing toward him.

"You cannot tell anyone about it because, should you do so, you will be hunted by every single fae in this world."

I step back—shock, fear, anger—all the emotions crash into me. "But I'm not his mate—not really."

"You are not fae," he explains. "Typically, when a fae marries a human, they turn them into a fae that same night to avoid their magic pulling from an empty vat."

I shut my eyes and shake my head, rejecting everything he's saying. "No. It's my disease. That's what's happening."

"Taranus is draining you, though not on purpose. Unless you complete the union and seal with another blood exchange, you will die."

"You said only a mate will die if their mate is gone."

"For fae, yes. But you, Ember, are not fae."

"Stop fucking saying that!" I scream. "I know that!" Tears stream down my face freely now, but I'm too damned frustrated to care. Ever since I got sick, everyone—and I mean *everyone*—has been telling me what I need to do.

You need this test, Ember.

You need this test instead, Ember.

Here, take this pill, Ember.

Time for hospice, Ember.

You're going to marry me, Ember.

Over and over and over again, it's been the same fucking story, and I am so... Damn... Tired. And now, that last forced choice is going to kill me faster than this disease. Unless, of course, I complete another blood exchange and have sex with a man I hate.

"Ember. You are not weak."

"I know I'm not! Do you know what it was like? Growing up alone? Having to fend for myself? Then, when I got sick, having to find a way to pay all of my medical bills, *alone*? Slowly dying, *alone*? Not once did I complain, not once did I break down because what was the point? Sure, I had my pity parties, but who wouldn't?"

"Ember!" he yells my name this time, his expression conflicted, as though he's torn somewhere between pity and anger.

Pity I do not want. "No." I turn away from him, emotions reeling, stomach burning, as I try like hell to ground myself in any sort of reasoning as to why this is happening.

And then—it hits me. I turn back to Rafferty. "You said you couldn't kill me, fine, but you need to take me home."

A muscle in his jaw twitches. "I do that and you'll die."

"But so will Taranus. Don't you see? This solves all of your problems."

Rafferty's upper lip raises in a snarl. "I will not sacrifice you. Not even for my world."

"I'm dying, anyway, Rafferty. If anything, you doing that is a mercy. Please." Tears stream down my cheeks. "Just take me home. I can die peacefully. Then you can take the kingdom. Maybe that's what this ridiculous prophecy has always been about. Not about me making the king in the sense of being a mate but of clearing the path for you. My death can make you king."

He shakes his head, backing away from me. "No."

"You don't get to choose for me, Rafferty. This is my life!" Tears burn my eyes. My throat is swollen with emotion even as I try to keep it together. I have to keep it together.

"More like your death!" he roars back.

I shake my head and rush toward him as desperation to have him see reason takes over. "Think about it, though. Doesn't it make perfect sense? My death means the crown is there for you. By binding himself to me, Taranus sealed his own fate."

"It doesn't make sense," he argues, shutting his eyes tightly and shaking his head.

"Yes, it does! Much more sense than me being some rumored queen."

Eyes blazing, he glares down at me. "No."

"Why not?"

"Because your death will *never* make sense!"

His words stop me in my tracks. But it's more than even that. The broken look on his face—the tortured expression—it tears me apart. It's no longer pity I see reflected in his gaze but rather something far more emotional. "Rafferty—"

"You cannot even begin to imagine what I feel for you, Ember. It makes no sense at all, but is nothing like anything I've ever experienced." He crosses the space toward me. "I have to keep you safe—protect you."

"And you have. You kept Taranus from making me immortal, Rafferty." I think of all the pain Taranus has caused and of how angry I felt getting my diagnosis. It always felt so pointless, me dying so young, but now it makes sense.

My life may not have changed the world.

But my death will.

"It can't end this way." He shakes his head. "All we need is a witch. She can break the connection—"

"Can she? You're sure? Or are you just grasping at straws?"

His silence answers that one. I step forward and reach up to cup his cheek with my hand. It's wet from the fresh tears falling from his eyes. "I made peace with death a while ago, Rafferty. This is how it was always supposed to play out. Desperately clinging to an idea will only stretch out the inevitable."

He reaches up and covers my hand with his much larger one. "No. I will continue saying no until you believe that your life is worth more to me than anything."

"Why?"

"Because you are everything to me, Ember of Austin. I have breathed you since the moment you first stepped into my dreams, and I will continue to breathe you until the day I die."

I'm speechless. "You breathe me, and yet, one kiss nearly sent you spiraling into a murderous rage." An exaggeration, sure. "We can't be together, Rafferty, and I won't complete the union with your brother."

"I'm not asking you to."

"No, you're just asking me to keep living in a world where I can't have the one thing I've ever actually dared to want." I inhale sharply, and my throat burns. "We can't be together, fine. I get it—but one thing in my life *will* be on my terms."

"My kind only mates once, and I had my chance."

"Maybe it wasn't your only chance," I nearly whisper.

"A second chance with a woman destined for death," he retorts. "Hell of a deal that is."

The whimper leaves my lips before I can stop it.

Rafferty rushes toward me, but I hold up both hands. "I'm not interested in whatever is about to come out of your mouth, and frankly, it's for the best."

"I didn't mean to be so crass," he says, softly.

"It's the truth. Never apologize for speaking the truth. You and me? We can't happen because that will give us both a reason to be selfish and not do what needs to be done. I'm dying. With or without you taking me home. It's really only a matter of time, at this point."

"We will find a way."

"No, we won't. Because even if we did, even if we fix whatever this is, it's still only a matter of time before he finds us. My death, however screwed the logic is, solves that."

Rafferty doesn't speak. He simply glares on. "So even with me telling you how I feel, you're still determined to let yourself die."

"This is so much bigger than us. Think of Flora. Of that man who was killed while I was sitting at a dinner table. Of all the people who have died since Taranus took over; can you really say my life is more important than theirs? Than this world?"

"Yes," he replies, no hesitation. "Because I would let this world burn if it meant saving you."

"That's not right."

"Maybe it's not, but it's how I feel. I love this

world, the people in it, but if I were forced to choose, I would pick you every single time."

He takes a step toward me, but I back away. "It's not right," I repeat. "Innocent people are dying."

"You're innocent."

"But I'm one person. They are—hundreds —thousands."

Rafferty turns away from me, giving me a full view of his bare back and the scars left behind from Taranus's mutilation.

Before I can stop myself, I'm walking toward him and reaching up to touch the jagged outlines. He shivers then stills beneath my touch. "He cannot keep doing to others what he did to you," I whisper. "It's not right. And for the first time in my life, I can make a difference. I can bring you—this world—peace. Please, let me do this."

"I cannot," he whispers. "I'm sorry, Ember, but even if you hate me for it, I will not deliver you to your world until I know—without a doubt—there is no other way."

He turns, and I withdraw my hand then look up into his eyes. Anger churns in my belly, igniting my blood and cementing the realization that I am truly alone in this world, too.

No matter what I tell him, what I want my choice to be, he is going to fight me. The shitty part is that he has the power to do just that since I know little about this world, and even less about how to get out of it.

"You're right," I tell him. "You are stealing my choice, my ability to control the outcome of my own life, and I do hate you for it."

Without speaking another word to him, I turn on my heel and march straight back to the fire I can still vaguely see through the trees. Every part of me knows that going home is the best answer for me.

It gets me away from here, away from Rafferty and Taranus, two brothers who couldn't be more opposite and yet both feel they have the power to control me. It saves this world from Taranus's bloody reign and hands the kingdom to a man who would rule fairly.

There really is no choice. No argument.

I just wish Rafferty could see it.

CHAPTER 31
RAFFERTY

F ire burns the forest around me. Heat licks
my sweat-slicked skin as I scan the area for
her. "Ember!" Heart pounding, I begin to
run, sprinting as I leap over fallen trees and the
bodies of the dead. "Ember!" Her name is a cry from
a tortured man.

"Did you really think you could control her?"

I stop and turn. Taranus stands behind me,
holding a blade in his hand. The left side of his face is
scorched, leaving little more than charred skin still
blistered. "Where is she?" I snarl, turning the blade
in my hand.

"Dead if we have any luck."

"What did you do?" I race toward him, stopping
when I'm only a few feet in front of him.

"I did nothing. You brought this fate upon us all

when you chose her over your world. Over your people. Some king you would have been," he spits back. "You claim I was the traitor. Really, you were nothing more than a wolf boasting the face of a sheep."

"If you hurt her—"

"You'll what?" he demands. "Kill me? Go for it. I'm already as good as dead."

———

I COME OUT OF THE NIGHTMARE WITH A POUNDING heart. Jumping to my feet, I scan the clearing for any evidence of a blaze. Of Taranus.

But there's nothing. Nothing but sleeping forms gathered around a dying fire. The adrenaline surge begins to die, so I lean back against the nearest tree and take a deep breath. I haven't dreamt of Ember since she showed up in that dungeon, what feels like decades ago.

My gaze drifts to the pile of blankets covering her slender body.

You're right. You are stealing my choice, my ability to control the outcome of my own life, and I do hate you for it.

Even now, as those words are nothing but an echoing memory, they gut me. But I'm selfish enough that I'd rather she hate me than no longer exist. All we need is a witch, and they can break the hold between her and Taranus.

I'm sure of it because, if they can't, if Ember really is here to die, how in the hell am I supposed to go on living?

Wide awake now, I take a deep breath and cross toward the tree where Fin is perched, keeping watch. "Fin? I can take over now," I call out quietly.

No answer.

"Fin?"

Once again, nothing.

An owl hoots overhead. Fear unfurls in my gut, a vicious beast reminding me of all that could have gone wrong while I was sleeping. I race toward the pile of blankets where Ember had been sleeping. Ripping the green wool away, I find nothing.

"Ember?" Panicked now, I turn in a slow circle.

She wouldn't have wandered off, right? Wouldn't have left? And surely, Fin would not have taken her! Unless—"No, no."

"Raffe? What the bloody hell is going on?"

Heelean's quiet voice is little comfort to me now as I piece together what likely took place. "Ember and Fin are gone," I tell her.

"What the hell do you mean *they're gone*?"

I close my eyes as I attempt to regain what little control I do have over the dark magic slithering beneath my skin. Reaching into my pocket, I withdraw a blade and slice open my forearm, the sting barely notable.

"Rafferty! What do you think you're doing?" Heelean rushes toward me, already holding a cloth in her hand. She attempts to bandage it, but I shake my head.

"It's the only way to keep control," I tell her.

With eyes wide, she stares up at me. I can see the moment she realizes what I mean. "The dark fae soul-matter."

"Yes. It's getting harder to control. Ever since—"

"Ember."

I nod. "And now she's—fuck!" I whirl and slam my fist into the nearest tree. Bones crack, knuckles bleed, but it's not enough. I want to take the whole damned forest down with me. Tree by tree.

"Why would she leave? And why would Fin take her?"

I swallow hard. "Taranus forced her into marriage."

"She's mated to him?"

Shaking my head, I walk over to where she'd been sleeping. "I got to her before he'd forced himself on her. They did not finish the tethering."

"Then what—oh, bloody hell. She's human."

"Yes."

"Which means that since they did not do the second blood transfer, that connection is killing her."

"Yes."

"So she went back to him? To save herself? That doesn't seem like her. And Fin certainly wouldn't—"

"She's not trying to save herself," I tell Heelean. "When Ember arrived here, she'd been on her death bed. Being here in Faerie stalled the disease killing her." I meet her gaze with a heart nearly as heavy as the day I discovered what happened to Niahm. "Ember is going back to her world to die because she believes that will fulfill the prophecy."

Heelean gasps and covers her mouth. "But how? The prophecy—"

"States that the true king will take her as mate," I finish. "Ember thinks that it's her death that will solidify the new king because her death will end Taranus's life. He took her as mate, an action that will result in *his* death."

"You believe she is sacrificing herself for this world."

"Yes. She asked me to help her. To take her home so she could die." The words are vile on my tongue; acid that burns my throat even as I speak them. "I told her no, that we would find another way."

"What other way?"

When I whirl on her, she throws up both hands. "Not that I agree with her, Rafferty, I'm merely trying to understand the thought process that would have her sneaking away from you in the middle of the night."

Sighing, I pinch the bridge of my nose. "I told her we could find a witch to break the connection."

"Then you would kill Taranus."

"Of fucking course," I growl, my temper igniting.

"Ember wishes to save you that pain," she says, softly. "What I can't understand, though, is why she would say no once you told her how you felt. Which, you did, right?"

I swallow hard. "I told her the truth."

"Which is?"

"That she is not meant for me."

"You bloody fool!" Heelean yells.

"What the hell else was I supposed to say? It's the truth!"

"You tell her that you can never be together then wonder why she runs off to die! You damned men, I swear, you wouldn't know your own ass from a hole in the ground, that's the damned truth."

"My destiny is to save her then help her find the one she is meant to be with. The one who will wear the crown."

"When the hell are you going to see that you *are* the one who is meant to wear the crown?"

"I am not good enough to be with her, let alone lead this world."

"Why is that, I wonder? Because you took on dark magic accidentally after your sister's death? Or perhaps it's because, even though you could have ended the war centuries ago, you chose not to because, in doing so, you risked unleashing a dark fae on this world? Bloody hell, Rafferty, for such a smart man, you sure are a dumbass."

My last moments with Ember run through my mind, watching her walk away, hearing her soft cries until she fell asleep.

"Why would Fin help?"

I turn to her. "Who do you know that has the most to gain with Taranus's death? Do you really think he'd pass up the chance to kill his mate's murderer?"

"No." She mutters a curse. "Dammit. This is a right mess. Do you at least know where she's going?"

"She mentioned that they'd found her near Mossy River."

"That's not terribly far from here," Heelean says. "We can likely reach it within the hour if we leave now. Once we reach the edge of the tree line, we can dematerialize there."

I start toward her, but she holds up a hand. "What is it?"

"If we show up and stop her from returning home, you'd damn well better have a good reason for it."

"She can't die."

"That is not your choice to make. If she was dying when you met, you need to give her a reason to live."

"Living isn't enough of one?"

"Not when dying would save the person you love."

I shake my head. "She doesn't love me."

"No? You sure about that? Because I'll be honest, you're lying to yourself so damned much I wonder if you'd even see the truth if it bit you on the ass."

"I already had a mate," I remind her.

Her expression softens. "Do you truly not believe you are worthy of a second chance?"

The words mirror Ember's so closely that they shatter another piece of my soul. "I didn't," I reply as I reach down and gather my blade. "But then I met her, and she changed everything."

"You love her, then."

"I do."

"Then why the hell are we still standing around?"

By the time we arrive at the edge of the forest so Heelean can dematerialize us, we're already far too late. Taking shelter in brush that shields us from view, I take in every inch of the scene before me.

A small clearing has already been set up as a battle camp with one giant tent erected in the middle and a handful of smaller ones surrounding it. Taranus's men patrol, marching in white and gold armor that glints beneath the bright sun.

How the hell did they know we were going to be coming here? Did Taranus suspect I would try to take Ember home?

Ember.

Frantically, I scan the area for Ember and Fin, but there's no sign of them. My gaze travels through the camp then to the trees just beyond. Is it possible they changed course and went back? Or is it—

"We found it, sir!" someone calls out.

The white fabric of a tent door opens, and Taranus strolls out. Far thinner than he was the last time I saw him, his gaunt face and pale hair showcase that he, too, is suffering from the bond not being complete.

Which answers my earlier question. Of course, he came here. He'd be so desperate to find her that this would be the best place to start looking. After all, why wouldn't I try to take her home?

Because doing so will kill her. I clench my hands into fists. Taranus didn't know about that part—didn't suspect his unwilling bride would already be dying. "Where is it?" he demands, marching up to a soldier whose back is to me.

When he turns to address his king, a low growl emits from my chest. *Conary.* "This way. It's small, barely large enough for a grown woman to slip through," he explains.

Heelean and I move carefully in the trees,

following their path as they move parallel to us through the clearing.

The moment my gaze lands on the shimmering space between two trees, that answer is confirmed. They found the portal. It slithers in the air, there but not really there. Honestly, unless the sunlight hits it just right, I imagine it's near invisible. Which explains how Ember managed to stumble into it at night.

Soldiers gather around it, all of them gazing intently. And who can blame them—an open portal between worlds? That's not something you see every day since those of us with wings can move freely between them without one.

Movement on the other side of the clearing catches my attention, so I shift my gaze just as a flash of orange comes into view between two bushes. *No.*

Fin moves to crouch beside her, both of them staring straight at the portal. *You fucker, I trusted you.* I glare across at him, willing the bastard to see me, but neither pays me any attention.

"We need to send someone through, see if she's there."

"There's no way she got past our lines, sir," Conary says. "My men have been combing this area since she left the castle."

"Then where the hell is she?" Taranus snaps. "Anyone?"

"She'll be here," a woman replies as she steps into my line of sight.

Rage burns my blood. *Not. Possible.*

Though, Lloren's dark hair and crooked nose are unmistakable, as is the dark magic that swirls around her like a constant blanket. I drove a blade through her damned heart, and yet she stands less than four yards from me. How the bloody hell is that possible?

My own heart lurches in response, so I clench my hands into fists.

End this with an order, my inner voice coos. *One. Word.*

"Do you believe she is still in this world?" Taranus questions.

"I do," Lloren replies. "In fact, I'd imagine she's nearby."

Fear claws at my throat. There's no way—

"Then shut the portal down," Taranus orders, gesturing toward it. "Close it for good."

"Your Majesty," Conary argues, but stops as soon as Lloren holds up a hand.

"Are you arguing with your king?"

"Shutting the portal could do more damage than good," he adds. "I merely wish for him to think it through."

"Shut. The. Damned. Thing. Down. Now!" Taranus roars.

"As you wish," Lloren replies as she bows her head.

Please don't move, I silently urge Ember as her eyes widen. She still hasn't seen me, but she's all I can see.

With my heart in my throat, I watch her expression morph from fear to determination. That's when I know I've lost her.

"No!" she screams and explodes from the brush, running into the clearing. "Please, don't shut it down!"

Fucker.

All eyes turn to her.

"Why if it isn't my bride."

"Don't shut it down, please," she begs, trying to inch closer to the shimmering space.

Something Taranus notices, instantly. "Grab her."

"No!" Fin roars as he rushes out in front of Ember, blade drawn.

Double fucker.

Taranus grins. "I'm surprised you're still breathing," he says. "Perhaps Meena meant less to you than you let everyone believe."

Fin's upper lip raises in a snarl. "Perhaps destiny is simply giving me more time to kill you before the Veil takes me."

Taranus chuckles. "Doubtful. Kill him. Bring her to my tent so we can finish this."

His men close in on them, and the restraints binding me snap. I leap from the brush. "Stop!" My order is laced with magic, light and dark colliding. Everyone stops moving and turns to face me. Everyone except Taranus, Lloren, and Conary, who continues toward Ember, not even breaking stride. He grips her by the back of her neck and rips her away from Fin, raising his blade.

Luckily, Fin spins and blocks the blow with his own.

Taranus's gaze narrows on mine a moment before he smiles. "You are truly losing it, aren't you brother?"

"You're the one who is going to lose."

"I have my wife, and soon, I'll be more powerful than ever. Lloren has seen it."

She stares straight at me with eyes so black I can barely see the difference in her pupils and irises.

"Your witch is not a Seer."

"Wrong. I've seen your destruction, Rafferty of Avon. Just as I foresaw my death and took precautions. Black magic has its benefits, wouldn't you say so? A simple rejuvenation spell helped my body shove that dagger from my heart."

Most of what she says falls on deaf ears, though, because all I can focus on is her mention of me. *Rafferty of Avon.* I know that voice.

She grins and snaps her fingers, transforming

from the woman who drew pleasure in tormenting me, to an old woman I've only seen one other time. In my camp as she foretold a prophecy.

It was all a lie.

All of it.

"There is no prophecy," Fin whispers. "'Twas all a lie to get Taranus to overthrow Rafferty."

"Of course, there was a prophecy," Lloren says. "It was just never meant for Rafferty."

Ember's eyes widen, and she looks from Taranus to me. In her terrified gaze, I see one thing other than fear: regret.

"Thank you for your message," Taranus says. "After Joaquin's return and bloody departure, we took precautions." Taranus reaches into the top of his tunic and withdraws an amulet. "This prevents you from taking such liberties with us."

But the magic in me can't be bothered to care. Prophecies are a problem for tomorrow. Right now, the only thing I can focus on is freeing Ember.

"Let her go, or so help me, I will cut your fucking heart out," I snarl at Conary.

To his credit, he actually looks concerned.

"Raffe—" Ember whimpers. "I'm sorry."

I don't say anything to her because any words I speak now would be a lie. It's not okay that she didn't trust me to find another way. Not okay that she's risked my life, Fin's life, and Heelean's life in this martyred suicide mission.

Taranus narrows his gaze at me then glances at Ember before barking out a laugh. "Unbelievable. You already have a mate, yet you dare to claim mine?"

"Ember is not your mate," I growl. "Not in any way, shape, or form."

"She is mine by right!" he roars back. "Lloren has Seen it!" he repeats, his fractured voice evidence of just how fucked he is should she not become a fae.

"A mate bond is about more than power, you sick bastard," Fin growls. "You both feel it, the inability to survive without the other."

"Kill him already!" Taranus roars the order, and Lloren raises her hand as black magic swirls around her fingers.

"With pleasure." She makes a move toward him but stops, gasping for breath. It's then I look down and see the scarcest hint of silver sticking out from her gut.

She falls forward, gasping, and Heelean glares down at her, holding the bloodied blade still in hand. "You see that coming?"

Taranus roars.

Conary brings his blade up to block Fin's.

And I head straight for my brother.

"Close the portal!" Taranus roars.

Lloren grips her abdomen and backs away before raising her hand. Heelean flies backward and into a tree then falls to the ground, unmoving. Lloren scrambles toward the portal, but I keep my focus on Taranus.

I can't kill him—not yet.

But I can restrain him until the bond is broken.

"You going to kill me, brother?" he snarls as I close in on him.

"Not yet." I raise my fist and slam it into his jaw. It shatters like glass, and he cries out, stumbling backward. "You always were the weak one. Do you know how many times I talked Ridley out of kicking your ass when we were children?"

I continue moving toward him, and the sound of metal against metal is an echo in my mind. One of Taranus's men rushes toward me, and I raise my blade, blocking the blow, then drop down and drive it into his gut.

He falls, coughing and sputtering, and I don't break stride as I turn back to Taranus.

Kill him and rule. She is dying, anyway. The dark thought seeps into my mind, and I instantly shake it off.

Because even now while my light and dark magic linger together as one, sacrificing Ember is not an option.

No matter how fucking pissed I am.

"Raffe!"

I whirl as Fin calls my name, only to see him on his knees with blood seeping through his tunic.

"Bring. It. Down!" Taranus orders.

Lloren nods, raises her hand—

Conary stumbles toward the portal with Ember in hand. "Rafferty!" She kicks out, trying to break free, and I rush toward her.

Her frantic fighting is no match for Conary's strength, though, as he meets my gaze and grins. "She's mine now. I'll be back for my throne." He jumps through, and Lloren's magic pummels the portal.

"No!" Taranus roars. "Stop!"

But it's too late.

The portal closes, shimmering to nothing but a spark until, finally, that dies, too.

My throat goes dry, and the sound of Taranus's roaring is blocked out by the pounding of my own pulse. I stare at the space as my heart seizes.

The portal— "Open it now!" I roar at Lloren.

She shakes her head. "I cannot."

I stalk forward, but before I reach her, one of Taranus's men appears behind her and grips her by the shoulder.

They disappear.

"Taranus!" I whirl on him, just in time to watch him disappear.

"No. This can't be happening." Rushing to the space where the portal was, I search for any sign of an opening, no matter how small.

Conary—to be trapped in her world, deathly ill, with Conary. I shake my head. The things he'll do to her.

I can't.

A deafening roar fills the clearing, sending birds to the sky in fear.

It's only when Fin rushes forward that I realize the scream is coming from me.

A broken man who just lost his one shot at redemption.

Keep reading with Cursed Fae!

DYING WOULD HAVE BEEN EASIER.

For five years I fought to survive the disease slowly killing me, not at all realizing that there are things so much worse than death.

Things that teeter along the lines of pain, torment– and the worse of them all–desperate longing.

Desperation for a man trapped in another world entirely. I crave Rafferty. His touch. His scent. Even his broody temperament caused by the dark energy infecting him. I see him when I close my eyes, moments before the nightmares take over.

Nightmares that remind me how small I am in comparison to what's out there.

In my moments of lucidity I know that something is coming for me. And it's far worse than anything I've seen.

Also by Jessica Wayne

Fae War Chronicles

Ember is dying.

But as she will soon discover, some fates are worse than death.

Accidental Fae

Cursed Fae

Fire Fae

Vampire Huntress Chronicles

She's spent her entire life eradicating the immortals.
Now, she finds herself protecting one.

Witch Hunter: FREE READ

Blood Hunt

Blood Captive

Blood Cure

Rejected Witch Chronicles

Coming back to life shouldn't be this hard...

Curse of the Witch

Blood of the Witch

Rise of the Witch

Dark Witch Chronicles

She traded her soul for the security of her friends. Now, she must cling to what little light is left, or risk losing everything.

Blood Magic

Blood Bond

Blood Union

Siren's Blood Chronicles

His enemies are vast. And they are coming for her.

Rescued by the Fae

Broken by the Fae

Healed by the Fae

Mated by Midnight

Barbarian. Beast. Murderer? One thing's for sure, nothing is as it seems in this crazy town.

Midnight Bewitched

Midnight Cursed

Midnight Claimed

Shadow Cursed

He can have her body. But never her heart.

Savage Wolf

Fractured Magic

Stolen mate

CAMBREXIAN REALM : THE COMPLETE SERIES

THE REALM'S DEADLIEST ASSASSIN HAS MET HER MATCH.

THE LAST WARD: FREE READ

WARRIOR OF MAGICK

GUARDIAN OF MAGICK

SHADES OF MAGICK

RISE OF THE PHOENIX: THE COMPLETE SERIES

ANA HAS SPENT HER ENTIRE LIFE AT THE CLUTCHES OF HER ENEMY. NOW, IT'S TIME FOR WAR.

BIRTH OF THE PHOENIX

DEATH OF THE PHOENIX

VENGEANCE OF THE PHOENIX

TEARS OF THE PHOENIX

RISE OF THE PHOENIX

TETHERED

SOMETIMES, OUR DREAMS DO COME TRUE. THE TROUBLE IS, OUR NIGHTMARES CAN AS WELL.

TETHERED SOULS

COLLATERAL DAMAGE

FOR MORE INFORMATION, VISIT WWW.JESSICAWAYNE.COM

ABOUT THE AUTHOR

USA Today bestselling author Jessica Wayne is the author of over thirty novels. During the day, she slays laundry and dishes as a stay at home mom of three, and at night her worlds come to life on paper.

She runs on coffee and wine (as well as the occasional whiskey!) and if you ever catch her wearing matching socks, it's probably because she grabbed them in the dark.

She is a believer of dragons, unicorns, and the

power of love, so each of her stories contain one of those elements (and in some cases all three).

You can usually find her in her Facebook group, Jessica's Whiskey Thieves, or keep in touch by subscribing to her newsletter.

Stay Updated:

Newsletter: https://www.jessicawayne.com/free-books-by-jessica-wayne
Website: https://www.jessicawayne.com
Readers Group: https://www.facebook.com/groups/jessicaswhiskeythieves

facebook.com/AuthorJessicaWayne
twitter.com/jessmccauthor
instagram.com/authorjessicawayne

Printed in Great Britain
by Amazon

42551485R00239